DECEIVED BY SELF

DECEIVED BY SELF

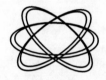

By William Mitchell Ross

To order additional copies of this book, contact:
Xlibris Corporation
1-888-795-4274
www.Xlibris.com
Orders@Xlibris.com
105776

ACKNOWLEDGMENTS

My special thanks to Monroe Police Chief Fred Kelley; John Douglas, a colleague at Saputo Cheese, Inc.; and my wife, Marilyn, whose patience with me during the writing process can best be described as biblical.

Death is a mystery. We don't like to talk about it and we rarely think about it unless it happens to someone we know. Fear of the unknown has a paralyzing grip on our psyche. We know that death is inevitable and inescapable, but by choosing to ignore it, it gives us a false sense of comfort and security. However, we must be prepared for death because it can come suddenly or it can take its own sweet time. When the time comes and we breathe our last breath, will the final punctuation to our lives be by natural causes, by accident, or by murder?

Keith Kranenbuhl steered his 1957 light blue and slightly dented Chevy sedan down Fourteenth Street barely slowing as he turned onto Sixteenth Avenue, tires squealing. The dents in his car were parking lot miscues from one too many beers after bowling league games. He needed to have them fixed. Yet another expense!

As he navigated his way down the tree-lined street, he was reminded once again that April in Wisconsin is an unpredictable and frustrating month. Everyone hopes for an early spring, but Mother Nature always teases them; warm one day and cold the next. An extra Green Bay Packers sweatshirt in the car trunk is a necessity.

This morning, Keith made his way to work through foggy and chilly weather. He needed to slow down because of the dense fog. He got a speeding ticket on Fourteenth Street last week on his way to work, but that wouldn't be a problem this morning. The ticket really pissed him off.

He bought the Chevy brand-new on his twenty-seventh birthday, nine years ago. He really loved the car; the envy of his friends and family. After its maiden voyage from showroom to home, he spit-polished it every week. The sun shone as brightly off the hood as a newly minted star in the night skies. The year 1957 held a special mystic meaning for cars back then, and to own this one was a dream that came true for him. His wife, Stacy, thought he was a little crazy buying this icon of a car, but she went along with it anyway.

Soon after the purchase, Keith insisted that Stacy sit beside him when he slowly cruised the local A and W root beer stand on Saturday nights. To say the least, she was embarrassed. His sophomoric behavior was appalling. Not only was he showing off the car, but he was also reminding everyone that he had married a high school cheerleader; his trophy bride! During high school, they did this cruising regularly in his dad's Ford sedan, but at thirty-six, "Uffda!" she would say.

Eventually, the cruising stopped when Stacy threatened to have her aging widowed mother move in with them. But not to be outdone, Keith proposed a compromise. On or near his son's birthday each July, they would go to the local drive-in movie theater and make love in the backseat of the Chevy. Just like the old days!

At first, Stacy laughed at this suggestion, but the more she thought about it, "Why not?!" After all, that's where their son, Brad, was conceived, and the place held many fond memories for her. Besides, when dating Keith in high school, making love to him under the stars at the drive-in was naughty and nice and romantic! She and her girl friends shared many stories during high school, and most of the more humorous ones took place during the second feature. They still laughed about it years later.

This morning, Keith had overslept and pressed on the accelerator a little firmer to hurry to the brewery to start his morning shift. He was late for work again, thanks to another Thursday night, bowling-league hangover. His plan last night was to make love to Stacy when he got home. He needed to get a good night's rest, but he passed out on the couch downstairs and never made it to bed. Stacy came looking for him at 6:00 a.m. and woke him up. He quickly changed his shirt, brushed his teeth, and raced out the front door and jumped into his car.

Keith was the dock foreman at the local brewery, and his job during the past eighteen years was to load beer trucks and to keep the paperwork readable and in order. Beatrice, in the front office, had fits if his record-keeping wasn't just so. Being late on a Friday morning was not a good thing. The trucks would be backed into his loading dock waiting for him. The drivers would be anxious to get early starts delivering beer to Madison and Chicago, as well as to local beverage marts and taverns.

As Keith pulled into the employee parking lot, he noticed that Fritz's car wasn't there. "Oh shit," he said to himself. Fritz was his assistant and he was counting on him to get the day's loading schedule under way. Keith turned off the engine and headlights and jumped from his car. He half-walked, half-ran along the broken sidewalk next to the two-story, white brick, brewery building. He was looking for black ice as he hurried along. A broken leg is all he needed! His unzipped faded leather Green Bay Packers jacket fluttered in the breeze. Twenty-five feet over his head, facing the street was a red and white faded sign featuring a long-necked beer bottle that said, "Leuenberger Brewing Co., 1845."

The early April snow that covered the sidewalk two days ago had almost melted. Keith felt more confident of his footing as he neared the entrance. He finally reached his destination and swung open the employees' door and disappeared inside. The familiar smell and aroma of brewers yeast greeted him.

Keith cautiously climbed the flight of stairs that welcomed him by pulling on the hand rail. The time clock was located at the top of the stairs on the second floor. At five feet ten inches and two hundred and twenty-five pounds, the climb up those thirteen steps was a challenge. He wasn't in very good shape for his thirty-six years and his paunch was well defined. He had had a mild heart attack two years ago, but he felt that his new heart medicine insulated him against that worry now.

Keith was a third generation brewery worker. His father, Fredrick, and grandfather, Nils, had made this same assault on these same stairs hundreds of times before him. But he didn't think about that as he labored up the stairs. His breathing was measured and his heart was pounding when he reached the top step. He instinctively reached into the right-hand pocket of his jacket and felt the familiar shape of the plastic bottle that held his heart medicine. He felt reassured. Then he turned and habitually touched a replica-sized beer bottle made from copper standing on a pedestal next to the time clock.

In 1910, the brewery caught fire and was badly damaged. During the major reconstruction and restoration repairs, new and larger copper vats were purchased. His grandfather Nils asked and got permission to melt down one of the discarded vats. He then proceeded to make a replica beer bottle statue, about two feet tall, from the copper. It was a work of art. The beer bottle was an instant success with the owners and employees during the re-dedication ceremony. It was then placed next to the time clock on a white marble pedestal. It was a reminder of the devastating fire. It also took on the aura of a good luck charm to protect the brewery against future fires. A new tradition was born. To protect and safeguard the brewery, each employee touched, rubbed, or massaged the copper bottle soldier with his hand when reporting to work. Even though Keith was in a hurry, he affectionately rubbed the bottle that had so many times reminded him of his departed Grandpa Nils.

It was now 6:25 a.m., and the only sound Keith heard was his own footsteps on the tile floor as he passed the dark and silent administrative offices. At the other end of the hallway was another staircase that would take him back down to the production floor. He pushed open the door with authority and worked his way around the beer-filling machines. He followed what seemed like miles of conveyor lines that delivered twelve-ounce sanitized beer bottles, at the rate of sixty-five bottles per minute, to the filling machines. The production area would spring to life at 7:00 a.m. with the clamor of clanking bottles and the beer aromas that he had come to love over the years that he had worked there.

The shipping and receiving docks were located adjacent to the bottling house for easy warehousing and the shipping of thousands of cases of beer. As he made his way to his desk, Keith noticed both shipping bays already had trucks backed into them; one of the drivers was leaning against his desk smoking a cigarette. "You overslept again, you little shit, Switzer," the burly unshaven driver blurted out as Keith reached around him and retrieved the clipboard from his desk.

He hastily threw his Green Bay Packer jacket onto the chair next to his desk. "Screw you," Keith replied with a grin.

The driver was wearing a Chicago Cubs baseball cap and a dirty T-shirt. He grinned back at Keith through tobacco-stained teeth but Keith ignored him. He was late and he had work to do. No time to talk baseball now. It was getting late and he had six trucks to load before noon. His head was throbbing. He hated hangovers. Even after last night's bowling fiasco with his team losing every game to Fritz's team, he was still able to get up and go to work. "Where the hell is Fritz?" he muttered to himself. "The asshole is probably at home puking his guts out!"

Over the past year, the pressure to brew more beer to increase sales and to make on-time shipping schedules was really on. Last April, the brewery hired a new sales manager, John Beckman, who had come out of retirement after a successful career at a big brewery in Milwaukee. Beckman and his wife, Martha, moved to Monroe two years ago to enjoy his retirement from the hectic pace of the beer industry. The lure of Green County cheeses and a family-owned brewery in historic Monroe was his dream retirement destination. At first, it seemed a little odd to Beckman that Monroe, being only a couple of hours drive from Milwaukee, could capture his imagination and re-energize him out of retirement.

At sixty-two, Beckman wanted to relax, spend more time with his wife, and travel to see the kids and grandchildren. But he soon grew bored with his retirement. He missed the daily challenges of traveling to see customers, selling beer, and the camaraderie of his colleagues. Martha loved Monroe and integrated well into the Swiss community. Martha's outgoing personality, knitting skills, and euchre-card-playing prowess made her a much sought-out person at the senior center.

Beckman started hanging out at the brewery and quickly made fast friends with the owner, Ernie Streiff. After several informal meetings and philosophical discussions about sales strategy, Ernie offered Beckman a part-time job as sales manager to help his struggling brewery. The opportunity fired up a renewed sense of self-worth for Beckman. Streiff gave him a lot of latitude and trusted his instincts about Beckman's abilities. Beckman wanted to explore new marketing ideas that he had to increase sales at his old job but couldn't get past the corporate culture of analysis and paralysis. Now he had his chance to implement some of his ideas and to prove something to himself.

The first thing Beckman did was to meet with all the employees and explain his plan. He preached the same mantra at all his subsequent weekly meetings—quality beer, delivered on time. He talked about the voice of the customer and reaching out to them. He told them that they should take pride in their jobs and pay attention to every detail. No job was too menial. The beer that they brewed and bottled was to be in the spirit and proud heritage of their brewery. The taste of old-world flavors would carry them into a very bright and prosperous future. He also insisted that the beer age five to six weeks before bottling to insure the best possible taste for the customer. To drive his point home, he created a sampler six pack of products and gave one to each of the employees to take home to try. It was the same product sampler that Beckman was going to deliver to current and potential new customers.

Beckman quickly had the employees excited and believing in themselves. With the extended brewing time and new marketing strategies, the orders came pouring in for the best beer brewed in southern Wisconsin and the United States. Beckman was true to his word and met with the employees every Monday morning to encourage them and to give them feedback on increased sales and to personally thank them. The resulting employee overtime and enthusiasm resulted in producing an extra ten thousand barrels of quality beer. For the first time in their working careers, all the employees each received a $100 Christmas bonus check from Mr. Streiff. The money was greatly appreciated.

As Keith was sorting through his beer orders, he could hear the first shift employees laughing and banging about in the bottling room. They were starting up the filling machines and conveyor belts. The sounds of empty beer bottles clanging against each other on the filling lines permeated the warehouse. Soon, the smell of beer would fill the air. He studied the sales orders on his clipboard as he walked over to his gas forklift located in the southwest corner of the loading area. The rows of palletized beer ran north and south in the warehouse.

The forklifts were lined up in a row like two monster machines ready to spring into action. Fritz nicknamed Keith's the "Beast." It had a temperamental starter that always gave him fits when starting up in cold or cool weather. While filling out the pre-trip log on the "Beast," Keith smelled the rich beer aroma wafting into the warehouse. He checked off the appropriate boxes: lights, tires, brakes, horn, and oil. He was convinced the starter had a short in it, but no amount of whining could get the maintenance guys to check it out. So his only recourse was to print in bold letters, "Fix the damn starter" on his daily trip sheet and wait another day.

He decided to load the Chicago truck first to get Charlie on his way. He looked at his watch and hoped that Fritz would be there soon. "Twelve pallets of classic pilsner, three pallets of bock, and three pallets of dark," he yelled to Charlie, but he only saw the back of him as he wandered off to the bottling area to watch the filling machines go round and round.

Keith was now ready to jump on the seat of his forklift to finally get his day under way when he heard his phone ringing. He looked at his watch. "Shit," he muttered to himself, "maybe it's Fritz." He hurried to the impatient phone on his desk.

It was John Beckman. "The owner of the Brass Tap in Chicago called me early this morning and increased his order. He wants another pallet of bock. Can we handle it?"

Keith rolled his eyes. *Beatrice is going to blow a gasket over this change,* he thought. *Not only am I late, but now Beckman has changed the shipping order!* He could feel tightness in his chest. "No problem, Mr. Beckman, I am loading the truck now."

"Thanks, Keith."

He hung up the receiver and shook his head. The last thing he wanted to do today was to face Beatrice with the change order. Her attitude was difficult enough for him to handle even without a hangover. A change order over the phone wasn't to be tolerated in her very structured accounting world.

As he went back to the waiting forklift, the extra pallet of bock was on his mind. Fritz had screwed up yesterday's order, and he hoped that he could deliver on his promise to Beckman. If he couldn't find another pallet of bock, then the Edelweiss Tavern would be short. He began to sweat a little and felt a bead of water run down his back. Suddenly, a cool breeze blew in from the loading dock and Keith shivered a little. "I need to get moving!" he said half aloud to himself. "Charlie is going to kick my ass if I can't get him out of here on time. Hitting Chicago traffic at the wrong time of the day could send him into a rage."

Keith jumped on the Beast and turned the key. Nothing happened! He jiggled the key and turned it hard to the left and then hard to the right, as if to teach it a lesson like some defiant child. Still, nothing happened. The old Beast was dead! He tried three more times. He then jumped off and lifted up the leather seat. He had seen Fritz do this a hundred times on his forklift. He hit the starter with the palm of his right hand in an attempt to bring it back to life. His hand stung like hell as he got back on the seat again. He turned the key hard right. No response. He jumped off and gave the Beast a kick with his foot. His face was flushed and frustrated and very red. "You son-of-a-bitch!" Keith yelled at the Beast.

"What the hell are you doing?!" a booming voice behind him reverberated in his ears. Keith jumped and spun around. He saw the fat-faced Chicago driver staring at him.

"What do you think I'm trying to do, you jerk?! I can't start this damn thing!" he screamed in frustration.

Charlie straightened his Cubs hat and gave him a little wry smile. He motioned for Keith to step back. He climbed onto the Beast and fondled the key. He looked like a big kid on a toy tricycle. Charlie seemed lost in thought when he very slowly turned the key to the right. The gentleness of his touch mesmerized Keith. Charlie's huge calloused right hand had swallowed up the key, but the tenderness of his touch didn't make any sense to Keith.

Suddenly, the Beast coughed and sputtered and sprang to life. Keith's jaw dropped in disbelief. "All she needed was a little TLC," Charlie said as he got off the seat. He then straightened his hat, winked at Keith, and swaggered back to the loading dock like some pompous parading aristocrat. "Screw you Charlie you lucky son-of-a bitch," Keith yelled after him but Charlie just kept on walking in the full knowledge of his greatness.

Keith jumped back on the fork truck and raised the forks a little and headed to the aisle of pilsner beer. With the grace and elegance of incessant fluid motion, his hands flew across the levers with practiced ease, and the Beast responded beautifully as if forgiving him for his earlier insults and impatience. Within thirty minutes he had the truck loaded and all the pallets squared off for shipment. He then signed the bill of lading and handed it to Charlie. "Gotta go," said Charlie, "the Cubs are waiting for me." Keith handed him a six pack of short fills and told him not to be late next week. Charlie grinned and laughed. "Go Cubs!"

One down and five to go, Keith said to himself as Charlie's truck pulled away from the dock. He scanned the next shipping order. "Damn that Fritz", he muttered. He climbed back onto the Beast and headed back into the aisle of pilsner beer. Once he turned into the aisle he suddenly broke into a cold sweat and felt nauseous. "What the hell?" he said. Then he felt a pain in his chest; "time for a heart pill!" he said to himself. "I am going to quit that damn bowling team – too much stress!"

He jumped off the Beast and headed to his desk and picked up his jacket. He reached into the right hand pocket and pulled out the plastic bottle. He popped open the lid of the nearly empty bottle and poured out a red and white capsule into his hand. "I'll need a refill on Monday," he said as he popped the capsule into his mouth and washed it down with the residue of yesterday's cold coffee he found in his chipped green and gold Packer coffee mug. "God, that coffee tastes terrible," he muttered to himself.

He headed back to the Beast and began to feel light headed and nauseous again. Suddenly his legs gave way and he grabbed onto the Beast. He slid down to the floor and put his head between his knees. He felt like he was going to faint. The pressure in his chest began to increase. "Oh shit," he said to himself, then like a bolt of lightning out of nowhere, Keith felt a sudden and unrelenting and excruciating crushing pain in his chest. He had shortness of breath and felt pain in his arm and his neck. He rolled over onto his side. "Oh God," he cried. He felt frightened and helpless on the cold damp floor. He stared at the stacked cases of beer. The familiar sound of clanging beer bottles as they marched along the filling line pierced his ears. Crazy thoughts flashed into his mind.

The image of Grandpa Nils suddenly appeared and then was gone. He saw Stacy in her wedding dress. He saw himself weeping at his mother's funeral. He saw his son, Brad, being born and then cheering for him at a high school basketball game. Were these images of life, his life or the end? The realization and sadness of the moment gripped his soul. April was supposed to be the month of new beginnings and new life. Had a cruel twist of fate just occurred in the warehouse? Was the cool breeze of destiny blowing through the warehouse this day really there to carry Keith to his everlasting flight? "Am I going to die?" he asked and then said, "Something is wrong here! The new heart medicine . . ." he whispered to himself through his agonizing pain. He lost consciousness.

Fritz ran to the shipping desk. "Keith is going to kill me for being late again," he said to himself. He spotted a truck driver coming toward him and asked him where Keith was.

"Over there somewhere. I am going to be late if I don't get my truck loaded!" He then pointed toward the southwest wall of the warehouse.

Fritz couldn't hear the engine noise of the Beast working the row. He went to investigate. As he turned down the first aisle, he spotted Keith on the floor. "Damn!" he shouted and ran to him. Keith looked very bad. He was pale and ashen and he looked to be in a great deal of pain. Fritz leaned over him and touched his arm. He felt chilled and clammy. "Keith, Keith," he yelled at him. "I am going to get help! Don't die!" Fritz jumped up and ran as fast as could to the warehouse phone and dialed the police department.

The brewery was located only three blocks from the police and fire departments and the voluntary ambulance service. Fritz was still on the phone to the dispatcher when he heard the sirens go off. He hung up and saw the truck driver staring at him. "When the police get here, tell them where we are," he said, and then he hurried back to Keith. Standing over him, Fritz felt helpless. *Should I find a blanket or try CPR or what?* His panicked mind wasn't working. He just stared at Keith.

A couple of production line workers noticed the commotion and ran toward Fritz and stood behind him. Fritz turned around and saw the concerned looks on their faces. Nobody said anything. The atmosphere had turned ominous. Then Fritz heard Beatrice's voice coming toward them. Another line worker had gone to her office and told her something was happening in the warehouse. As she stood beside Fritz, she whispered, "Oh my God."

Keith wasn't moving. His vacant eyes stared into nothingness. Beatrice began to weep softly. She sensed the seriousness and gravity of the moment as the others did.

The surreal sound of the sirens became louder and louder, and then the dark mood was broken by the sound of Police Officer Kennickson's voice as he made his way to the assembled group. He asked everyone to stand back and kneeled over Keith. Then an ambulance driver appeared and kneeled beside the officer. They began to work on Keith while another volunteer brought in a gurney. As gentle as they could be, they lifted Keith onto it. The gurney then bumped along on the uneven warehouse floor to the waiting ambulance.

The ambulance pulled away and exited the warehouse parking lot. It bounced along as it maneuvered across the ruts in the driveway. Back on the street again, it turned north and headed for the Monroe Regional Medical Center. The sirens wailed and lights flashed as Keith and his hopes faded as he sped toward his destiny.

Officer Kennickson pulled Fritz aside to ask him a few questions. Ernie Streiff appeared and asked the employees to return to their work stations. He told them he would notify them as information became available on Keith's condition. Beatrice was still upset and weeping. Ernie took her by the arm and guided her back upstairs.

Fritz told Kennickson everything that he knew, starting with finding Keith and his subsequent actions. Kennickson wrote down Fritz's statement in his notebook. "Poor bastard," he said when Fritz had finished. He had known Keith and his family for a long time. Growing up in a small rural city of ten thousand people did that to you. He also knew that Keith's family was cursed by heart disease. Keith's grandfather and father had died suddenly and tragically from heart attacks, and now poor Keith was being rushed to the hospital. Kennickson saw the tears in Fritz's red eyes and put his arm around his shoulder. He was satisfied that he had all the information he needed for his report and put his notebook away. He told Fritz he was going to the hospital and headed back to his squad car.

Fritz stared after him as if in a trance, and then his mind started to engage again. He picked up the phone on the shipping desk. He wiped his face with the sleeve of his shirt. He needed to call Stacy. "Hello, Stacy?" Fritz said into the phone, trying to control his shaky voice.

After what seemed like an eternity, Stacy said, "What do you want, Fritz?"

"You better get over to the hospital right away," Fritz said. "Something has happened to Keith."

"What's happened, Fritz? Tell me!" Stacy demanded in a panicked voice.

"I don't know. He sort of keeled over in the warehouse and was having trouble breathing." Stacy hung up. He turned away from the shipping desk and went to the loading dock. He felt his sides and stomach churning and aching. He leaned over the edge of the dock plate and threw up.

CHAPTER 2

Gregory Denton relaxed on an over-stuffed, button-backed, burgundy antique chair with his feet up on a matching hassock. He had a smirk on his face. His slim, six-foot body fit comfortably into his semi-prone position. He was in good health. He was proud of his physique, being that he was in his mid-thirties and had no paunch. He displayed an air of confidence. He was dressed in his blue plaid, flannel pajamas with a red cotton blanket wrapped around him. His profile featured a long face with a pointed nose, brown eyes, and high cheekbones. His chocolate brown hair was cut short, giving his features a sculptured, distinctive look.

On a circular oak table beside him was a Victorian-style Tiffany lamp that he had inherited from his mother. Its overlaid, etched glass shade was crafted from hand-rolled art glass using the Tiffany's copper-foil technique. It featured graceful, wrought-iron scrollwork and a cast base. The lamp had twin pull-chain sockets. He greatly admired the lamp.

He was fascinated by her story of taking an adventurous trip to New York City to buy it. The romance and enthusiasm of her trip, as she retold it to the family, convinced Gregory that someday he had to have it. And now there it stood, in all its beauty, in his Milwaukee apartment. It was one of his prized possessions.

From his chair, he stared out of the window of his second-floor apartment across East Juneau Avenue. It was 7:00 a.m. and he could see the overcast skies breaking up and the hint of the early morning sunlight starting to appear. The traffic was getting noisy as cars honked at one another, traveling to work or wherever they were going on this final day of the work week.

Today was his scheduled day off from his job. He was one of four pharmacists working at Milwaukee General Hospital. His tidy one-bedroom apartment was located on the south side. A small city park was located across the street, which gave him the enjoyment of a pastoral garden view. He hadn't slept very well since his return from Monroe a few hours ago.

Gregory was born in La Crosse, Wisconsin, and raised in Monroe. He was an only child. He was adopted by his Aunt Marge and Uncle Ben Denton soon after he was born. His unmarried mother, Ellen Johnson, gave him to her twin sister to raise after a family crisis that centered on abortion and religion.

After giving up her child to Marge, Ellen abandoned them all and chased after her dreams in Chicago. But one failed relationship after another finally brought her back to Monroe when Gregory was fifteen years old. Ridden with guilt and remorse, she tried to reconnect with her son, but the rebellious teenager would have none of it and tormented her. Her attempts at reconciliation also put a strain on Marge and Ben.

The interesting thing about Ben was that he had a twin brother named Wes, and they grew up on a farm outside of Monroe, near Clarno. There were six siblings in their family, but the twin boys were special. Six months after the Denton twins were born, another set of identical twin girls were born in Monroe; Ellen and Marge Johnson. They also received special attention and treatment from family and friends.

The two families attended the same church. Growing up with the Denton twins and spending much of their time together as youngsters led to dating in their teenage years to no one's surprise. They had great fun with their friends, making them guess which twin was holding hands with whom. In the end, Ben married Marge and Ellen turned down Wes. It seemed that Ellen had no intention of marrying a farmer.

During his younger years, Gregory proved an exceptionally bright student. He was always on the honor role and excelled as an A student. He went on to the University of Wisconsin in Madison after high school. He graduated with a degree in pharmaceutical science with honors. After graduation, he accepted a job at Milwaukee General as a pharmacist in part to get away from the stifling small-town life he felt in Monroe. The two-hour drive from Milwaukee to Monroe suited him just fine. Over the years, he had come to enjoy the independence and the freedom of his bachelor lifestyle.

His aunt and uncle visited him about once a month under the pretense of shopping in Milwaukee, but the visits were normally short and pleasant. He thought it was cute the way they always seemed to ask him, in their own slightly embarrassed way, if he was dating anyone special. He thought the notion of future grandchildren was the sub-text of their inquiries, but his answer was always the same, "I am dating, but no one special." His response time after time must have frustrated them. It also bothered them that he would not invite his mother to visit him. The abandonment he felt still gripped his psyche and had turned his heart cold against her.

Then the unexpected reality of life took him by surprise. His aunt Marge died two days after he celebrated his thirty-second birthday. A head-on automobile collision with a drunk driver abruptly and tragically ended her life.

A year later, his uncle Ben checked himself into the hospital. He was not feeling well and complained about blurry vision. He had fallen two days before but had not lost consciousness. After a thorough examination, he was diagnosed with CML, chronic myelogenous leukemia; six months later, he died. The suddenness of these two deaths unnerved Gregory. He had a hard time coping with these deaths; the only two people who truly loved him.

But now as he stared out at the traffic, a small sinister smile crept crossed his face. "Brilliant, just simply brilliant," he said to himself and then he laughed out loud. He jumped up from his chair and started dancing around in a circle, laughing hysterically. After a few moments, he quieted down.

He needed a cup of coffee, so he walked the short distance to the kitchen. He found the kettle and filled it with tap water and put it on the stove, turned the front burner to high, and then he went to the cherry wood cabinet above the kitchen sink and retrieved a jar of instant coffee. He measured out a heaping teaspoon, dumped it into his coffee mug, and then he sat down on a kitchen chair to wait. The water made gurgling sounds as the steam began escaping from the curved spout.

Gregory had never paid much attention to the everyday mundane chore of brewing a cup of coffee. Living alone, he had a set routine and went about his business without thinking too much about what he was doing. But today was different. Soon the kettle whistled, and Gregory made his first steaming cup of coffee for the day. He learned to drink his coffee black during his college years, and that morning, he found it very comforting. He made his way back to his chair and placed the cup of steaming brew on the oak table and snuggled in once again under his blanket. He told himself he needed to run through his fateful trip to Monroe the night before one more time. He prided himself on attention to detail, so he carefully and meticulously began to replay last night's trip in his mind.

As he slowly sipped his coffee, Gregory's dull brown eyes stared into nothingness. His wrinkled and pinched brow started the process of clearing and focusing his mind. He had left his apartment at 8:15 p.m. with his television left on and the volume turned up just enough to be heard outside his apartment in the hallway. He seldom saw his neighbors due to conflicting work schedules and hours, but in case of any inquires later he felt this detail was important. He then made his way to the underground parking garage and got into his shiny black Corvette sports car. The smell of the leather seats excited him. He loved the smell of leather and was looking forward to the drive.

He exited onto Juneau Avenue and worked his way to the freeway and headed south. The traffic was light. He knew the way to Monroe by heart. As a child, his uncle often took him to Milwaukee to see the Braves play baseball.

As he drove, he noticed the overcast skies and the threat of freezing rain. He purposefully stayed within the speed limit, and after leaving the city limits he increased his speed. He would have to be careful as he sped down the highway because of the deer. His uncle hit one once on this same road, but Gregory had been fortunate and only had one near miss. This night he hoped that his luck would hold.

As the miles melted away beneath his smooth riding radial tires, the trip to Monroe was uneventful. He rode in silence rehearsing his plan in his mind. Everything was a go, and he felt comfortable that he could abort his plan if anything unforeseen happened.

He passed the 'Welcome to Monroe' sign as he entered the city limits and quickly found a parking space two blocks off the square. Gregory looked at his watch, 10:45 pm. Two hours and thirty minutes on the nose. "So far so good," he told himself. He sat in his car and reviewed, once again, what he was going to do during the next ten to fifteen minutes. He was very confident of his mission and reminded himself that he could stop at any time without consequences.

He had worn a dark nondescript flannel shirt with faded blue jeans and an old baseball cap. His hand reached into his shirt pocket and he felt for the bottle that held the lethal red and white capsule. He was ready. He got out of his car and locked it and headed to the square. He walked at a normal pace as his heart raced.

The Swiss Pin Bowling Alley was located on the south side of the square. It had been built after World War II for the returning GIs and opened in 1947. It featured eight bowling lanes and a bar, and it became an instant success. It was very popular with the locals. Renovating a vacant shoe store and fitting in the bowling lanes into a row building had proved a little tricky, but common sense and practical engineering carried the day. It was a little cramped for space, but no one complained. Ownership had changed hands several times over the years, but it never closed because of the popularity of the bowling leagues.

The familiar smell of stale cigarette smoke and spilled beer greeted all the patrons who entered the premises. The "Pin's" colorful history over the years included numerous bowling tournaments, fist fights, and two marriage ceremonies. Gregory's uncle, Ben, had taught him how to bowl there at an early age. Bowling was the only sport he had any success at, so it seemed a fitting place for his mission.

Gregory also knew that Keith had a passion for bowling and never missed Thursday night league, except for deer hunting season, of course. As a testimony to his passion, Keith's bowling trophies were scattered all around his house like mini shrines.

Gregory reached the front door and slipped in unnoticed. Due to the harsh Wisconsin winters, he had to pass through a double set of doors before he was safely inside. The stale smell of cigarette smoke greeted him as he stood and surveyed the bar area and alleys. No one turned to look at him. The bar to his left was very busy with noisy customers. The sound of bowling balls making thudding noises and winging their way down the lanes, pins flying everywhere, and very loud chatter filled the room. He felt very warm; he was sweating. Then he turned to his right and looked along a coat rack that measured ten feet long.

He slowly made his way along the rack, examining each coat, and suddenly there it was: Keith's Green Bay Packers jacket. He took a quick glance around, and then reached into the right-hand pocket and grabbed the bottle that he knew would be there. Then he hurried past the bowling lockers and into the men's room located against the west wall. It had only taken seconds. Once inside the men's room, he was alone.

He went into one of the three stalls and locked the door. He sat down on the stool and carefully put on latex gloves and wiped the bottle clean. He popped the lid open and saw that it was nearly empty. He took the capsule from the bottle in his shirt pocket and put it into Keith's bottle. It was identical in color and size to the rest of the capsules. He replaced the lid. He could feel his heart pounding in his chest.

Suddenly, the restroom door burst open, and a bowler rushed in and went straight to the urinal. Gregory froze. The loud sighing sounds from the guy as he relieved himself made Gregory smile. The thought of someone pissing away not knowing the drama that was unfolding behind him was almost comical. When the man was done, he exited almost as fast as he had burst in.

Gregory listened intently for a few seconds; then he left the stall. He exited the bathroom and looked around. The bar was still busy with bowlers, and no one seemed the least bit interested in him. He made his way back to the coat rack and adeptly replaced the bottle into Keith's jacket pocket. Then he quickly left the building through the same doors that he came in and was once again on the sidewalk. He took off the latex gloves and stuffed them into his pocket. He looked up and down the sidewalk and only saw a couple of teenaged kids smoking cigarettes at the far end of the block. He hurried back to his car, unlocked it, and got in. He relaxed and let out a big sigh.

The ride back to Milwaukee soothed his nerves. The deed was done. He felt confident that all went according to plan; almost too easy. He dialed in his favorite AM rock and roll station and listened to the stereo sound in his car. He watched again for deer and saw some shadows in the darkness beside the road that made him anxious.

Before he realized it, he was pulling into the underground parking garage off Juneau. During the drive back, he had been on some sort of auto pilot and he couldn't remember many of the details of his return trip. Had he really driven through Beloit? He must have. He parked his car. No one was around. "Perfect," he said to himself. Once back in his apartment, he turned off the TV and got ready for bed.

Sleep wasn't forthcoming. He tossed and turned most of the night. He dozed off for a while before he finally got up. Now he sat in his chair waiting for the phone to ring with the news. His mother's best friend was a spinster woman named Ada Klausner, and the call would undoubtedly come from her. She was known as a character of sorts around Monroe for her radical ideas and outspokenness. Ada and Ellen had grown up together in Monroe and were more like sisters than friends. Upon Ellen's return to Monroe, they became close friends once again.

After Ellen died, Gregory inherited her house. Ada was adamant that she should buy her friend's house. After long and contentious negotiations, Gregory finally sold it to her. She, in point of fact, just wore him down. Ada's reputation for her eccentric personality, that some folks thought a bit daffy, carried the day for her and she got her price.

Along with the house, Ada assumed the responsibility of keeping tabs on Gregory. At first, Gregory objected to this intrusion into his life, but after a while, he accepted it and he enjoyed the drama of it all. Ada told him that she owed it to Ellen's memory. She would call him once or twice a month and chat about the goings-on in Monroe. These phone conversations were a bit one-sided and colored by her take on life, gossip, and politics in Monroe. Gregory was a good listener, which suited her just fine.

But today, he was waiting anxiously for her call. Any news concerning Keith Kranenbuhl would be reported with excitement and furor. He may have to wait a couple hours or days, which he was prepared to do, but the call would come. He was sure of that.

After he finished his coffee, Gregory showered and got dressed. He turned on the television to catch up on the news and weather. He made himself another cup of coffee. He didn't have an appetite, and nothing seemed good to eat. He decided to do some grocery shopping at the market a couple of blocks from his apartment. He had to maintain his routine and self-control. Nothing out of the ordinary; just maintain his cool.

He put on a light jacket and put his checkbook into the inside pocket. He headed to the front door. As he reached for the door knob, the telephone rang. Gregory's heart jumped a foot! The call he was waiting for startled him. He made his way to the phone on the desk in the living room and answered in as calm a voice as he could muster, "Hello," he said. "Hi, Ada, what's new?"

CHAPTER 3

It was Monday morning and Detective Samantha Gates, of the Monroe Police Department, had seated herself in the last pew on the west side of the First Christian Church of Monroe. Her parents had wanted a second son and planned to name him Samuel, after her grandfather. As a back-up, if the child was a girl, the name Samantha was chosen, after her great-grandmother. Either way, the child was going to be known as Sam. So, as a young girl, her family and friends called her Sam.

Her elder brother, Philip, was also named after a family member. As Sam grew older, she realized that all her family seemed to be named after each other. Sometimes it was difficult trying to keep the names straight. After she moved to Monroe, Sam joined First Christian Church, and she volunteered whenever her work schedule permitted. Today was her day off, so she told Helen Rupnow, the chairman of the Worship and Church Life Committee, that she would help serve lunch after the Kranenbuhl funeral service and help with clean-up.

Sam was five feet ten and a half, lithe, with blue-green eyes, and wore her chocolate brown hair short. Her legs easily reached under the pew in front of her. She always thought of herself as a little overweight, but her height seemed to compensate for that. Her short haircut was easy to maintain, quick with no fuss. She had a round angelic face that masked her firm resolve and determination. Today, she felt very comfortable in her black cotton dress. On her wrist, she was wearing a watch that her grandmother left her when she died. In her long slim fingers, she held a copy of Keith's funeral program. She glanced at the watch and thought about her grandmother.

Kranenbuhl's funeral service was scheduled to begin at 11:00 a.m., and the church began filling up with mourners around 10:00 a.m. The visitation was the night before, but people kept coming in this morning to view the body and then retreated to the pews and whispered to one another. The sanctuary was lit with candles. The smells of fragrant sprays of colorful spring funeral flowers surrounded the pulpit and altar at the front of the church. Another spray of flowers was near Keith's open casket, which was surrounded by pictures and his bowling trophies. It was going to be a standing room only funeral.

The brick, Victorian High Gothic-style church was vintage late nineteenth century, featuring steep gables and pointed windows. The architecture was northern European, including a very high steeple with a cross at its apex and was well known as the highest point in Monroe. The cross could easily be seen above the terraced trees for several miles outside the city limits.

The church trustees had a slightly different view of the steeple and cross since it was also the favorite target of lightning strikes during fierce thunderstorms. The congregation willingly and cheerfully raised the money for repairs after the strikes, making many wonder if the damage was really a message from God.

Sam liked the church because of its light, airy, and pleasing style. The sun shining through the stained glass windows transported her into a rainbow of colors. As she waited, she enjoyed the peace and quietude of the moment. Then her mind began drifting back to another time.

She was born in Silver Bay, Wisconsin, thirty two years ago. Silver Bay was located twenty-eight miles south of Milwaukee on Lake Michigan in Racine County. Her father, Earl, was a police officer for the Silver Bay Police Department. Her mother was a stay-at-home mom. Her elder brother, Phil, was two years older and had spent a troubled youth at home. He never seemed to get his life together, which put a strain on the entire family. He was always in trouble for one thing or another. Her father was the disciplinarian of the family, and he and Phil never got on.

Earl started calling his new daughter Sam almost from the day she was born. Growing up, Sam idealized her dad and tried to please him. She would shadow him everywhere he went. It was a special thrill for her when Earl took her to the police station to visit with the other cops. The tall men in uniforms always made her feel special and important.

Sam and Earl would go on long walks together through many of the small parks around Silver Bay and sit on park benches to talk. The city parks overlooking Lake Michigan were her favorites. Earl usually did most of the talking. Sam was a good listener and took great pleasure and delight in the many stories he told her about being a police officer. She especially liked his stories about helping people with problems. Sometimes he would get irritated when he talked about the personnel conflicts and politics within the police department, but he always ended his narrative with a "whatever."

It was on one of those sunny afternoon walks with her dad that Sam decided to become a police officer. She was only twelve years old at the time, but she knew what she wanted. Being a bright student, she started reading anything available about police work and constantly quizzed her dad about his job. He would bring home reading material from the station for her to study. He was very proud of his daughter as she poured herself into her newfound passion, devouring page after page.

As Earl watched his daughter's passion grow daily, he couldn't help but think about the insurmountable obstacles that blocked her dream. The likelihood that Sam would ever wear the uniform was remote. There were precedents, of course, in other bigger cities, but the odds were stacked against her. It was a man's world, after all, high on hairy-chested testosterone. If by chance, she realized her dream and wore the badge, she would be an outlier. And this notion worried Earl. But for now, he went along with her dream.

Her mother, Sharon, protested her new interest in police work and tried to dissuade her. But she instinctively knew that Sam was very much like Earl in one respect, stubborn!

Then suddenly, at age sixteen, Sam's life changed forever. On a Friday night, Earl was working the second shift filling in for scheduled vacations, when he pulled over a car for speeding. He called in the license plate and it checked out. It hadn't been reported stolen. He approached the driver's side door and asked for a driver's license and registration, a normal traffic stop on any other night. Two gunshots rang out, killing him instantly. The car sped away, leaving Earl's lifeless and contorted body sprawled on the cold earth. The worst night of Sam's young life was about to begin.

Police Captain Cal Thompson called the house at 10:30 p.m. and asked Sharon if he could stop by. Sharon hung up the phone and sat down on the couch in the living room. She had a pain in her chest and her stomach ached. She started to sob as she waited for Thompson to arrive. She knew what the call meant. Earl had talked about it many times. Sam heard her softly crying and joined her on the couch. Her mom's face was buried in her hands, and tears flowed like raindrops through her fingers onto her lap.

She put her arm around her mother. Sam asked her what was wrong, but she couldn't speak. Sam was frightened and she felt light-headed. After several minutes, Thompson arrived, and Sam opened the front door for him. He hesitantly walked into the living room with his hat in his hand. He had visited this house many times and was very familiar with it, but tonight, he felt like a stranger trespassing on sacred ground. He looked into Sharon's sad red eyes and told her how very sorry he was. She let out a low moan and just stared into the carpet.

Thompson gave a brief explanation of what had happened to Earl. He said that a witness saw the car speeding away from Earl's patrol car with two young white kids in it. The witness was sure that he could identify the car and gave a partial license plate number. They ran the plate and contacted the owner, who wasn't aware that his car had been stolen. The police were urgently following up. Thompson was sure that they would make an arrest soon. In the meantime, he wanted to know if Sharon wanted a police officer to stay with her. She declined. Both she and Sam were in shock. Phil was spending the night at a friend's house and refused to come home after Sam called him.

The next few days were a blur for the family. The death of Earl, their patriarch and protector, left a huge void in their lives. The question of where to go for comfort and guidance left them totally lost. Having a very small extended family was a problem; they all lived out of state.

Fortunately, a casual lady friend of Sharon's felt sorry for them and stepped up to the plate to help. She reached out to the family and organized a plan. Her first suggestion was to contact Pastor James Cihlar at St. Martins Church in Silver Bay. He would give Earl a proper Christian funeral. Having no church affiliation of their own, the family quickly agreed. In fact, they didn't even have a Bible in their home, and Sharon and Earl never talked about the possibility of his death. Looking back, it seemed odd to Sam that her parents never talked about it. Other cops were killed in the line of duty, and they discussed that. Maybe the thought of it was too much to contemplate. They didn't even have a will.

Pastor James could have been anyone's benevolent grandfather, complete with white hair, smiling face, and natural wit. He met with the family and immediately put everyone at ease and explained the steps that needed to be taken. He arranged for the funeral home to take care of Earl's body, and then he talked the family through a funeral service and what was expected of them. Pastor James picked out the hymns and the funeral service biblical texts. He helped to procure a gravesite. Throughout this ordeal, Sharon and

Sam were numb with grief and appreciated all his help and attention. The tears never stopped flowing from Sharon.

Phil was another story. He had disappeared again and kept his distance. Sam called around and found out that he was staying with one of his loser friends and told him what was expected from him out of respect for his father. Phil came late to the funeral and sat with them during the service. After the graveside burial, he quickly abandoned his family once again and disappeared back into his world of addictions.

During her time of grief, Pastor James took Sam under his wing. Both Pastor James and his wife, Harriett, agreed that Sam reminded them of their daughter Julia, who was working in the Peace Corps in South Africa.

After the funeral, Pastor James counseled Sam and she grew to trust him. The time they spent together found Sam doing most of the talking. She poured out her nonstop feelings of anger and grief. The pastor was a very good listener and reflected back to Sam much of her feelings. They slowly worked their way through the why questions. She found much-needed comfort in these discussions and strongly bonded with the good pastor as if he was her own grandfather. He always made himself available and took the time to give her special attention whenever she needed it.

During the ensuing weeks, many hours were spent talking about the meaning of death and the celebration of Earl's life. He talked to her about faith, hope, and love. Pastor James taught her how to pray and explained the power that prayer had to heal. Sam began to attend his church and soon joined the youth group. During the next couple of years, the ache in her heart lessened as she felt a spiritual awakening of her soul. She really believed that Earl was in a better place.

Sam tried to get her mom to make an appointment to visit Pastor James, but she always refused and stayed pretty much to herself. Sharon was clearly depressed and didn't want any help. In her darker moods, she cursed God for what happened to Earl. She angrily rejected Christianity and severely criticized Sam for her newfound faith. How could a loving God let her husband die? As far as Sharon was concerned, there was no God!

As Sam's view of life improved and the bounce was coming back to her step, Sharon asked her why she seemed so happy. Sam told her about the visceral feeling of her newfound religion. It had given her a new outlook as well as a changed perspective on her own life. Sharon just shook her head at this explanation and went into her silent world, retreating back to the familiar demons that dwelled within her.

The one thing that Sam couldn't do was forgive the killers of her dad. When she visited his gravesite, she secretly promised him that she would find them and bring them to justice. Little did she know that this promise would shape her life and her future career as a police officer.

Sam finished high school and went to the University of Wisconsin in Madison to major in criminal justice. Through friends, she was able to keep track of Phil. He had become a full-blown alcoholic and was doing drugs. He was constantly on the move, working at marginal jobs, living in squalid conditions in one house after the next.

Sharon never recovered from the loss of Earl. Even after the counseling that Sam insisted upon, she couldn't get her life together and her health declined. She lived alone and isolated in the old house in Silver Bay, barely making ends meet, living on Earl's pension and Social Security.

Suddenly, the sound of the organ brought Sam's thoughts back to the church. Mary Tollakson started playing familiar hymns. The sweet organ music featured old favorites "Abide with Me," "Be Thou My Vision," "In Heavenly Love Abiding," and "The Day Thou Gavest, Lord, Is Ended," setting the woeful mood. Sam's pew was full and she noticed that the church was at standing room only. Conversation quieted down with Mary's playing. Two older people, a man and his wife who Sam didn't know, were sitting next to her. The woman smiled at Sam in an exchange of pleasantries.

As the undertakers slowly walked to close the casket, Keith's elderly mother suddenly rose from her seat and quickly made her way to the casket. The two men stopped and waited for her. She paused in front of the casket for a moment and then reached into her purse and removed a coin. She placed it inside the casket and returned to her seat with tears streaming down her face. The casket was then closed with years of practiced military-like precision.

Mary Tollakson stopped playing and the church became very still. Pastor Carl Peterson, dressed in his black clergy robes, stood at the pulpit and gently gazed at the family seated in the front pew. His slow, deep commanding voice started with a short prayer. He then read from the obituary that appeared in the paper next to Keith's smiling face. A short meditation followed with a quotation of Dietrich Bonhoeffer's hymn lyrics on faithful angels: "Surrounded by God's silent, faithful angels, we wait expectantly for what may be. God is with us from evening until morning and will remain through all eternity. When silent death comes knocking on our doorstep, then let us hear the full triumphant sound. The world we cannot see breaks through earth's bound'ries and all your children sing the glorious song. Surrounded by God's silent, faithful angels, we wait expectantly for what may be. God is with us from evening until morning, and will remain through all eternity."

The family members then took turns reading scripture and poems. Fritz was the only non-family member to speak, and he struggled through a prepared text about best friends and love. He tried to tell a funny story about Keith when they went to the Badger Inn and Grill near Lamont at closing. After bar time, the place was locked up and the patrons would go into the back room to bet on mouse races. On one particular evening, they stopped at a pet store on the square and bought a white mouse for fifty cents. On the way to the bar, the mouse somehow escaped its flimsy cage. Keith shrieked in terror as the mouse climbed over him and headed to the backseat, causing Fritz to drive into the ditch. At that point in the story, his eyes teared over and he couldn't finish and sat down. Stacy had heard the story thousands of times, and she smiled and nodded to Fritz as he passed her on the way back to his seat.

Cheryl Kubly was known as the songbird of Monroe because of her beautiful singing voice. She sang with all the passion, drama, and commitment that lifted all who heard her to new heights of pure musical enjoyment; and that endeared her to the hearts of all her fans. Her proud mother once boasted that a voice like Cheryl's is only heard once every hundred years.

She slowly made her way to the front of the church. Cheryl had grown up in Monroe and was a classmate of Keith. She began her singing career in this church, and then moved on to a very popular high school quartet to the delight of her many admirers. Her solos would soften the hardest of hearts when she sang. She majored in music at UW and left for New York after graduation to pursue her dreams on Broadway. She was cast in one off-Broadway musical that ran only six weeks. After that disappointment and much frustration, she returned to Monroe to continue singing at weddings and funerals.

Now she stood next to a free standing microphone. She looked beautiful in her crochet knitted two piece beige dress that clung to her slim figure. After a brief musical intro, she started singing "Going Home," a haunting hymn arranged from a melody in Antonin Dvorak's Ninth Symphony.

Without warning Sam's eyes welled up and tears spilled out over her cheeks in uncontrollable streams. "Going home, going home, I'm just going home. Quiet-like, slip away, I'll be going home," Cheryl sang. The music flowed from her lips like a gentle breath of wind from Heaven's gates.

Soft tissues suddenly appeared among the mourners as they dried very wet eyes and cheeks. This very poignant and emotional hymn had been sung at Earl's funeral.

Sam hadn't come prepared for her response to the hymn. She accepted a Kleenex from the woman sitting next to her. She wept quietly and continually throughout the entire hymn. The woman gave her more Kleenexes. Sam found it startling that this beautiful hymn could transport her back so quickly to the darkest moment of her life.

The service ended with Pastor Carl's announcement that after the graveside service, lunch would be served in the basement of the church. The undertakers rolled the coffin to the side entrance; the family followed. Then everyone else filed out of the church to the sounds of more organ hymns. Ada and another woman were handing out sprigs of rosemary to everyone as they left the church; a sign of the resurrection.

Sam made her way to the church basement and reported for hostess duty. The committee ladies had outdone themselves. The luncheon buffet of ham sandwiches, salads, cheese trays and desserts was ready. The smell of freshly brewed coffee was wonderful and plastic glasses full of red punch were poured and ready for the kids. Sam helped herself to a cup of coffee and stood behind the serving table with her back to the wall. She noticed that when Ada came into the room, she briefly looked around. She spotted Sam, made eye contact, and then made a beeline straight to her.

Ada walked with a quickened pace and a sense of urgency in her stride. Something was on her mind and Sam knew she was about to hear it.

Ada only stood five feet tall, not much taller than an adolescent child. She was slightly hunched over, showing the first signs of osteoporosis. She had a pleasant face and short brown hair that was accented by her natural gray highlights.

Sam had to lean over as Ada began to speak. She whispered into her ear, "Detective, we need to talk." As she stood on her tiptoes, she said, "First it was Ellen and now poor Keith." Sam straightened up with a quizzical look on her face. Ada just stared at her. Then she looked around to be sure that no one else was within earshot. She looked up at Sam again and spoke in more determined tones. "Trust me. I know that something is not right but we can't talk here. If I call you for an appointment, would you come over to my house? I have my suspicions about Ellen's and Keith's deaths!"

Sam heard the desperation in her voice. Sam nodded and told her that would she accept her invitation. Ada smiled, turned, and left as suddenly as she had appeared. "I will call you!" she said as she walked away.

CHAPTER 4

After the church service, the women volunteers finished serving lunch at Keith's funeral. Sam was told by Helen Rupnow that they had plenty of help for clean-up and she was free to go. The funeral brought back many painful memories for Sam, so she felt a powerful need to be by herself. Since it was only 1:30 p.m., she decided to drive up to Devil's Lake to relax and gather her thoughts.

She went to her apartment and changed into comfortable clothes. She slipped into a pair of blue jeans and an oversized red polo shirt. She laced up her tennis shoes and locked the door behind her. She drove north to Madison and then to Highway 12, which took her to Baraboo. It was a beautiful day for her journey.

Devil's Lake State Park is located near Baraboo, Wisconsin, situated along the Ice Age Trail. When the early American settlers came into this territory, they discovered the beautiful lake. The Black Hawk Indians living there called it Spirit Lake, a rough translation for the pioneers who didn't speak the language. Those early settlers changed the name to Devil's Lake because they felt that it would attract more people. They rightly surmised that the name change would engender a curiosity about the place, and the small settlement thrived.

It was 3:30 p.m. when Sam drove into the park and parked her car. She selected one of the many trails that surrounded the lake. She hiked along it until she came to her favorite place that overlooked the lake. She perched herself on a flat rock about ten feet above the trail and gazed out over the calm lake.

As she sat silently, Sam reflected on Keith's funeral and her life. She had only been in Monroe for about a year. She left the Silver Bay Police

Department after an incident that could have ended her police career. After the move to Monroe, a church acquaintance told Sam if she wanted a place to get away and to be alone, the lake was a perfect spot. The woman was right. Sam had frequented the park many times.

As she now looked down at the hiking trails from her rocky perch, she didn't see much activity and enjoyed the quietude. The lake was glassy smooth, and some robins were prancing and dancing around on the trail beneath her. The longer she sat there, the more nature seemed to come alive. The trees swayed effortlessly back and forth in the breeze. She watched little creatures rushing about, going from bush to bush and up and down the trail; the air around her smelled fresh and sweet.

The wild flowers were showing off their magisterial beauty as they soaked up the sun. Other birds soon joined the robins. She watched a blue jay, two cardinals, and a gold finch circling around her. In the distance, she could hear the tap-tap-tap of a woodpecker. She noticed a yellow-throated Vireo perched on a nearby branch, looking at her. The bird didn't seem the least bit afraid. Sam felt like she could almost reach out and touch it. She felt very much in the moment. The sun felt warm on her face. It touched her with a sense of friendship and calm. The solitude was hypnotizing, and soon her thoughts drifted off to happier times.

After her undergraduate work was completed at the University of Wisconsin, Sam applied for and was accepted into the masters program in criminal justice. While in graduate school, she dated a couple of times, but she was more driven to complete her degree and abandoned any idea of close personal relationships. She discovered that hanging out with a group of friends was uncomplicated and fit into her lifestyle as a student. Her goal was to graduate with honors.

Sam had a part-time job with the campus police department during her studies, but she found the work mindless and not very challenging. She also felt a gender bias from her male coworkers and quickly learned that she had to be mentally tough to survive in a testosterone-driven job. The incessant flirting and crude remarks really got on her nerves. If she didn't need the money, well, that would have been that.

Then with one semester to go until graduation, one of her professors, Dr. Eric Nelson, told her about an internship in London, England. The program was for serious students focused on a career in law enforcement. The course consisted of observing police work at the Scotland Yard. It would be a semester course, finished off with a paper submitted on "Police Procedures and Techniques in the UK." He suggested that Sam apply for the internship. He offered to write a letter of recommendation for her from the University of Wisconsin. Sam felt pleased and honored that he would single her out and recommend her. She was very surprised when she was accepted into the program. She reasoned that her 4.0 grade point average probably played a part in the selection.

Sam arrived in London full of anticipation to start the program. She was housed in a quaint and charming hotel on Oxford Street and shared a small flat with another female intern from New York City. She fell in love with the city and its cobblestone streets and upscale specialty shops and outdoor cafes.

Sam was assigned to the homicide unit at Scotland Yard and reported to Chief Inspector Justin Piers, who immediately handed her over to a Sergeant Dan Oliver. Oliver was on the fast track in the department, being promoted to the rank of sergeant at a young age. In fact, he was only two years older than Sam.

Totally consuming herself with this opportunity of a lifetime, Sam arrived to work early and stayed late. To the chagrin of Oliver, she asked thousands of questions. Normally, interns just observed the inner workings of the police unit and fetched coffee or tea and sweets for the officers and then wrote a paper at the end of the semester. The interns were expected to remain quiet and not interfere with ongoing police cases. The interns were generally a pain in the ass for the police and were constantly underfoot, but it was politically expedient to humor them.

Sam couldn't wait to get to the office each day. Rain or shine, she was always early. She soon found herself following one case in particular, the murder of a police officer during a covert drug operation. Sam had quickly become friends with Oliver. After the morning briefings, she would get him a fresh cup of coffee and ask him endless questions about suspects and police procedures. He took all this personal attention in good humor. As they visited, he shared his personal opinions on how the investigation of the slain officer was going and how he would try to solve the case. This was another opportunity for Sam to learn how deductive reasoning was used at the investigative level.

Sam was also fascinated by British slang, a much different culture to what she experienced growing up in Wisconsin. Phrases like, "Do a runner," "Driving the porcelain bus," "Get one's knickers in a twist," "Dodgy," and

"Duck and dive," and other such words and phrases just added to the romance of a different culture with different values.

She also learned from Oliver that solving a case involved more intuition and common sense than by-the-book methods. Using one's imagination was vital to solving murders. Keeping a personal notebook and a flow chart of interviews with suspects, along with the details of the case, was absolutely required in order to see the whole canvas. That was the secret to solving crimes, according to Oliver; seeing the whole canvas. Sometimes your intuition took you into bizarre places, but these hunches needed to be eliminated to clear one's mind and stay focused.

She and Oliver spent so much time together that an affair seemed inevitable. They tried to be discreet, but everyone seemed to know about it. Even her roommate from New York was seeing somebody. Sam worried that Oliver's career could be in some sort of jeopardy, but he told her not to worry about it. Anyway, all his chums were jealous and that was fine with him. Nevertheless, the everyday work schedule and nightly romance was like a fairytale. After Sam's return to the United States, she and Oliver stayed in touch for a while, but their long-distance relationship faded and they both got on with their lives.

Suddenly, Sam became aware of voices coming up one of the trails. It was a father and his little girl. Sam pegged the child to be three or four years old. They were holding hands and her long blonde hair swayed back and forth on her forehead as she skipped along bouncing and singing. The little tike was very entertaining to the great delight and pleasure of her dad. He was smiling and laughing. When he spotted Sam, he waved a friendly greeting and Sam waved back. The one thing she liked about the lake setting was that people were friendlier and took the time to wave to one another. When the little girl spotted Sam, she grinned and blew her a kiss. They all laughed.

As Sam watched them disappear down the trail, her thoughts turned to her dad. How many times had he taken her on walks in parks along Lake Michigan when she was a child? His hand seemed so warm, big, and gentle compared to her tiny hand. Sam felt very safe and secure when her hand was safely tucked away into his. But now, she felt a great sadness in her heart.

The abrupt and untimely death of Earl had unnerved everyone in her family. Her mother was a wreck and Phil had retreated into an Aladdin's lamp of lost hope. All of Earl's future plans, dreams, and desires were wiped out in a split second as the deadly shots rang out that fateful night. For sixteen years, she had known his love; then death took it all away. He was buried in his dress uniform. He would have liked that. But the question that haunted Sam was "Where is the justice when good people die violently?"

As she sat alone on the rock staring at the lake, Sam thought about what the future held for her? What genes and character traits that Earl had passed on to her would shape her personality and future? She was very aware that she was intensely driven to follow in her dad's footsteps in police work and to make him proud of her.

Pastor James had counseled her on the meaning of death in a religious sense, and she accepted this and was able to move on with her life. But she also had unfinished business. She felt an intense desire to find Earl's killers and bring them to justice. She didn't view this resolve as revenge but to right a wrong and to bring closure to his death. This sense of justice had given her the passion to pursue police work, and she knew that she would never rest until justice was served, no matter how long it took.

During the time she spent with Oliver in London, he had sensed a certain kinship with her in the pursuit of justice. He also saw a certain tension about her, but Sam remained quiet when he questioned her about it. He respected her privacy and didn't press her. He did however leave the door open if Sam ever wanted to talk about it.

As she sat and pondered on that cold hard rock, Sam could see that her life was slowly slipping away. The years were passing her by as she worked long hours to protect herself from the loneliness that she felt. She lamented that she didn't have anyone to share her joys and disappointments with. She didn't have a love life. All she had was her job, her mother who was slowly wasting away, and a passion to find justice for her father. Was her life just slowly creeping along some endless path? Was she walking in the shadows waiting for her life's candle to slowly die out? The beautiful day turned gloomy and she suddenly felt depressed. Sam got up and made her way back to her car. Maybe her visit with Ada would get her mind off the past.

CHAPTER 5

Monroe Police Chief Brandon Johns waited patiently in the foyer outside the law office of Roger Nussbaum. Nussbaum volunteered his time to the city as the chairman of the Police and Fire Commission. Johns was summoned to a brief meeting with him at 10:00 a.m. The law offices of Nussbaum, Beck, Webster, and Thoman LLC were located on the east side of the square facing the courthouse. The secretary at the front desk confirmed his appointment upon his arrival and offered him a cup of coffee. He declined. Johns found a comfortable chair and settled himself into the soft leather.

As he waited, he heard the striking of the bells from the courthouse bell tower. It rang out ten times. In the early days of Monroe, the sound of the bells announced both the start and end of the work day. In its day, the clock was set to railroad time to insure accuracy. Johns counted the ten strikes to amuse himself, as if to say that he was on time. Nussbaum was never on time and he took some pleasure in having other people wait for him. The meeting that day particularly irritated Johns because he had a busy schedule and Nussbaum didn't respect that. It seemed to Johns that whenever he was summoned by Nussbaum, his own work schedule flew out the window.

Nussbaum was appointed to the Police and Fire Commission fifteen years ago by the mayor of Monroe. He quickly got himself elected chairman and held that honor over the subsequent years. If he hadn't been a lawyer, he probably would have been a career politician. He loved the public arena, and he often had his picture in the Monroe Press for one thing or another. Being a member of the Wisconsin Bar Association, he cast his net north to Madison and tried to be on any law enforcement committee he could find that was appointed by the governor. Being close to the governor and the political power base in Madison gave him a huge adrenaline rush.

When the former police chief retired and moved away from Monroe six years ago, Nussbaum orchestrated the appointment of Johns to the position. Johns was a lifelong resident of the city and was a detective within the police department. Other officers applied for the position, but Nussbaum was looking for a chief that would easily identify with the younger officers and forge the future of the department under Nussbaum's direction. He used his political acumen and charm to persuade the Police and Fire Commission members to vote for his choice after the usual candidate searches and interviews had ended. After the appointment, Nussbaum made it clear to Johns that he owed him his loyalty as the new police chief. Johns saw through this charade and threat and often wondered how he would handle it if he crossed the boss.

Johns shifted his weight in the chair and felt the pressure on his beltline. He had gained some twenty pounds over the past couple of years due mainly to the stress of the job. Every year, more and more paperwork was required of his department from both the state and federal governments. He hated paperwork.

The latest irritation came from the governor. He wanted more community-friendly policing where the cops were supposed to be best friends with all the citizen voters. Nussbaum quickly endorsed this idea, to the chagrin of the police department. Keeping nine uniformed police officers in line to be everyone's best friend was laughable at best and ran counterculture to the department. The officers were out policing to catch the bad guys and to keep the community safe, not to win popularity contests. Currently, any citizen complaint about a police officer was treated as a major crisis within the department and took valuable time and resources to resolve. Johns had to become a politician himself in order to reassure and satisfy the mayor and the aldermen and the Police and Fire Commission. He told them that all was well within his department. If he found cause for any complaint, he personally would take care of any disciplinary action that was warranted.

At the urging of his wife, Johns gave up smoking three months ago. He was able to do it, but the price he paid was found in his waistline. Another belt loop lost! He went from a size 38 pants to a size 40. He had become a junk food addict. Sitting in that soft, cushioned, leather chair in his tight pants was getting very uncomfortable.

Johns looked at his watch and decided that he needed to reschedule his appointment with Nussbaum. It took him two tries before he could get out of his chair. He went up to the secretary/receptionist at the front desk and stared at her as she typed her heart out. She looked up at him.

"If Mr. Nussbaum is too busy to see me today, maybe I should make another appointment," he said. "It's already 10:45 and I have phone calls to make and an appointment at noon. I am the speaker at Kiwanis today. Since this is the only Thursday I have available on my calendar for the next two weeks, I can't be late."

Just as she reached for the phone, Nussbaum burst out of his office.

"Hello Chief!" he bellowed. "Good to see you. I hope you haven't been waiting long."

Johns winched a little and then he subconsciously rolled his blue eyes ever so slightly. "Not at all Mr Nussbaum, I was just telling your receptionist about my noon appointment at Kiwanis."

Nussbaum smiled broadly at him. "Come on in and sit down. I just got off the phone with the governor's office. Alice, would you be so kind to get the chief and me a fresh cup of coffee." She pushed herself away from her desk and got up rather rudely and disappeared down the hallway.

Johns felt Nussbaum's hand on his back as he guided him to his office and into another soft leather button backed chair. Johns sat down and felt a slight twinge in his back from already sitting too long. Nussbaum's office was the only one in the building that had a nice view of the square. Johns glanced out the window and saw people walking down the sidewalk. He sighed as Nussbaum closed the door.

"I have some great news and I needed to share it with you today," he said as he walked back to his dark mahogany desk. Behind him were rows of law books lined up on expensive cherry bookcases.

His desk looked massive and impressive against his five foot eight and three quarters height. It was all the further he got in life he explained, and would then laugh at his own joke. Johns never found this funny.

Nussbaum liked looking down on clients and visitors whenever possible as he was doing now at Johns. Even his desk chair was slightly higher than the visitor chairs that were strategically positioned in the front of his desk. This little ruse gave him a subtle height advantage over his clients.

"And by the way don't worry about the Kiwanis meeting," Nussbaum said. "I called Tim Martin and told him something urgent had popped up and he needed to excuse you today and I said to reschedule you for another time. I hope you don't mind?"—"

"No, sir," said Johns weakly. He felt his face get warm and flushed.

There was a soft knock at the door, and Alice entered carrying two cups of fresh steaming coffee on a tray. Nussbaum stood up as she handed each of them a cup and then she hastily retreated.

Nussbaum sat down at his desk and looked at a picture of himself and a smiling governor Bartholf standing together on the state capital steps. The picture was angled in such a manner that visitors could see it. A picture of his wife and kids was next to the governor. He took a sip of the black coffee and set the cup down. He paused and then spoke to Johns as if he was about to give the speech of his life.

"The reason I called you here this morning was to inform you that the governor is going to take a hard stance on violent crime in the state of Wisconsin this year and plans to use this as a platform for his re-election campaign. To show the voters that he is serious about crime, he is creating a blue ribbon commission of twelve members to lead the charge. He wants the committee to study the problem and to come up with recommendations. He wants to tell the voters that if he is re-elected he has a plan to reduce crime by ten percent."

He stopped talking and took a sip of coffee and waited. Johns didn't know what to say so he remained quiet.

"The chairman of this new committee will have excellent media exposure across the state, including television, radio, and newspaper coverage. The governor wants this to be very high profile stuff and wants committee progress reported in the press and on the local nightly news. In other words, both the governor and the committee chair will become familiar household names and faces as they rail against crime. Isn't this a great opportunity for me?"

Johns started to say something, but Nussbaum was hitting his stride and raised his hand to cut him off. "The governor is picking his team from cities with populations of over eight thousand people with proven track records of low crime statistics. Our statistics here in Monroe have been below the national and state average for the past fifteen years. Violent crime in Monroe is almost nonexistent, and we haven't had a murder since Joyce, what's her name, shot her husband twenty years ago claiming he was a burglar." Nussbaum paused and laughed at his own little joke. "Thought he was a burglar, ha-ha-ha. That woman had no imagination!!" He hooted again. "And, I have it on good authority that the governor has chosen me to be on the committee. And more importantly, the governor is looking at either me or a lawyer from the Wisconsin Dells to chair the committee." Nussbaum shifted his weight in his chair as sipped his coffee. "I want to chair that committee!" he suddenly exploded.

The volume of his voice made Johns jump, spilling some of the black liquid on his pants.

"I will do a damn fine job. The governor will be proud of me, and who knows what the future could bring me after that. It would be good for me and the city of Monroe. It would put us on the map, a robust boon to the community, and the chamber of commerce would love that!" Nussbaum was pumped up and talking very fast and gasping for breath. Johns smiled at the grandiose figure sitting in front of him. "I am going to make my pitch to the governor for the chairmanship and that's why I called you in."

Johns sat up in his chair. "What's on your mind?" he asked.

Suddenly there was a sound of a soft knock on the closed door. Alice stuck her head in and announced that a Mr. Aleksandrowicz was waiting and was about to leave if he didn't have a word with Nussbaum right away. "Damn, I forgot about him," Nussbaum said. "Johns, I will be back to you shortly, don't leave!"

Johns watched him as he quickly made his way to the door and disappeared. As he glanced around the room, he could smell a whiff of stale cigarette smoke. He then looked at the picture of Nussbaum's family and shook his head. The police know many things about the prominent citizens of their community and Nussbaum was no exception. Johns knew that he swigged bourbon in the middle of his working day; he knew that he cheated on his wife; he knew that he only loved himself; and he knew that Nussbaum was working and stressing himself into a coronary.

Just as suddenly as he left, Nussbaum returned and began speaking as if he had never left the room. "I have been touting our low crime statistics during several meetings in Madison over the past year, telling everyone that we are hard on crime in Monroe and that we have excellent closure rates. But I have one nagging thought in the back of my mind. Remember when Ada Klausner wrote us letters last year and made a public nuisance of herself over the death her friend, Ellen Johnson? She had wild ideas and she thought the death was suspicious. But as you recall, Ellen's family doctor, Dr. Gehringer, signed the death certificate as heart failure."

"I remember," Johns said. "Ellen had a history of heart problems, and the doctor said that he was convinced that she had died from heart failure and it was nonsense to think otherwise."

Nussbaum stared at the picture of the governor and himself again and said, "Do you think Ada was satisfied with this explanation?"

"I doubt it," answered Johns. "You know perfectly well that when Ada makes up her mind about something, she usually sticks to her opinions. And she is a woman to be reckoned with if she feels strongly about something. And the death of her best friend would do it."

Johns paused and looked up at the ceiling. His memory quickly flashed back years ago when Ada threatened a lawsuit if she wasn't admitted to the Monroe Gun Club. Nussbaum was the club's president at the time, and he and Ada had many spirited discussions about the sanctity of a men's only club. She became very outspoken to any one who would listen to her and wrote letters to the paper.

After one heated exchange with Nussbaum, she devised a plan. She would storm the men's locker room and give those overweight, pompous men with their chauvinistic attitudes a severe shock. So, one very warm evening after a rigorous day of shooting competition at the club, she sneaked into the men's locker room and hid. At the appropriate time, she dashed out, bare-chested, into the center of a room full of naked men, screaming at the top of her lungs and pointing to her breasts, "Size doesn't matter, size doesn't matter!"

Chaos and mayhem followed immediately as the men dived for cover, grasping wildly for towels or anything else within reach. The adjectives from the startled men were loud and descriptive. She leaned over backwards and laughed out loud at them and then raced to the nearest exit and disappeared.

After she left the locker room, Green County Judge Myron Dietmeier stood tall with a towel around his waist and a frown on his face. He walked up to Nussbaum and told him to not even think about pressing charges. He didn't want to hear about this incident in his courtroom! Nussbaum was no fool. He knew he was beaten and surrendered. The next day he sent Ada a letter welcoming her to join the gun club.

However, his ultimate humiliation occurred when she beat him in the pistol shooting competition and took the trophy home. He had previously won the competition three years in a row. But shortly after her victory, Ada resigned her membership in a letter stating excessive drinking, boredom, and bad language in the club. Nussbaum never forgave her. But, the thought of it all made Johns smile.

Suddenly, Johns was aware of Nussbaum staring at him. "Look, Johns, I don't want that woman messing up my chances for this appointment. Do you understand what I mean? We all know she is a little daft, and we all know that Ellen Johnson died from natural causes. I know I can count on you to keep her in line. Understood?"

Johns didn't say anything. He just nodded. *Why was he worried about Ada anyway?* he asked himself.

Nussbaum got up from his chair and wandered over to the window and looked out onto the square. He seemed to be lost in thought for a moment and then turned back to Johns. "Just one more thing," he said. "How is Detective Gates working out? I know I sort of thrust her into your department, but as you know, it was a favor for a friend of mine in Madison."

Johns shifted once again in his chair. He was feeling very uncomfortable. *What was he after?* he thought. "Sam is doing okay," he said. "The officers have welcomed her, more or less. As you recall, they were a little upset at first about her being the first and only female detective in the department, but those feelings have softened somewhat once they realized that she had the right stuff to do the job."

"Anything else I should know?" Nussbaum asked.

"I think she is a little bored. She worked a couple of homicide cases for the Silver Bay PD before she came to us, and that seems to be her main interest and passion, given what happened to her father."

"Can we trust her?" Nussbaum asked.

"Yes, I think we can." Johns paused. No comment from Nussbaum. "Right now, we have a problem with some kids stealing license plates and Sam is working on that."

Nussbaum relaxed and smiled. Just the kind of crime he liked; small town stuff with no real consequences. "Okay," he said. "Keep me posted on her activities. She has a bit of a reputation of going her own way if she gets interested in something. I just don't want anyone rocking the boat here in Monroe."

And that was that. Nussbaum dismissed him with the wave of a hand. Johns got up and Nussbaum walked him to the door. "I know I can count on you, Brandon," he said in a condescending way as Johns left his office. He felt much relieved to be out of Nussbaum's office, but at the same time, he felt a little bewildered. *"Why this sudden interest in Ada, and why should it matter?"*

CHAPTER 6

The Monroe Police Department consisted of a chief of police, a captain, a detective, and nine uniformed officers. The officers worked three rotating shifts, giving the city twenty-four-hour police protection, seven days a week. At the moment, they were short-handed because the captain injured himself chasing a juvenile over a fence. The officers found plenty of humor in his plight and unmercifully teased him about it. All their desks were crammed together in a small room, except for the chief. He had his own office.

Sam sat at her desk looking over some paperwork. She was alone in the room and lost in her thoughts. In her right hand, she held a couple of stick pins. Her desk was located in a large room with several other desks closely packed together. No privacy there. A gold-framed picture of her parents sat facing her on her desk. In the picture, her dad was standing tall in his dress police uniform with her mother seated next to him. Looking at this picture of Earl during happier times gave her some comfort even after the most trying of days. She thought he looked quite handsome in his uniform.

She got up from her chair and went to a street map that she had borrowed from the city engineer's office. It was hanging on the wall next to her desk. She studied the map for a moment and then pushed in two yellow stick pins identifying the locations of the latest license plate heists. "Kids," she muttered to herself. "I will hunt you hardened criminals down and prosecute to the full extent of the law!" Then she laughed at herself and out loud. She quickly looked around, but no one else was in the room.

Since coming to Monroe, she had found it to be a great city with many friendly people. She especially liked to take short walks around the downtown square to look at the majestic Romanesque Courthouse and the old arcane buildings that were long on history. She was grateful for a second chance here, but she also knew that if things worked out, she would be moving on some day. She hoped to land a job in a bigger city in the Midwest.

She stared at the stick pins on the map and found them all clustered around a three block radius of the square. "Well, the pattern is certainly there. We just haven't been able to catch them," she said to herself. She returned to her desk, picked up a legal pad, and began working on a plea-for-help article that the Monroe Press had agreed to print. She was asking the community for any information that they might have to come forward and identify the culprits.

The phone on her desk suddenly rang and made her jump. The dispatcher informed her that Pastor Carl was on the line and wanted to know if she wanted to take the call.

"Hello, Pastor Carl," she said, "what can I do for you today?"

There was a slight hesitation on the line, and then the pastor spoke in a voice just above a whisper, "Thank you for taking my call, Samantha. I was just wondering if you could stop by the church parsonage at your convenience to see me. I have a somewhat, well you know, a personal matter that I would like to discuss with you."

"Has something happened that needs investigating?" she asked.

"Oh no, nothing like that," he quickly responded. "I just need to seek your advice on something in confidence. I thought that you would be the best person I could contact."

After squinting her eyes and wrinkling her nose, Sam quickly thought about the rest of her day's activities. "Would you like to meet today?" she asked. "I could come by to see you at three this afternoon. Should I meet you at the church or the parsonage?"

"Please come to the parsonage," the pastor said, "and thanks again for seeing me."

She hung up the phone. Sam looked at the picture of her dad and thought, *You were spot on about this part of the job. It is all about helping your fellow man.*

Sam went back to composing her article. She heard Chief Johns's loud voice coming from the hallway that led to the front door of the station. He was escorting a visitor out. Then she heard his footsteps on the linoleum floor as he made his way back to the briefing room. He entered the multipurpose room and walked over to Sam's desk.

"Sam, why don't you come to my office and fill me in on what you have been doing to catch the license plate thieves? I need a break. And since you are the only one here to bother . . ." He didn't finish his sentence. Sam grinned at him, got up, and followed him back to his office.

In Sam's opinion, the chief's office was too small and claustrophobic. From the initial impression of his hovel, he seemed a haphazard administrator. His office looked like a landfill full of papers, books, receipts, newspapers, keys, pens, pencils, coins, umbrellas, file folders, and used Styrofoam coffee cups. The floor had narrow paths in order to navigate to his desk. He had a picture of his wife and two children on the top of a bookcase behind his desk.

Sam saw that there were only two chairs in the office that faced the chief's desk. One of them was stacked with papers and the other one was sort of presentable, being that it was cleared of obstructions. She stepped over a garbage bag filled with who-knows-what and made her way to the empty seat. She heard an object go crunch under her foot as she advanced. She thought it sounded like something plastic. She sat down.

"Sorry about the mess," was the chief's predictable opening line that had become an inside joke at the department. First impressions are everything, so anyone who ventured into this hovel of an office knew immediately that the chief was not a neat freak. But, amazingly, he could lay his hands on any folder, file, or scrap of paper he needed.

As the chief settled back into his black leather chair, he smiled at Sam and asked, "So how are you doing on the license plate mystery?"

Sam told him about the city map and the stick pins that located where the thefts had occurred. She had identified the target area around the square. She went on to say that she had requested extra patrol passes in the area from the second shift officers. But the plates continued to go missing anyway. The kids seemed to know where the police cars were at all times, and it had turned into a cat-and-mouse game for them.

The aggrieved complaining citizens, who only lost their front plates, were basically good natured about it all, but they all wanted their plates back. Then she told the chief about contacting the newspaper and her plea-for-help article.

"Well done, Sam," Johns said. "After your article hits the streets, you should get a phone call or two identifying the culprits. I would guess they would range in ages twelve to fifteen. And once you solve the case, I suspect that you will find those missing plates hanging in some kid's bedroom like prized trophies. Of course, their parents will be totally amazed, shocked, and astounded. Not to mention the guilty looks on their faces." He laughed after he said it. "For the most part, the folks who live around here like helping the police whenever possible, and your article should do the trick."

Sam looked over the chief's shoulder at his closed Venetian blind. She saw dust everywhere. After he confronted the cleaning lady about moving some of his stuff, she avoided his room like the plague and it showed. He tried to apologize to her but the damage had already been done. He was reminded by the other officers that you don't treat the cleaning lady like a suspect. "Remember, she only vacuums in straight lines!"

Johns had a window behind his desk that looked out onto the street, but in the year that she had been there, Sam had never seen the blinds or the window open. *Dark and dusty*, she thought. No wonder he never spent much time in his office.

"How was Keith's funeral?" he asked.

Sam turned her attention back to the chief. "Pastor Carl did his usual good job and had a very fine service. Like every good pastor, he could make us laugh and cry. As always, the music was especially moving and beautiful." She skipped over the part about her teary-eyed moment.

"After the service I helped to serve lunch. An interesting thing happened though. Ada Klausner approached me when I was standing behind the serving tables and whispered something about wanting me to stop by her house. She wanted to discuss the death of Ellen Johnson and her suspicions about Keith's death as well."

Johns suddenly sat up in his chair. "What did you tell her?"

"I told her that I would stop by next week. Was that okay?" she asked. Sam felt uneasy and a little concerned by the chief's sudden change in demeanor. Johns could see that he startled her and settled back into his chair.

"Do you know anything about Ellen's tragic death?" he asked.

"No, not really, but I have heard that Ada has a reputation and is quite the character."

Johns thought for a moment and then said, "Let me fill you in. I have been following Ada's adventures for a very long time. You wouldn't believe the complaints and gossip about her that has come into my office."

He leaned forward putting his elbows on his desk and folded his hands together, making a steeple with his index fingers. He looked at Sam and began. "Ada and Ellen had known one another since childhood. They grew up together and were more like sisters than friends. After high school, they went on to the University of Wisconsin in Platteville. They both graduated with teaching degrees. Ada moved back to Monroe and taught English in the public school system until she retired. She could be a very outspoken and abrasive woman who never pretended to hide her personal opinions about stuff. She had a reputation, but she didn't seem to mind." Sam was listening intently.

"When she turned thirty-one, a very bizarre event occurred that was both humorous and sad at the same time. Ada decided that she needed a husband and jumped into bed with a Norwegian bachelor farmer named Ned Anderson. Ned and his three brothers farmed north of Monroe with their parents. Why she picked Ned to marry was a mystery. He had an agricultural degree from the UW, and some speculated that his education had been a major influence on her decision. It was also rumored that his family had money, but they all claimed to be farmer poor, if you know what I mean. Ned was easily recognized around town for his big honker nose and premature gray hair; a family trait. He also had a reputation of eating like a high-powered Hoover vacuum cleaner."

Sam snorted and laughed!

"Well anyway, they started dating and somehow she talked him into marrying her on her thirty-second birthday. Some folks said that the date would be tied to both her birthday and her wedding anniversary for Ned's sake.

The same age as me, Sam thought.

"As things turned out, they had a very stormy courtship that became the talk of the town. Ned was receiving a lot of sympathy and advice from his friends, but it seemed he couldn't say no to her. Ada made all the wedding arrangements and invited the entire city to the First Christian Church for their special day. All that was required of Ned was to show up in his rented suit."

Johns paused and saw the look on Sam's face. "Yes, you guessed it. Somehow, Ned got up the courage and left Monroe the morning of his wedding, leaving Ada standing at the church in her mother's white wedding dress. Needless to say, she was furious and humiliated. She filed a lawsuit against Ned for breach of promise that the county judge dismissed out of hand. She never married after that humiliation." Johns paused to let his narrative sink in for a moment. Sam remained silent and just sat in her chair listening to him.

"Okay, back to Ellen then. At the end of her senior year at college, she got pregnant. Being an immature party girl, she desperately wanted to abort the child. But through family intervention, it was decided that her twin sister,

Marge Denton, would adopt the boy and raise him. Ada wholeheartedly supported this plan and Ellen agreed. After the birth, Ellen moved to Chicago and continued her party life of men and booze. She desperately longed for love, but her drinking got in the way, and she continually confused sex and love. For fifteen years, she abandoned her family in Monroe. Her only contact was Ada. She took absolutely no interest in her son.

"Then one day, Ada got a call from a social worker in Chicago. She explained that Ellen was in jail on a variety of charges and needed help. Ada rushed to her rescue, paid off her debts, and offered her a room in her house. Ellen came back to Monroe and went into counseling. She had a tough go of it as she tried to straighten her life out. She fell off the wagon a few times and seemed to have contentment one day, then suddenly she was consumed by rage and madness the next. These personality swings drove Ada crazy. However, she hung in there with her until she was cured and sober.

"Nelson's Real Estate Company gave Ellen a chance by hiring her as a secretary/receptionist. They must have felt sorry for her and also hung in there with her until she eventually kicked the alcohol out of her life.

"She repeatedly tried to make amends with her family and her son, Gregory. But things were difficult, especially with Gregory, who would have nothing to do with her."

Sam stirred in her chair as Johns continued.

"Ada had a strong constitution and was always in excellent health. Ellen, on the other hand, was born into a family that had hereditary heart problems. Both of Ellen's parents died from heart attacks in their sixties. And as Ellen grew older, she had two mild heart attacks in her sixties."

Sam felt the muscles in her long legs cramping up a little. She stood up and stretched and then sat down again.

Johns continued, "Then, a little over a year ago, Ellen died. She was alone in her house at the time. She died while sitting in an overstuffed high back chair, watching television.

Her family doctor signed the death certificate as "heart failure." Ada went nuts. She claimed that she had left Ellen at 6:30 p.m. that same evening for a school board meeting, and according to her, Ellen was in good spirits and doing fine. Ada insisted on a second opinion as to the cause of death. She couldn't and wouldn't believe that the death was from "natural" causes. She wrote scathing letters to the mayor, to me, to the Police and Fire Commission, and to the county coroner. We interviewed Dr. Gehringer, and he stated that it was a waste of time and money to do an autopsy given Ellen's documented history of heart problems. And besides, Ada had no legal status to back her request.

"She appealed to Gregory to authorize the autopsy, but he refused. He said he was satisfied with Dr. Gehringer's opinion."

"I wrote her a letter to that effect, which she sent back to me, and I won't go into the graphic detail of her comments. She still hasn't gotten over Ellen's death and she is still brooding over it."

As Johns was filling her in, Sam's mind kept asking the question, *Why was the chief giving her all this information?* For some reason, he probably thought it was important. Having no history with Ada and her odd behavior, maybe he was giving her a heads-up as to what to expect when they met.

Johns stopped his monologue and looked at Sam. "So, there you have it. Do you have any questions?" Yes, she had a question, but let it pass. "If anything of interest comes up during your meeting, please let me know so we can discuss it," he said. Sam nodded and said she would.

"Anything else happening, Sam?" Johns asked.

"Pastor Carl called and wants me to stop by to see him about a personal matter. I have the time, so I told him I would see him this afternoon."

"Just one more thing before you leave," Johns said. "We need to deliver some court records and other documents to Milwaukee tomorrow, and I was wondering if you could do it. The documents need to be dropped off at a police station in Milwaukee. I know today is Friday and you probably have weekend plans, but I am in a jam. We are short-handed because two of our officers are sick, and no one else wants to make the trip. You can take an unmarked vehicle. How about it? Will you do it?"

"You mean I can't take a panda car?" Sam said with a wry smile. Johns grinned back at her.

"I was going to Silver Bay this weekend to visit my mother. If you don't mind, could I stop to see her on the way back?" Sam asked.

"No problem. The packet of papers and the address for delivery will be at the front desk in the morning. And thanks again."

Sam stood up, stepped over the piles of papers on the floor and left. As she disappeared down the hallway, Johns followed her with his eyes and wondered how her visit with Ada would go. He also wondered how she would react if any of Ada's accusations and doubts interested her. Chasing down kids for stealing license plates is one thing, but the slightest whiff of a possible suspicious death was something else entirely.

CHAPTER 7

Pastor Carl sat in the living room of the church parsonage waiting for Sam. The two-story, three-bedroom brick home was located at the rear of the church property that featured a small flower garden plot located in the back yard. He had already ground fresh coffee beans and put on the coffee pot to perk. He found some chocolate chip cookies that Mary Tollakson had given him. He had arranged them on a plate that now sat on the coffee table in front of him.

In the refrigerator was a tray of Green County cheeses. The local custom of serving various cheeses to visitors dated back to the early immigrants of Monroe as their way of welcoming guests into their homes. He had a selection of aged Cheddar, Colby, Monterey Jack, and Baby Swiss.

The living room was arranged with a sofa and three comfortable chairs facing the coffee table. It was a practical and friendly conversational arrangement for impromptu church meetings or just entertaining guests. A picture of his wife and two girls was prominently placed on a desk along the west wall of the room. The wood floors and floral wallpaper gave the room a formal appearance. As he waited, Pastor Carl was thinking about how to approach Sam with his unsettling thoughts.

A few days after Keith's funeral, Keith's son, Brad, came to visit him at the church. Pastor Carl was surprised to see him. He hadn't seen him for long time, that is, until he started making the arrangements for the funeral. Keith and Stacy seldom attended church. After his confirmation, Brad was seldom seen at church again. He was now a senior at Monroe High School and had been accepted at the University of Wisconsin in Madison for the fall semester.

The visit with Brad was a painful one, centered on Brad's grief and the sudden loss of his dad. He told Pastor Carl that he felt guilty about not knowing his father better. He had put his own friends ahead of his family. He talked about a fishing trip that Keith had planned for just the two of them to Canada, but he got a better offer from some friends and blew off the trip. He talked about being busted for under-age drinking and how his dad handled it. The more he talked about Keith, Pastor Carl saw the deep pain and anguish in the boy's heart.

Brad was grieving the fact that he had taken his dad for granted and never told him how much he loved him. He just knew and believed that Keith would always come home from work every day, walk through the front door, and sing out to the family that he was home. Now the front door was closed and silent and the silence was haunting. Brad was left with unfinished business. He was longing for his dad's outstretched hand, a word of praise or just an embrace; anything to affirm the love between them.

The other thing that he shared with Pastor Carl was how very little he knew about his dad. He always thought that Keith would be there for him. But now he and his mom were all alone. He said he felt like the little boy who would wait by the front door for his daddy to come home. Tears exploded from his red eyes when he confessed his grief to Pastor Carl.

Brad also wondered what Keith's thoughts and feelings were about life and family and other stuff? Brad knew that Keith was a hard worker and enjoyed his job at the brewery. He knew that Keith loved him and his mother, but he seldom said the words. He also knew that Keith was very proud of him going to college. College was a far and distant dream of Keith's. Brad would be the first college man in the family. He knew that Keith worried about the cost of him going to college, but they never sat down and talked about any of this.

Brad wanted to know what it was like growing up with Grandpa Nils, but again, he never asked. He had questions that would go unanswered forever. That's what sudden death does to families—unanswered questions, the guilt of not saying good-bye and not asking for forgiveness for past transgressions. And now that Keith had died so young, what would Brad's remembrances be? What would he tell his future wife about his dad and what would he tell his future children about their grandfather?

Pastor Carl felt Brad's pain in his own heart. He assured Brad that his feelings were genuine and real and showed the love he had for his dad. Pastor Carl hoped that his words were comforting to Brad; he referenced several Bible verses and passages for him. After their meeting, Brad promised to come back to see him again. It was the last time he saw Brad in church. *Why?* he asked himself.

As he reflected on his words to Brad, Pastor Carl began thinking about his wife, Susan. His conversation with Brad had brought back painful memories for him as well. He and Susan were married twenty-eight years before she died from a brain aneurysm last year. As he sat and pondered, he recalled the day of her death as if it had happened yesterday.

It was a day like any other. They had finished dinner and cleaned up the kitchen together, washing and drying the dishes. Susan then went into the living room and picked up the phone. Pastor Carl got on a second phone as she called their daughters. Both Rachel and Beth lived in California. Rachel and her husband, Bill, lived in San Francisco with grandson Jake, and Beth lived the single life in San Diego. As usual, Susan did most of the talking while he listened in.

She called Rachel first, who was expecting her second child and was making plans for the glorious event. After a rather lengthy call, she hung up and then called Beth. Beth was a social worker for the State of California. She loved the West Coast and managed to scrape by financially. She always joked that she was paid in sunshine and not in living wages. Talking to the girls always lifted Susan's spirits.

After the calls, as they were getting ready for bed, Pastor Carl took a phone call of his own. One of his church parishioners had been rushed to the hospital. He quickly changed into his proper pastor attire and kissed Susan good-bye. "See you soon," he shouted as he flew out the door.

When he returned three hours later, he found Susan snuggled in their bed with her head on the pillow. She looked as if she was sleeping. In the dim light, he called to her to see if she was awake. No sound came from her lips. He couldn't hear the soft breathing rhythms of her slumber as he gingerly made his way into bed. He reached over and touched her arm as it lay on top of the covers. It was cool to his touch!

The coolness of her arm sucked the breath out of him. "Oh my God!" he shouted. His mind froze up. He just stared at her. He couldn't move. She looked so alive and natural as her head rested on her pillow. She looked calm and beautiful. He couldn't take his eyes off her. He finally managed to get up and stood over her as if he was suspended in surreal time.

Then his senses started to kick in. The contented and peaceful look on her face, as she laid so still forever emblazoned itself into his memory. It wasn't a death mask. It was the face of someone sleeping. Her lips lacked the breath to tell him that she loved him. Only later did the county coroner tell him that she had died in her sleep and that she felt no pain.

After the funeral, the girls reluctantly left for the West Coast, promising to keep in touch. But as time passed, Pastor Carl's family, friends, and parishioners seemed to slowly fade from his life. The visits from the Monroe folks became less and less frequent, and the routine of ordinary life settled in once again. The sadness and pain in his heart remained as the days turned into weeks and months, and he missed her more than he could have ever imagined.

Susan was buried at the Green Lawn Cemetery in Monroe. Once a month, he would faithfully take fresh cut flowers to her grave and read the inscription on her tombstone, "Susan Peterson, Loved by all who knew her and too well loved to ever be forgotten."

During those visits, he would sit on the grass with blue skies above. Sitting beside her grave, he reminisced about their life together. He thought about the flowers that she cared for and loved; and now she lay under the earth with the colorful flowers above. She was a beautiful woman and would be forever young. Sometimes he could hear the ringing of the clock tower chimes from the square so clearly that they seemed to be calling to him. He would watch as the Monarch butterflies landed on the flowers with their different destinies. The one would fly away and the other would stay.

Sitting there among the other tombstones made him sad. Some of the names etched on the granite were familiar to him. The pull of a small town is found in a cemetery with the names of family and friends; a cemetery of relations.

Some of the graves were maintained and manicured with roses and different varieties of hostas that where planted immediately in front of the gravestones. Some of the graves showed neglect, and the weeds told the story that some of the sleepers were forgotten. *What a terrible thing to happen to someone,* he mused, *to be forgotten and erased from memory.* Pastor Carl vowed to never forget his beloved Susan. Sometimes his throat would choke up as his grief tried to smother him.

As he made the pilgrimages to the cemetery, he reflected on their life together. He slowly began to realize how little he really knew about his wife as a person. *"How well did I really know her?"* was the question that started to plague him. He took it for granted that she would always be there for him, a good minister's wife. She never complained. She took charge of the house and raised the two girls. She was very helpful around the church and prided herself on her colorful flower garden at the parsonage, which she showcased to the community without being boastful. Susan once told him that human relationships required weeding and pruning and cultivating, just like her flower garden.

But his reality was one of service and duty to the church. He was constantly attending to the needs of his flock. That consumed much of his time, and he spent many hours away from home. He was on call 24/7, and his parishioners loved him for that. If any of them had a problem, they could always count on Pastor Carl. *But what about Susan and her needs?* he asked himself. He couldn't recall a single time when she asked him for help. If he was perfectly honest with himself, he didn't know her at all. He had a hard time recalling special occasions like birthdays and anniversaries. Was he so entrenched in his work at the church that anything Susan planned went unnoticed? A strange thing to admit after twenty-eight years of marriage, but this revelation had him perplexed. Was he so self-centered and focused on his needs and the needs of others that he had abandoned his own family? Even now, he didn't feel particularly close to the girls and little Jake and the baby.

The day after his talk with Brad, he started going through some of Susan's things. He had put off this task and found numerous reasons to avoid it. He didn't know exactly why, but he felt the time had come and he needed to sort through her stuff. Perhaps just to feel close to Susan and try to put some closure to her death. As he was looking through her chest of drawers in their upstairs bedroom, he found a picture. It was under some papers and notes that she had in the upper right-hand drawer of her bureau.

The picture seared his brain as he stared at it. His hand started to tremble, and he had a queasy feeling in his stomach. It was a picture of Gregory Denton!

It was obvious that the picture had been taken out of their second-story bedroom window. From the window, they could look down and see into the backyard of Ellen Johnson's house. The photo was a close-up of Gregory. He was dressed in blue jeans and tennis shoes. He wasn't wearing a shirt and held a hedge clipper in his hand. It was a profile shot of his head and body as he stood over an overgrown bush. From Gregory's demeanor, Pastor Carl had the impression that he wasn't aware that his picture was being taken. He slowly turned the picture over, and on the back, Susan had written the initials J.S.

Pastor Carl hastily started looking for other pictures among Susan's things. What else would he find? He made a thorough search of the chest of drawers but found nothing. The discovery of that single picture started him down the singular path of irrational thinking. *What did it mean?* He was thinking the unthinkable, *Did Susan and Gregory . . .?* He could not finish the thought.

He realized that he was acting foolishly and needed help to explain what it all meant. He hoped that detective Gates could help him.

Suddenly the doorbell rang, breaking Pastor Carl's reverie and announcing the arrival of Sam. He jumped up and made his way to his stained glass, oak front door. He welcomed Sam in and thanked her for coming. He ushered her into the living room and motioned her to sit in one of the wing-backed chairs. "Would you like a cup of fresh coffee?" he asked. Sam accepted and he disappeared into the kitchen.

Sam looked around the living room at the flowered wallpaper and a thick beige rug on the shiny wooden floor. This was her first visit to the parsonage, and she imagined that Susan had had a lot to do with the warmth and charm of the house. Sam liked the shiny hardwood floors in the hallway and the well-placed throw rugs. She also liked the high ceilings with crown molding, which reminded her of the church. She noticed Susan's picture with the two girls on the desk along the wall.

Pastor Carl returned with a silver tray that held two cups of coffee. On the tray was a matched set of a small cream pitcher and sugar bowl. He carefully placed the tray on the coffee table. He retreated into the kitchen again and returned with the cookies and a tray of cheeses with a miniature fork resting to the side. Sam smiled to herself when she saw the tray. The one thing that she had learned after coming to Monroe was that when visiting folks, a tray of delicious cheeses would always appear with coffee and sweets. Pastor Carl seated himself on the sofa. Sam gladly picked up her steaming cup of coffee and took a sip. He smiled at her as he picked up a cookie.

"I imagine that you must have felt it a little strange hearing from me this morning," he began. "Afterwards, I realized how cryptic my call must have seemed."

Sam looked at him over her cup and smiled. Pastor Carl looked a little pale and somewhat nervous.

"Whatever we talk about today will be in confidence," Sam reassured him. "I am here to help if I can." She could see the tension in his shoulders relax a little.

"Thanks," he said. "Please help yourself to a cookie."

Sam took a cookie from the plate and settled back into her chair. As she munched on it, Pastor Carl told her briefly about his talk with Brad and the subsequent events leading up to his finding the picture. As he talked about Susan, Sam could feel the familiar pain in her own heart over the loss of a loved one. Sam thought to herself just how human we all really are when a sudden death tramples on our lives. As he spoke, Sam had a hunch that there must be a very plausible explanation to this picture mystery.

When Pastor Carl had finished talking, Sam asked to see the photo. *So this is Gregory Denton*, she said to herself. "What is your take on this photo?" she asked.

Pastor Carl drew a deep breath, "I don't know. Susan never mentioned it to me, and my imagination has been torturing me ever since I found it."

"Do you think that Susan and Gregory knew one another?"

Pastor Carl sat straight up and stared at Susan's picture on the desk against the wall. He felt his face growing warm. Sam had asked him the same question that he had been asking himself. "Are you asking me if it was possible that they were somehow involved? Romantically involved maybe? Having an affair?" he said in a low voice. He then slumped back into the sofa. He looked like a beaten man. The burden of this doubt was suffocating him. He couldn't go to the grave not knowing. He silently cursed himself for admitting out loud his greatest fear. But, he had to know!

So this was the purpose behind his phone call, Sam thought. *He is in distress not knowing what to believe. After all the years being married to a loving wife, he is now questioning their relationship.* Sam shifted in her chair. "We can't make any assumptions without the facts," she gently said. "There could be a very reasonable and simple explanation here. If you like, I can make some inquiries for you."

Pastor Carl's face winched and his brow tightened up. "What kind of inquiries are you thinking of?" he asked.

Sam could see that she needed to explain herself. His reaction demanded it. "What I mean to say is that I will look into resolving the picture mystery in a very discreet manner," she explained.

"Thank you, Detective. I would prefer that no one knows about this," he responded in a more relaxed tone of voice. Then his face immediately brightened as if he was suddenly relieved from some burdensome worry.

Sam looked at the back of photo. "Do the initials J.S. mean anything to you?"

Pastor Carl just shook his head. "I have no idea," he said.

"Where does Gregory live?"

"I think Ada mentioned Milwaukee to me once. Yes, I believe that is correct."

"Do you by any chance have his phone number?"

"I can get it for you. Ada had given it to me as an emergency contact." Pastor Carl stood up and walked to the desk in the living room. Sam's eyes followed him and then she stood up.

"The chief asked me to take some documents to Milwaukee tomorrow," she said. "If time permits, perhaps I could drop by to see Gregory and try to clear some things up. Would that be okay with you?"

"That would be wonderful," responded Pastor Carl. He jotted down Gregory's phone number and handed it to Sam.

"Now, if I can keep the photo for a while, I would like to see the upstairs bedroom where it was taken." Pastor Carl escorted her to the wooden oak staircase that led to the second floor. She listened to the stairs creak as they ascended, reminding her of her childhood home in Silver Bay.

CHAPTER 8

Gregory slowly opened his eyes. He was lying in bed snuggled under the covers when something, a strange sound, awakened him. Peering out his bedroom window, he could see the vast darkness of the night. He felt secure and safe snuggled in under his warm bed covers. He glanced over to his alarm clock radio on the nightstand to see what time it was. The radio wasn't there. He sat up and was suddenly fully awake and alert. He thought he heard the noise again, a slight moaning sound. He got out of the strange bed and put on his robe and slippers. Only then did he fully realize that he was in Ellen's house in Monroe. *What am I doing here?* he asked himself.

He slowly descended down the staircase to the first floor. He called out, but no one answered. It seemed that he was alone in the house. The moaning sound was slightly louder now. *What the hell?* he asked himself. *Perhaps it is the wind blowing against the house.* He located the light switches and turned them on as he proceeded through the house. Once in the kitchen, he heard the sound again and ascertained that it was coming from the direction of the basement cellar door just off the pantry. He made his way past the oak kitchen table and put his ear to the door and listened. The sound was more audible. His curiosity was overwhelming. He felt like he was being pulled and even summoned to the sound by some invisible force. At the same time, he felt afraid.

He noticed a sliding dead bolt on the door that secured it. After releasing the bolt, he turned the doorknob and pulled. It didn't budge. The door was old and the hinges were rusted. He put both his hands on the doorknob and pulled with all his might. The hinges squeaked, and the door opened under protest.

Once he got it fully open, he peered down into the darkness. He felt the cool musty air on his face. There was that sound again. He turned the basement light on but only saw the dim light of a single bulb at the foot of the stairs. *The other bulbs must be burned out,* he thought. He gingerly grabbed onto the loose handrail and ever so slowly descended the steep open back stairs down into the cellar.

Once he was at the bottom of the stairs, he surveyed the cellar. Through the poor lighting, he could make out a dusty old furnace and discarded objects lying about. Only half of the basement floor was concrete, leaving a dirt floor along the east wall. The ceiling was low. It was dark and gloomy with cobwebs hanging everywhere. He felt another draft of cool air on his face and felt more frightened; like a scared child. He wanted to turn and run back up the stairs to safety but he couldn't.

His eyes adjusted to the dim lighting. The corners of the cellar were creepy and dark. He tried to identify the strange shadows he saw. The damp walls were dreary and daunting.

Then he heard the moaning sound again and thought it was coming from the direction of the dirt floor about ten feet away. He was sweating profusely and feeling a little light headed. He instinctively knew that he should get out of there! *"Why didn't I bring along a flashlight?"* He heard the moan again. And once again his curiosity overcame his fear. "Is there someone there?" he called out. "Are you injured?" No response.

As he made his way slowly toward the sound, Gregory suddenly saw movement out of the corner of his eye. He immediately tensed up and froze. His heart accelerated and he felt the rapid pounding in his chest. He could feel cold sweat running down his forehead and back. He turned toward the distraction. All he could make out was his own shadow on the wall. The crooked shadow had a surreal look to it. He moved his hand up and down and the shadow followed. "I need to get a grip!" he scolded himself.

As he inched along, he came to a place where he could see that the dirt was disturbed. It was next to the wall. The dirt was mounded up like a shallow grave. The moaning was definitely coming from beneath the dirt. He was drawn to it like some bizarre siren call. The moans continued to beckon him as he moved in closer and closer. It was like he was being drawn in by an invisible magnet.

Gregory was now committed; no turning back. His body was tense and his muscles ached. Then he heard the moan again. He stared down at the mounded dirt. After a few moments, he knelt down on his knees. *"Should I run and get some help?"* he questioned himself. But at the same time he didn't want anyone there until he was sure of what he would find.

He summoned up all the courage he could find and slipped his bare hands into the cool earth. He began digging slowly with his fingers. With the adrenaline pumping madly through his veins, he found that he could see surprisingly well in the dim light. As he removed dirt from the mound, he suddenly became frantic and started digging with more vigor. His mind became a blur. The dirt flew in all directions as Gregory's sweaty palms and fingers probed and removed the stale, damp earth like a giant mechanical earth mover.

Suddenly he felt what he perceived to be a human skeleton. A part of a human form, a woman, was taking shape under his fingers as he furiously excavated more and more dirt. Then he saw it through the duskiness of the cellar. A hand! He slowed his pace as he unearthed an arm by her side! He saw a faded and rotting white cotton dress on the female corpse as she emerged from her shallow grave. Her other arm was lying listlessly across her bosom. He cleared more and more dirt away until he uncovered her face. His mind was frantic and obsessed, but his hand movements slowed and were surprisingly calm as he cleared away more dirt.

The sweat was pouring profusely off his face. He saw the remains of her long, gray, disheveled hair. The stench of decaying flesh nauseated him as he stared at a wretched, emaciated, pale body. The bizarre sight of the bones of some poor creature lying in a bed of earth puzzled him. *Who is she? Do I know her?* he anxiously asked himself as he stared into the recessed sockets of her sightless eyes.

Suddenly and without warning, she sat upright in her deathbed! Instantly, surprised by shock and fear, his head snapped back and the hairs on the back of his neck violently tingled! Gregory instinctively jumped up and stood rigid. He was unable to move! Terror seized his body! He was turned to stone and couldn't move. He tried to open his mouth to scream, but nothing came out. Staring at the living corpse had paralyzed him. Then the corpse turned her face to look at him. Those hellish and bottomless eyes stared straight through him. His eyes were riveted on her ravaged face. Her pitiless gaze passed through him. He felt nauseous. The putrid smell of death permeated his nostrils. This unearthed ghoulish creature reeked of decay. The corpse opened her mouth. The only audible sound he heard was a hellish rattling in her throat!

Gregory screamed. He felt his legs moving as sheer terror overtook him.

He flew to the stairs. His heart was pounding and beating so hard and fast he thought it would explode and burst out of his chest. He lost his slippers as he raced to the stairs. The pain he felt on his bare feet was excruciating as he dashed back up the rickety old steps two at a time.

When he reached the top step, he was gasping for air. He felt suffocated and he couldn't breathe. He reached for the doorknob and pushed against the door with all his might. It didn't budge. He started pounding on the door as hard as he could and was screaming at the top of his lungs. Suddenly, he realized that he was locked in. This sudden comprehension had him shaking like a terrorized cornered and frightened animal. He glanced back down the stairs and saw the woman standing there, staring at him in the ghostly dim light. The mysterious woman in a faded cotton dress with no eyes! He began banging on the door again for all his worth. His hands were bloody and his face was covered with dirt and sweat. He was biting his lips so ferociously that his crimson blood was flowing down his chin staining his pajamas red.

His strength began to fail him. His legs no longer supported his weight. He felt faint. He collapsed on the top step breathing heavily and exhausted leaning against the door. He suddenly felt a cold hand grab his ankle! Gregory screamed so loudly that the terrorizing sound of his voice echoed off the cellar walls!

The sound of his own voice screaming from fright woke him up! He sat bolt upright in his bed with his eyes wide open. He threw the covers off and grabbed his knees and pulled them under him. He was shaking uncontrollably. Rapid breathing and his accelerated heart beating raced through his body. His pajamas were soaked from sweat and clung to him. He had wet himself! It took a full five minutes to reorient himself to his own bedroom in Milwaukee. As his senses kicked in, Gregory's mind raced madly, *Am I going crazy?* He just sat in his bed another ten minutes trying to calm down and to make some sense out of what just happened. *The most God-awful nightmare of my life!*

After he quieted down, he got up and took a hot shower. Disgusted, he pulled off the sheets and threw them into the laundry hamper next to his bed.

He went into the kitchen and put on the kettle to boil and got out some instant coffee. His hands were still shaking. He went to the living room and sat down heavily in his easy chair. His face tensed up and he became angry at himself. "I lost control! My nerves gave out!" he shouted at the empty room. "It must have been that damn phone call!"

Around 7:00 p.m. the previous evening, he had received a phone call from a Detective Gates from the Monroe Police Department. She introduced herself as Sam Gates. *An odd name for a woman detective*, he thought. She asked if she could stop by to see him and chat. She had a personal matter that she wanted to discuss with him. She hoped that he could shed some light on it for her. She didn't say what the problem was, but it should only take a few minutes. They agreed to meet at the Yellow Iris Café on Oakland Street at 1:30 p.m. that afternoon.

Gregory suddenly felt chilled and went to the bedroom and got dressed. As he was dressing, the kettle started whistling. It was time to brew his coffee. After filling his cup with the steaming coffee, he went back into the living room and collapsed into his favorite chair again. He stared out of his window onto Juneau Avenue. His mind was churning and spinning with unanswered questions. He concluded that he had to keep his cool; rational and logical thought was needed for his meeting today with the detective.

He convinced himself that if the meeting had anything to do with Keith, they wouldn't be meeting at the Yellow Iris for a light lunch. They would be meeting in a police station playing some sort of psychological games with each other. *If it isn't that, what could it possibly be? Whatever it is, he needed to act as normal as possible and be as helpful and cooperative as he could.*

But after his nightmarish dream, Gregory felt that being normal today would be a challenge. He didn't feel any particular guilt about murdering Keith, so why was the guilt or whatever it was come back to haunt him? *Or could it be . . .?* he didn't finish his thought. He had heard once that dreams were trying to tell us something, and if so, what did this one mean? Well, anyway, he needed to put it out of his mind. His more immediate concern was to go over his murderous trip to Monroe once again in his mind to see if he missed anything. He picked up his coffee, took a sip, sighed, and felt exhausted.

CHAPTER 9

am had just passed through Beloit and headed north to Milwaukee in her unmarked police car. Officer Kennickson had teased her about being a "kiss ass" when she picked up the car. The chief obviously had made the rounds asking for volunteers before Sam accepted the paper transport assignment. Dressed in her off-duty casual clothes, khaki pants, light blue cotton blouse, and sunglasses, she felt very comfortable and relaxed. As she accelerated and matched her speed to the cars around her, she looked like any other car heading north going five to ten miles over the speed limit. She had plenty of time to get to the Milwaukee County Jail to drop off the papers.

As she cruised along the scenic highway, she enjoyed looking at the farmland and lush green rolling hills steeped in history. From her school days, she recalled the early Indian tribes and the French explorers that traveled through the same area. She saw dairy farms and Holstein cows. Even the skeletons of old barns held a special charm of earlier days. The pastoral setting relaxed her.

Her mind began to wander as she cruised along. Her phone call to Gregory Denton the day before was a bit awkward. Having a police detective call to set up an informal and impromptu meeting on the spur of the moment must have seemed somewhat disconcerting to him. Little wonder she heard the nervousness in his voice. He was nice enough on the phone, and he knew where the Yellow Iris Café was located. He didn't hesitate to say he would meet her there. She didn't ask him if she was messing up his day or any other plans he might have had. It didn't really occur to her that he may have had other plans. If the meeting was inconvenient, maybe he should have told her or, again, maybe not. The police can be intimidating to anyone who wasn't used to being around them. Perhaps she should have given him more information about the meeting. He had to be wondering what the urgency was even when there really wasn't any, except for Pastor Carl's angst, of course.

Her dad used to say that Sam lived too much in a world of action. Even as a little girl, if she thought something needed to be done, she just plunged right into it. She rolled up her sleeves and got her hands dirty. Her attitude was to get the job done now and worry about the consequences later. She could probably write a book on some of the unforeseen consequences of her life. But on the other hand, her intuition and impulses had led to their share of successes.

She could see clearly now that this was the attitude she had when setting up her appointment with Gregory. She wanted to show him the picture Pastor Carl had given her and to get his take on it. Was there an affair, which she doubted, or wasn't there an affair? Who was J.S.? How would he react to these personal questions? She needed to get to Silver Bay by 4:00 p.m. to see her mother, so she had to keep an eye on the time.

She was also a little curious about her appointment with Ada. Ada had certainly gotten her attention. Was there more to the story than natural causes concerning the deaths? According to Chief Johns, Gregory didn't want an autopsy done on his mother while Ada was so insistent upon it. Ada may be short of stature, but she was long on attitude and seemed to generally get her way with people. If grief was stopping Gregory, that was one thing. But wouldn't he want to be certain as to the cause of death? Maybe he would or maybe not? She filed that thought away for another time.

Even though she was enjoying the ride, she started to feel a little time pressured. She checked her watch; so far, so good. She didn't want to be late. She told herself again that she needed to be gentle with Gregory during their meeting and to apologize for the short notice. After all, he didn't have to agree to meet.

Suddenly she felt the need for a cup of coffee. She checked her watch again. A ten-minute stop would be okay. She pulled off at the next exit and drove to a gas station and convenience store. As she was pulling out of the station with her coffee, she did a double take when she saw a gray-haired lady pumping gas. The elderly lady reminded her of her mother. She was the same height and body type and had the same hairstyle as Sharon. Only the car was different. *Do all old people morph into one another as they age?* Sam wondered to herself.

Sam waited for the traffic to clear and once again pulled back onto the interstate and headed north. The lady at the pump had startled her, and she was immediately transported to Silver Bay. It had been a month since Sam last visited Sharon. They talked on the phone, but the visits to Silver Bay were a drag on Sam. Sharon hadn't moved on emotionally since Earl's death. The visits to see her mom depressed her.

The same repetitious and boring conversations would be waiting for her. "Why did Earl have to die? Life isn't fair. Nobody loves me. I don't have any money. I am always sick. Why does Pastor James keep calling me? What's going to happen to me? Will Sam look after me in my old age?" All these lamentable questions couldn't be answered, because Sharon didn't want to know the answers. She just wanted somebody to take care of her like Earl did. She was all alone and clinically depressed, and her only entertainment and companionship was her television set. Her self-imposed isolation was accented by lonely nights in an empty house, and it was taking its toll.

Sam's mind drifted to happier times before her father's death as she cruised along the smooth highway. Her childhood was very happy. Both her parents doted on her with lots of love and affection. It was like being raised in Camelot.

Both Sharon and Earl were the taskmasters, and that's where Sam learned the value of hard work, accomplishment, and high self-esteem. Her mother always reminded her that being a girl didn't mean that she couldn't compete and be as good as the boys, and she took great satisfaction in Sam's accomplishments. Earl was more relaxed about his expectations of Sam, but he never missed an opportunity to praise her and to tell her how proud he was of her. Sam thought she had the perfect parents.

But death is the greatest interrupter of life; Earl's death. That fateful morning began like any other. Sharon had a husband and she had a dad. The day started out like a thousand other mornings; the routine of life just playing itself out. When Sharon kissed Earl good-bye that day, how could she know it would be for the very last time? When she got the phone call that Earl needed to work a double shift, it wasn't anything new. He had pulled double shifts before to help out the department.

But like a thief, death came and stole a huge part of Sam's life. It was like being trapped in a nightmare without waking. She became a prisoner to her own dark demons and frustrations. The loss of her beloved dad was more than she could understand and deal with. Her rich and fulfilling life had turned into a tragic and solitary existence. The light around her became darkness. She departed Camelot.

The more Sam thought about her visit with Sharon that afternoon, the more depressed she became. She had envisioned a strong mother–daughter bond as an adult. But Sharon's emotional state made that impossible. Before Earl's death, Sam thought of her Mom as all-knowing, all-powerful and the nurturer. But now Sharon had become a stranger to her; an unknown woman or maybe an enemy. She would call Pastor James later to see if he was available to meet after her visit. She just felt like she needed to talk to someone and the good pastor was always there for her. The thought of seeing him put a smile on her face.

After she entered the city limits, Sam found the police station and slowly drove up to the side door. An officer immediately came out from behind a re-enforced pane glass door and walked over to her car. "We have been waiting for you," he said. Sam handed him the envelope through the car window.

"Do you have time for lunch?" he asked. "We are bringing in some sandwiches."

"No thanks," responded Sam, "I have an appointment at one-thirty and I can't be late."

"Okay," the officer replied. "And thanks again for bringing up these papers." Sam smiled at him and backed up her car. She exited the parking lot, turned right and headed to the Yellow Iris Café.

CHAPTER 10

G regory arrived early at the Yellow Iris Café on Oakland Avenue for his meeting with Detective Gates. He was surprised that the detective knew about the restaurant, being she was from Monroe. He had lucked out finding a parking space right in front of the café. Normally he would have to park two or three blocks away. But today, he could keep an eye on his car from the café window. It was a beautiful day in May with the temperatures in the mid-seventies.

It was 1:15 p.m., and the hostess seated him immediately. He requested a table near the window. The lunch crowd was dwindling, and only about three-quarters of the tables still had patrons. He had expected more of a crowd on the weekend, but now he felt that this would make his conversation with the detective more palatable and relaxed.

The Yellow Iris Café was famous for its coffee and sandwiches. The food was excellent and a bit upscale for the neighborhood. All the tables had white linen table cloths and yellow silk irises for centerpieces. A small candle was placed beside each flower for evening dining. Gregory looked over the menu card. He hadn't eaten all day. After that horrid dream last night, he had lost his appetite and was unable to eat. Two pots of coffee had sustained him so far today. He was feeling ravenous. The menu featured gourmet sandwiches, salads, soups, muffins, fruit breads, fruit juices, and a variety of coffees. He took a sip of water from the frosty glass in front of him and glanced out of the window. He could clearly see his car and had a good vantage point to watch for the detective's arrival.

Gregory had rehearsed all morning what he would say if the detective questioned him about Keith. He didn't want to appear too defensive, and he planned to give mundane yes and no answers, if questioned. But why would she want to question him about Keith? It didn't make any sense to him. There was absolutely nothing to tie him to Keith. Maybe his imagination was getting the best of him. He needed to calm down.

Nevertheless, if she pressed him, he was ready. He would tell her that he got home from work Thursday evening. He was not feeling very well and decided to stay home all night. He had a light supper and nursed a splitting headache. He fell asleep on the sofa in front of the television set. Around midnight, he got up, switched off the set, and went to bed. He was alone, so there was no one to vouch for him. He thought this was a straightforward and plausible statement of his movements. And if anyone checked up on his story, the bit about leaving the television on during his absence was brilliant. He felt confident he could pull this off. His adrenaline was giving him a boost. He would be as cooperative as possible and not offer too much information. He had to keep his nerve. The police were trained to interview people and look for inconsistencies in stories so he had to be careful. He had read once that the act of observing affects the thing being observed, so he had to be on his guard.

Looking out the window again, he saw a tall woman wearing khaki plants striding along the sidewalk. He instantly knew that it was Detective Gates. She was taller than he imagined and sort of cute, in a pedestrian sort of way. Sam entered the café and looked around. Gregory stood up and waved. She instantly recognized him. He was definitely the same man in the photo that she was carrying in her pocket. She smiled at him and hurried over to his table. He looked a little slimmer than she had imagined from the photo. He had chocolate brown hair—trimmed and neat looking.

She stuck out her hand, "Hello, I am Detective Sam Gates," she said, "and you must be Gregory Denton."

Gregory blushed a little at this bold and straightforward introduction. "Yes," he said.

He motioned to the chair across the table from him. "Please sit down."

Sam settled herself into the chair. "I thought I was going to be late. The traffic got snarled up on the way here and I had to park three blocks away. Sorry," she said.

Gregory felt his armpits getting a little damp, but at the same time, he felt this meeting was going to be okay. Sam's folksy introduction had put him somewhat at ease.

He asked Sam how she knew about the "Iris".. She told him that she grew up in Silver Bay and that her dad used to bring her there for lunch on his trips to Milwaukee. Earl loved the house specialty, "Abbey's Estate Coffee." He told her it was the best cup of coffee in the state of Wisconsin. Sam picked up the menu board and scanned it.

"Are you ready to order?" she asked him. Gregory waved the waitress over and Sam ordered a half-sub beef and cheddar sandwich with horseradish sauce. Gregory ordered a bowl of veggie barley soup with warm parmesan bread and a Rubin sandwich with a slice of Havarti cheese. Then they each ordered a cup of Abbey's famous coffee.

After the waitress left, Sam put her elbows on the table and looked at Gregory.

"I feel I must apologize to you for the way I spoke to you yesterday. During my drive here, I thought about my call, and I concluded I must have seemed a little rude."

Gregory didn't say anything, so Sam continued. "The reason I wanted to see you is that I am here on behalf of a friend of mine, Pastor Carl Peterson. He is agonizing over a discovery he made and has asked for my help."

As Sam spoke, Gregory felt his body relax even more, and he settled comfortably into his chair. "I know Pastor Carl," he said. "He and his wife lived in the church parsonage behind my mother's house."

"Yes, that's right," responded Sam. "As you probably know, his wife Susan died last year. Well anyway, he was recently cleaning out some of her things and found a picture of you."

"He found a picture of me?" Gregory quickly responded. He was quite surprised at Sam's revelation. He had no idea where this was going. The waitress appeared with two cups of coffee.

After she set them down and left, Sam continued, "The discovery of the picture really puzzled Pastor Carl and triggered off some really discomforting thoughts and imaginings. I brought the picture with me in the hopes you could shed some light on this little mystery."

Gregory's brown eyes followed her hand as she reached into her shirt pocket and retrieved the picture. She then handed it over to him. She noticed that he accepted it with a calm hand and relaxed fingers. He thoughtfully stared at it for some time. Sam could clearly see the puzzled look on his face.

Sam was studying his facial expressions as carefully as she could without staring directly at him. She was looking for any atypical body language that he may exhibit. She looked at his eyes, facial expressions, and any little body movements that she had been trained to observe. He seemed a little nervous, but she thought that was normal. After all, he was sitting at a table with a police officer that he had just met. From time to time, she noticed some of the other diners looking at them. She dismissed the casual looks as people just looking around at other people; just another human trait of curiosity. She thought that Gregory also felt the intrusion. She couldn't discern anything in his manner other than his expression of surprise as he examined the picture.

After a little while, he asked, "Who took this?"

"We assume that Susan took it out of the second-story window at the parsonage," she said.

"But why did she take it?"

"That's the question that is bothering the good pastor."

Gregory looked at the picture once again. "Well, I am clearly standing in the back yard of my mother's house. It must have been a warm day for yard work since I don't have a shirt on," he said. He then turned the picture over. He immediately focused on the initials J.S. but didn't say anything.

"Do the initials J.S. mean anything to you?" Sam asked him.

Without looking up, he shook his head and simply said, "No."

Sam could see that he was trying to puzzle out who or what J.S. meant.

"Can you put a date or a time to this picture?" Sam asked.

"Well, not really. I remember that my mother was ill and wanted me to come down to her house to do some yard chores for her. However, and this may seem a little strange to you, but I do remember talking to Susan Peterson during one of my visits. It was probably the only conversation I ever had with her. You see, there is a cedar fence that divides our property and the church property. She came though the gate unannounced and said she was looking for mother. But as I thought about it later, I think she really came to see me. She was friendly enough, but asked me some rather personal questions."

"Typical for Monroe, I suppose," Sam said. Gregory paused in his narrative and smiled.

The waitress arrived with their food and asked if they wanted more coffee. Sam was surprised to see that her cup was empty. "Yes, thank you," she said. Once the coffee cups were topped off, the waitress left them.

Gregory took a big bite out of his Rubin sandwich and looked at Sam. "Sorry, I haven't eaten all day," he said.

"That's okay," Sam replied as she watched him chew his food.

Gregory continued, "She wanted to know if I was dating anyone. She didn't exactly put it as bold as that, but it seemed to me that was her main interest during all her chatter. I told her I was dating someone, but of course, that wasn't true. I didn't think it was any of her business. Then after some more small talk and pleasantries, she left."

"So that's all you remember?" Sam asked. "You didn't see her again?"

"Of course not," he replied. "Why, do you think differently?"

"No, but I had to ask."

Gregory looked a little offended. "Look," he said, "I am as surprised as Pastor Carl is to see this picture. I have no idea why Mrs. Peterson took it, but at the same time, I must say I find it rather fascinating."

"Do you?" Sam responded.

Gregory's face turned a shade of red. Sam could see that he was getting a little upset with her. He may have thought that she was too accusatorial toward him during her questioning. However, she was satisfied that Gregory could not shed any new light on this mystery picture, other than the fact that she didn't think that he having an affair with Susan. And about this point, Sam was quite sure. Her intuition told her that much. Gregory gave the picture back to her. They finished their lunch in silence.

Sam decided to change the subject to Monroe and asked Gregory some open-ended questions about growing up there. She wanted to get the conversation free flowing again. He seemed to settle down, and they talked in more casual tones as they sipped their coffee. From the small talk, he told her the story about his aunt and uncle raising him. He didn't go into any detail about the relationship between himself and his mother. He then offered that he hadn't been back to Monroe since he sold his mother's house to Ada.

When they were finished, Gregory motioned to the waitress and asked for the check. Sam looked her watch. She had an hour to get to Silver Bay to see her mom. The time had really flown by. No problem, she would get there in plenty of time. Gregory offered and then paid the check. They walked out together.

"Thanks again for meeting with me and thanks for the lunch," she said. "You have cleared up some questions for me. Now I must try to find out who J.S. is," she said.

"It was nice meeting you," said Gregory as they shook hands. "Good luck."

As she turned to go, she took a couple of steps and suddenly stopped in her tracks. *Oh shit!* she said to herself. She turned around and saw Gregory opening his car door.

"Hey, Gregory," she half-shouted. Gregory looked up surprised and saw Sam coming toward him. "I am really sorry about this, but I did have another question for you and I only just now remembered it."

"Okay, if you must," Gregory grinned at her.

"I am seeing Ada Klausner next week, because she has some concerns about the death of your mother."

Gregory's eyes narrowed and the skin on his forehead pinched. "It seems that Ada either can't or won't let go of my mother's death until her damn curiosity is satisfied!" he said with sudden irritation.

She saw that Gregory's face, for a very slight moment, had a strange, almost contorted look to it. She noticed that his right eye started twitching, and the color rose in his cheeks. Then he quickly recovered and stared at Sam.

"Are you sure that you are completely satisfied that your mother died from heart failure, natural causes?" Sam asked.

"Yes, I am!" Gregory exploded. "Ada has made quite a fuss over my mother's death, and everyone knows that she is in some kind of denial about it. I think her grief has altered the circuitry in her brain and has challenged her perception of reality! Did you know that she calls me fairly regularly to gossip about Monroe?" His voice was trembling and rising in volume. "Well, anyway, she can be quite tiresome at times, and I think she should just let it drop and let my mother rest in peace!"

Sam was very surprised at this outburst of emotion. As she looked into his intense eyes, she suddenly had the feeling that there was something more to the story than what he was saying. Maybe Ada was getting on every body's nerves with all her meddling, or maybe not.

She noticed that a miniscule muscle in Gregory's right eye had a steady, almost imperceptible tic, during his spirited commentary. Could this be an autonomic response of someone with guilty conscience? His face was flushed and his breathing and heart rate was up. Sam had to caution herself against jumping to conclusions concerning micro expressions. However, she did find it interesting.

"Okay, thanks," she said. "I just wanted your take on Ada."

"Well, now you have it!" Gregory screeched. Sam backed up a step and didn't say anything else. She noticed that a young couple had stopped on the sidewalk and was staring at them.

"Nice car," she said as she turned to go. Gregory didn't respond. She could sense his eyes staring through her back as she headed down the sidewalk back to her parked car. *A little too cool and controlling at lunch,* she thought to herself. *He chose his words very carefully until the mention of Ada and his mother, and then he let his guard down.* She once again had to caution herself to stick to the facts. There was something about Gregory that she didn't like. Perhaps her meeting with Ada would be very interesting after all.

CHAPTER 11

Sharon Gates sat in front of her television watching reruns of old Westerns. Her days had morphed into reliance on television for noise and entertainment. She hadn't picked up a newspaper or magazine in years and watched the six o'clock news for the news of the day. It didn't interest her. *Why does the news only report the bad stuff that is happening?* Sometimes she would turn the sound down and just watch the pictures.

She was having trouble sleeping at night. Any little noise or disturbance had to be investigated. With the streetlight next to the house shining into her living room, navigating around the furniture in the dark was no problem. When the windows were open, she could hear the leaves rustling when the wind picked up. Stormy nights with thunder and lightning frightened her. Tree branches making scratching noises against the windows alarmed her. If she was hit by a lightning bolt, who would know?

Cats made her sneeze and she didn't trust them. As she kept her vigilant watch at night and stared out the picture window, she marveled at how many cats there were. She knew that they must have different colors, but at night, they all seemed black to her.

Kids walking past her house on the sidewalk after midnight were disconcerting. *What if they were checking out her house? Did they know she lived alone?* The sound of their loud voices made her nervous.

Also, the different phases of the moon caused spooky shadows. In the wind, the shadows seemed to come alive. She felt panic throughout her whole body as she checked and rechecked the locks on her doors. After all this nocturnal activity, she would fall asleep exhausted on her living room sofa.

The interior of her house hadn't changed much since Earl's death. The furniture, rugs, lamps, and pictures were all frozen in time. They all remained in the same places they were that fateful night. Sam suggested that she should buy some new furniture and other things or at the least rearrange the furniture. Sharon stubbornly refused and left things the same.

It was as if she expected Earl to suddenly show up one day and walk through the front door. When Earl was alive, her life was complete. She relied on him for everything. He was a rock, the foundation that her life was built on. But now she was alone. The empty dinner plate she set for him every night only deepened her despair. If only he would come home! She harbored that delusional and hopeful thought in her heart and it consumed her.

On the coffee table next to her sat a vodka martini. She took a sip as her program droned on. She wasn't paying any attention. One of her favorite shows, a game show, was starting at five o'clock and she hoped that Sam would be gone by then. "I can't be interrupted and miss my show," she said to herself. She took another sip and heard a light knock at the front door. Sam walked in.

"Hi, Mom," Sam said and then walked over to her and gave her a kiss on the cheek. She immediately noticed the glass of vodka. She then went to the television and turned it off.

"Why did you do that?" Sharon protested.

"We can visit better without all the distraction and noise," Sam replied as she sat down on the sofa.

"Why are you here?" Sharon asked.

Sam patiently reminded her about the documents that she transported from Monroe to Milwaukee. Sam noticed Sharon's unkempt hair and the smell of body odor. She looked like she hadn't changed her wrinkly cotton dress in a week. The house needed a good airing out. "Are you feeling okay?" Sam asked.

"Sure. Why shouldn't I?" she responded in an irritated voice.

"I still think we should bring someone in either part-time or full time to help you with the housework," Sam said.

"I don't need any help, Samantha!"

Sam could see this conversation was already heading in the wrong direction. She sat quietly for a moment thinking of something to say.

Sharon spoke up first. "Besides, Mrs. Yost brings me my groceries once a week and looks in on me. Who else do I need?" Sam had arranged for Mrs. Yost, a widowed lady living in the house next door, to check on her mom from time to time and to help do her grocery shopping. Sharon's self-imposed imprisonment made this arrangement necessary because she never left the house. Sam had tried to get her out of the house for short shopping trips, but once they were out, Sharon made a fuss and wanted to go home again. When Sam tried to convince her that getting out was good for her, Sharon refused.

"How long are you staying?" Sharon asked. "My program starts at five o'clock!" With that announcement, Sam suddenly felt more deflated and depressed.

"Should I fix you something to eat?" Sam asked.

"No, I am not hungry," she shot back.

Sam loved her mom, but seeing her like this was difficult. Sam felt helpless and isolated living two hours away in Monroe. With the demands of her job, it wasn't very easy to get to Silver Bay as much as she liked. Besides, Sam's social life only centered around a few friends in Madison. To balance the three was very stressful.

It was obvious to Sam that Sharon's mental state was deteriorating. Living alone and isolated in this old house was taking its toll. It was also clear to Sam that her mom's quality of life was at low ebb and her life in the house had to be a daily struggle. The realization that Sharon would need to be institutionalized was becoming more and more apparent. Caring for and dealing with a depressed and irrational elderly parent was beyond her abilities.

Sam glanced over to the mantel above the fireplace and saw Earl's picture. His smiling face looked back at her. One of his favorite sayings was "Old age is the only disease that mankind hasn't found a cure for." The thought of it made her sad.

As Sam surveyed the room, she saw two new additions since her last visit. One was the wedding picture of her folks that had been in the bedroom. It was now located on top of the television set. The second thing she noticed was the vodka martini sitting on the table next to Sharon. "How much is she drinking?" Sam asked herself.

"How's Phil?" Sam asked. "Has he called you?"

"Phil who?" she asked.

Then Sharon got up and turned the television back on.

"Well, I guess that's that," Sam said. She got up and went into the kitchen. It was a mess. The kitchen table was covered with dirty dishes and fossilized food. The kitchen sink was also piled high with dirty dishes. Sam rolled up her sleeves and spent the next thirty minutes cleaning up and taking the trash out.

She was just finishing up when the phone rang. Sharon ignored it, so Sam picked it up in the kitchen. "Hello," she said.

"Hi Sam, this is Pastor James. I was driving by your mother's house a few minutes ago and I saw what I presumed to be an unmarked Monroe police car."

The sound of his voice was like a breath of fresh air in the stale house. She felt her spirits lift and told him how nice it was to hear his voice.

"Look Sam," he said, "I have some time to kill. Do you want to stop by the church office for a visit before you leave? I would like to discuss your mother if that is okay with you? I could order pizza and we could dine in at my office."

Sam didn't hesitate. "I'll be there!" She hung up the phone and went back into the living room. Sharon was staring at the television.

"I am leaving now mom. I will call you, okay?" Sharon didn't respond. Sam went over and kissed her on the cheek.

I will need to call Mrs. Yost tomorrow and ask her to keep a closer eye on her, she thought.

As she slowly walked to the front door to let herself out, Sam felt the weight of sadness in her heart. She turned back and looked at her mom. Sharon had lost herself in her personal grief and was living without hope. She was isolated, lonely, bored and depressed. Taking her anger and resentment out on Sam was an ongoing melancholy that Sam had learned to live with. The ache she felt in her heart, as she stared at her mom, never went away. It was always there, simmering away on the back burner of her mind. Sam worried that her mom could become suicidal if things got much worse. The very thought of it sent shivers down her spine.

CHAPTER 12

Pastor James Cihlar stood next to the desk in his office. He had just ordered supper from a local pizza joint and replaced the receiver on his phone. "The pizza will be delivered in thirty minutes to forty minutes," he said to himself. He walked over and checked the small utility refrigerator in the corner of his office. The refrigerator was well stocked with fruit juices and an assortment of pop. He returned to his desk and started to tidy up a bit. By nature, he wasn't a neat person, and his desk showed it, much to the chagrin of the church secretary. But he was used to these last-minute attempts to rearrange his papers in tidy stacks before meeting people in his office. Sam wouldn't be fooled though. They had spent many hours together in his office after Earl's death. They talked about life's mysteries and tried to make sense of his death. It seemed so long ago now. As he was cleaning up, he smiled to himself and realized that Sam would easily see through his pretentiousness at tidiness.

He settled his rotund frame into a well-worn leather chair behind his desk. As he waited, he slowly swiveled his chair around and assessed the state of his office. He needed a new carpet and some new furniture. The carpet pre-dated his ministry at the church and was threadbare and stained.

"At least it isn't a shag carpet," he chuckled to himself. A little fresh paint on the walls wouldn't hurt either. All his furnishings were donated from somewhere else and looked it. The notion of buying anything new for his office seemed to be against some sort of unwritten church doctrine.

He felt that his assessment of church polity was somewhat correct after meeting with the chairman of the church finance committee. Mr. Krupke harbored some very conservative views about the financial plight of the church, so Pastor James had to accept the fact that any upgrades or improvements to his office would come under the heading of a miracle at St. Martins.

During some of his quieter moments, he reflected on his ministry at the church. The congregation was getting older and more conservative as the years rolled on. At times, he even questioned his personal commitment to St. Martins. From time to time, the fanciful thought of living life as a solitary monk in some impoverished monastery appealed to him and at the same time made him laugh. In some ways, he felt that he was living that life now, at least the impoverished part. But the thought of living in isolated religious orders appealed to him, especially when meeting with the church trustees. They constantly bemoaned budget woes and the anticipated financial collapse of the church. The old refrain that he often heard in these meetings was "Well, we can't even afford two gallons of paint for the good pastor's office!" He wanted to print the quote in the church bulletin but decided against it. Maybe he would just print it in bold lettering and hang it on his office wall and then campaign for some new paint.

His reverie was interrupted by a knock at the door. "Come in," he said. The door to his office slowly opened and Sam looked in. He got up from his chair and went to greet her.

"Hi, Sam," he said, "you look wonderful." He then gave her a grandfatherly hug. "Come and sit down." He motioned her to sit in one of two chairs located in the front of his desk. The high back chairs were made of well-worn leather and very comfortable. Years of pastoral counseling had broken them in nicely. Sam sat down and Pastor James turned the other chair around to face her. He smiled at her as he sat down.

"Thanks for stopping by," he began. "It's been a while since we have seen one another. I want to hear about all your adventures in Monroe."

Sam smiled and sunk back into her chair. Pastor James reminded her of the grandfather that she never had. Instinctively, she knew that she could trust him. Looking at his short white hair and soft pale blue eyes, she realized that she needed to talk. She needed to unpack some personal feelings and other stuff in her life. "I ordered a pizza and it should be delivered here fairly soon," Pastor James said. "Can I get you something to drink?"

"How about a beer?" she instantly responded. Pastor James gave a start and then noticed Sam smiling at him with a twinkle in her eye.

"Oh, it's been that kind of a day, has it?"

"Okay, how about a pop then?" she said.

Pastor James laughed as he got up and went to the refrigerator to get the two drinks. He handed one to Sam. They clanked their bottles together and toasted each other. As Sam slowly sipped her drink, she looked at him. She felt very secure being here in the presence of the man who she credited for saving her life from sadness and despair.

"How has life been treating you?" Pastor James began.

Sam took a deep breath and reflectively looked down at her hands. "Where should I begin?" she pondered. Suddenly there was so much that she wanted to share with him. "As you know, I still miss my dad terribly every day," she began. "Being around cops day after day in Monroe is a constant reminder of him. I miss our walks together and I miss talking to him about stuff." She hesitated and sipped her drink. "I still blame myself for the tragedy at the Silver Bay Police Department. I wished I could have talked to Dad before I made the biggest mistake of my life! Now I must live with another death."

Pastor James leaned forward in his chair and said softly, "You know what happened wasn't your fault. You just got caught up in a bizarre situation and you followed your instincts and conscience. You couldn't have seen the suicide coming."

Sam's first job out of college was with the Silver Bay Police Department. She was hired mostly out of the department's respect for Earl. "Earl's Girl" is what she was called when she started there. What the department didn't know was how ambitious and smart she was. Sam worked long hours and had virtually no personal life. She was driven to do her best for the department. During her off-duty hours, she tried to follow up on any leads that could shed light on the kids who shot and killed her dad. The case was still officially open, but Sam was the only one showing any interest in it. It was very frustrating for her. Every thought, lead, and idea she had just led to a series of dead ends.

Being new in the department, she impressed her colleagues after she caught a couple of lucky breaks and solved two important cases. The first case was the murder of a woman who was killed by her ex-boyfriend, and the other was the rape of a fourteen-year-old girl. Using her imagination and detection methods, she made the arrests. Her skill and instincts interviewing suspects and persons of interest were remarkable. She had developed a knack for sorting out who was lying and who was telling her the truth. She learned that she could intimidate witnesses using a variety of facial expressions and gestures. She found this technique most helpful when assuming everyone was lying to her until proved otherwise. Her methods led to convictions in both cases.

Shortly after the celebrations of her successes waned, one of the three detectives in the department announced that he was leaving. He had accepted a job offer to be the new chief of police in a city in northern Wisconsin. After he left, Sam applied for his job and got the promotion. Her fast-track promotion was at first resented by some of the other officers, but later, she was accepted after showing her mettle. Sam put in even longer hours and had some more successes. She was never condescending toward her fellow officers and they respected her for that. That was until she came back to the station late one night and found a horrific situation.

Officer Brian White, a twenty-year veteran of the department, was having what appeared to be a mental breakdown as he sat alone at his desk in the squad room. He held his head in his hands and was weeping uncontrollably.

It was well known within the department that he was having marital problems. His erratic behavior and his heavy drinking were troublesome. The other officers constantly covered for him. They suggested to him that he should get counseling and take some time off to sort things out. But White desperately tried to hold it all together by living the life of a macho cop. That image demanded all the strength and control he could muster. It wasn't surprising that he thought seeking counseling was a sign of weakness, and besides, cops were supposed to be strong problem solvers, not a problem.

Then one day, his wife suddenly moved out, taking the two kids with her. He returned home after his shift late one night and found a note and an empty house. After that, things just got worse for him. He freaked out. Three days later, he was involved in the arrest of a heroin-addicted mother. She was well known to the police. They had responded to several domestic abuse calls at her house. The police had filed a complaint with Child Protection Services concerning the two kids living there, but the agency had failed to take any action.

On the night of her arrest, one of her children was missing. After questioning her at her home, they arrested her and took her to a holding cell at the station. The police took her five-year-old daughter to her aunt's house. She still wouldn't tell them where her baby was. She insisted on seeing a lawyer. She started acting irrationally, so they put her into an isolation cell. The more White thought about the missing baby, the more irrational his thoughts became. He convinced himself that he could make her talk and tell him the whereabouts of the child.

After everyone left the station, he raced home and retrieved a pet mouse that his son had left behind in his room. He brought it back to the station and went directly to the holding cell. He opened the door and saw the woman huddled on her bunk bed lying in the fetal position. He demanded once again to know where the baby was. She cursed him and gave him a defiant look. He took the mouse out of his pocket and held it by its tail. He grinned at her. "Tell me, you little bitch," he shouted at her. She shrieked in horror. The mouse was desperately trying to free itself from White's grip. He threw it at her and he slammed the door shut. She screamed in terror and panic and had a psychotic breakdown. White looked at her through the cell window and just wandered back to his desk, sat down, and stared at the wall with eyes glazed over.

As Sam came back to the station that night, she saw White weeping and in a state of shock. No one else was there. He was mumbling something about the holding cell. Sam went to investigate. She opened the door and jumped back as the furry little rodent raced between her legs and out into the hallway. She then saw the prisoner frozen like a statue on her bunk bed. Her face was ashen and her eyes had a blank stare. Sam hurried over to her and touched her arm, but she only groaned and was unresponsive. Sam raced to her desk and phoned for emergency help.

The cover-up started immediately. A protective wall of silence was constructed around Officer White. "We must protect White" was the covert message. "He is the victim here." The rationale was that he could only take so much personal and emotional stress in his life. He lost control that night. The blame was shifted to the mother of the lost baby. The unwritten code of loyalty and trust must be maintained within the department.

Sam struggled mightily with her conscience and with her loyalty to a fellow police officer. She didn't have her dad to counsel her and to give her the answers she needed. She wrestled with her conscience and then made a decision. She felt sick about it, but she also felt a moral responsibility. She filed a report with the department that led to White's immediate suspension and a formal investigation.

Two days later, White shot himself. The subsequent incident report concluded that he accidentally shot himself while cleaning his gun. An "accidental death" report gave his estranged wife and kids his full pension and financial benefits. No one questioned the findings, and White was given a proper burial with full ceremonial honors.

The fallout from the suicide caused the whole police department to go into a prolonged depression. Morale dropped to an all-time low. As a group, they blamed Sam. She was ostracized and ignored. No one spoke to her. But on some level, the officers knew that White had crossed the line and Sam did the right thing. But loyalty was everything, and betrayal couldn't be forgiven.

Sam needed help. She went to Pastor James for personal counseling. After a few sessions, he feared for her welfare. She wasn't sleeping well and had lost weight. He contacted a political friend in Madison for a favor. He pulled some strings and arranged for her to interview and to be hired at the Monroe Police Department.

As Sam sipped her drink, she looked up at Pastor James with a tear perched on her cheek, poised and ready to fall into her lap. "I could have handled the situation differently," she said.

Pastor James shifted in his seat. "Look, Sam," he began, "it isn't your fault," he said with authority in his voice. "You had no idea White was going to kill himself. And if you think you betrayed him, how about the woman? Didn't she have the expectation of safety once she was in police custody? She trusted the system to protect her and it betrayed her. When you get right down to it, who was the real victim here?"

"I know," Sam said, "but it is all so sad and I miss not being here in Silver Bay. I also feel that I let my dad down."

Pastor James could feel her pain. She was still trying to articulate her feelings of guilt and shame in White's death. She hadn't found the closure she needed. He sat in silence. "Sam," he said in a gentle voice, "you did the right thing, given the situation. None of us are protected from our feelings, and second-guessing ourselves is a waste of time. We can't change what happened in the past. We must learn to accept it and move on. When you doubt yourself, then your problems can really overwhelm you. Remember, you only have control over your judgment and intuition. You did the right thing at the right time." Sam gave a slight nod of her head and dried her tear. She felt embarrassed crying like that in front of him.

They heard a knock at the office door and they both looked up. The pizza guy popped his head in. "Hi, Pastor James. I have your super duper and hear healthy dinner in my hand," he said and then laughed. His silly manner broke the somber mood in the room. Pastor James jumped up and opened his wallet. He walked over to the pizza guy and said, "Thanks, Bobby. Here is the money for the pizza and some left over for your charming personality."

Bobby grinned at him and handed over the pizza. "It's always nice doing business with your lordship," he said, "and thanks for the big tip. Maybe I can get into medical school!"

Pastor James laughed and said, "If you are going to be a brain surgeon, maybe you could practice on yourself." They both laughed and then Bobby spun around and disappeared back into the hallway. "And to think he was in my confirmation class," Pastor James said out loud. Sam laughed.

Pastor James retrieved some paper plates and napkins stored in the cabinet above his refrigerator and served up the pizza. "Thanks," Sam said. They both ate in silence. The pizza tasted great to Sam. She was more famished than she thought.

"How's your mother doing?" Pastor James asked. Sam filled him in on her observations from her visit that afternoon. "What are you going to do?" he asked.

"I don't know. Phil is useless and I can't count on him for any help. Mrs. Yost is helping, but she can't provide the care that Mom needs. I suppose if things get any worse, I will have to move her to Monroe," she said. The sound of her own words gave her pause. Saying the words out loud seemed to have a different and more sobering meaning to her. She continued, "It is really hard on me seeing her in all her pain and depression. I really appreciate you phoning her and trying to see her, but she is in a dense fog and I can't see it lifting anytime soon."

"Well, if you can think of anything more I can do, just let me know," he said.

Sam nodded, "Okay, thanks."

Pastor James finished his slice of pizza and asked, "So, how's life in Monroe?"

Sam wiped her face with her napkin. "I can't thank you enough for getting me the interview there," she said. "The people are really kind and friendly. I am going to a very nice church. Pastor Carl is great and everyone loves him. He is a bit sad though. He lost his wife last year and is just coming to terms with it. In fact, I am working on clearing up a concern of his at the moment and I must call him as soon as I get back tonight."

"Do you want to call from here?" Pastor James offered. "Is there anything I can help with?"

Sam hesitated, "Thanks, but the call can wait. Pastor Carl has a puzzling question about a photo he found, but I think his imagination is getting the better of him. He is perplexed about his late wife. And he is also married to his parish work which might be part of his problem."

"Now, that sounds familiar," Pastor James interjected. "And I don't know how a photo can be so troublesome. There probably is a very innocent explanation behind the mystery picture." He sat back in his chair and tried to contain his curiosity. "Remember, we ministers are also human beings, so go easy," he said.

"Oh, don't worry about that," Sam responded and didn't say any more about the picture.

"How's the job going?" he asked.

Sam sighed, "Well, we have a crime wave in Monroe. Some kids are stealing license plates and I have been put in charge of capturing those hardened criminals before they wreak any more havoc on our law-abiding city."

Pastor James laughed. "Do you have any leads?" he asked.

"I am putting an ad in the local paper requesting help from the general public in apprehending them."

Pastor James caught his breath, coughed, and began to laugh wholeheartedly.

Sam stared at him. "What was so funny about that?" she asked. But by now, the tears were screaming down his face. He looked so ridiculous that Sam started laughing at him. It took a full five minutes before they both stopped laughing.

"What was so funny?" Sam asked.

"I don't know," he said. "Whoever heard of a police detective placing an ad in the paper to apprehend juvenile offenders?"

"Maybe you should come to Monroe and find out for yourself. Then maybe the idea wouldn't seem so funny."

"Okay, I apologize. I shouldn't have laughed, but the idea of it really tickled me and it conjured up some absurd thoughts," he said.

"I forgive you," Sam said. She glanced at her watch. "I need to be going. The chief will wonder what happened to me if I don't get the squad car returned to the station tonight."

"When will I see you again?" he asked.

"Well, that depends on Mom. If things get any worse, I will be back sooner than later."

"On your next visit to Silver Bay, please stop and see me. I would like that."

"Okay," Sam assured him.

"Do you have time for a short prayer?" he asked.

"I would really like that." Sam folded her hands and bowed her head. Pastor James always started with a short silent meditation before he launched into prayer. The silence would last for about a minute. The quietitude was welcome, and it gave Sam the time she needed to relax and focus on his prayer. Pastor James then prayed for her and her mom and for Phil. The prayer was very personal, soothing, and comforting. He ended his prayer with, "Deo gratias. Amen."

"Amen," Sam whispered.

CHAPTER 13

Chief Johns was seated comfortably in his chair behind his desk. Another weekend had passed by too quickly. He enjoyed the time he spent with his wife and kids and all the constant activity. He wasn't called into work, which made the weekend especially nice. A 24/7 job has its drawbacks when it came to his family life, but his wife had learned to live with it. It was Monday morning. As he read the police reports in front of him, he was pleased to see that it had been a quiet weekend in Monroe. After he put the reports down, he appreciated that it was just routine stuff and no arrests. No additional paperwork was required from him. He had a fresh cup of steaming coffee in front of him and took a sip. He then surveyed the piles of papers on his desk that needed attention. He let out a big sigh and felt the very familiar feeling of disdain looking at the stacks. The paperwork was always there, like some freak of nature. No matter how hard he tried to keep up with it, it just kept coming and landing on his desk. It reminded him of how white-capped ocean waves would leave their deposits on a beach.

Over the past couple of years, his attitude concerning this influx of paperwork had changed. It now took second and third requests to get his attention. He tried to delegate some of the more mundane stuff, but he got little to no interest from anyone on his staff. It seemed that everyone was overworked these days.

He was waiting for Jake Neuberger, a reporter from the Monroe Press. He was stopping by to get the latest weekend news for the police blotter section of the newspaper. Jake was usually very punctual and would be there at eight-thirty. The police blotter was very popular along with the obituaries, and together they kept the circulation numbers up for the paper. In a small town like Monroe, calling a cop to get a cat out of a tree or someone hitting a deer on a county road usually got the attention of the press.

His thoughts were interrupted by the sudden ringing of his telephone. "Hello," he said cheerfully.

"I have Roger Nussbaum on the line for you," the dispatcher said, "and he doesn't sound like he is in a very good mood. Do you want to take the call?"

As the call was being passed through to him, Johns wondered why Roger hadn't called him on his direct line. "Hello," he said as pleasantly as possible.

"What the hell is going on?" the voice on the other end of the line boomed.

"What are you talking about? Has something happened?" Johns asked in a bewildered voice.

"I just got off the phone with Gregory Denton and he is furious. He wants to know why we are re-investigating the death of his mother. I assured him that we were satisfied with the doctor's report as to the cause of death and that we were not investigating it. Then he went on about Ada's suspicions and Detective Gates. He said that Gates questioned him about Ellen's death Saturday afternoon. Is that true?"

Johns stared helplessly at his coffee cup. "I don't know anything about it, sir, but I will talk to Gates."

"Good!" he boomed again. "I thought I made myself perfectly clear to you about this whole business. Ada and her rants and ravings are bad enough, but now Gates? Listen to me carefully, Johns. I want you to talk to Gates about letting the past be in the past. I can't afford any screw ups. In the next couple of weeks, the governor will announce the chairmanship of his crime committee, and I plan to be the guy! Do you understand me?!"

Johns couldn't remember the last time when Nussbaum was in such a state. It seemed that the governor's appointment that he wanted so badly had taken on a life of its own. "Okay. Don't worry. I will talk to Gates and get it all sorted out."

"I am counting on you. I am counting on you!" Nussbaum repeated himself and abruptly hung up.

Johns sat back in his chair and let out a sigh. He took another sip of coffee and set the cup down absentmindedly. He stared over his desk at nothing in particular and tried to puzzle out the phone call. It seemed to him that he had two problems. The first, of course, was that Sam interviewed

Gregory concerning Ellen without telling him, and the other was Nussbaum's insistence concerning the circumstances of Ellen's death. So to Ada's point, without an autopsy, how would anyone know for sure?

He personally had no reason, other than Ada's suspicions, to think that the death was anything other than what it seemed. Dr. Gehringer was convinced after he examined the body that heart failure was the cause of death. Even Gregory didn't question his judgment. So why does Ada think that Sam, being new to the department, would investigate the death? As far as he knew, Ada didn't even know Sam except maybe from church. And then, Sam had never brought up her name to him until after the funeral.

Johns didn't usually believe in coincidences, but he found that the convergence of both Ada's and Nussbaum's concern over Ellen's death interesting. Their reasons were totally different, and their personal agendas seemed to be polar opposites. But maybe, there was something more to this than he had originally suspected, or maybe everyone was wasting everyone else's time and energy.

"A penny for your thoughts," Sam said as she stood in the doorway.

Johns jerked his head up in surprise. "Was I that obvious?" he asked.

"You were in a land far, far away." They both laughed. He motioned for Sam to sit down. Once again, she had to maneuver her way around the cluttered obstacle course to find an empty chair before she sat down. As she glanced around the little office, it had a different feel to it. Something was different. She felt a soft cool breeze on her face. She glanced over to the window and she heard a cardinal singing outside. *He opened the window*, she said to herself.

"Fill me in on your weekend," Johns said.

Sam started her narrative with the paper transport and the unscheduled coffee stop that triggered off thoughts of her mother. No comment from Johns. Then she launched into her meeting with Gregory. Johns leaned forward in his chair, staring at her, and listened intently. She started with the mystery photo that Gregory said he didn't know anything about it. She believed him. When she got to the point in her story about asking Gregory's opinion on the death of his mother, Johns stopped her.

"Why did you question him about that?" he asked.

"Well, I knew that Ada wanted a meeting with me about it, and I felt that Gregory needed to know. This is a small town, after all, and I am sure that word would get back to him anyway. So, I was just letting him know what I was doing in advance."

"How did he react to your questions?" Johns asked.

"Funny you should ask that," Sam answered. "I got an unexpected response. He got very angry and upset and went off on me. It was like I had pushed one of his hot buttons. I quickly ended the conversation after his angry outburst. However, I will say that he was in some sort of state. He probably felt threatened by the question, so his best response was to attack Ada."

"It might interest you to know that he called Roger Nussbaum this morning, and he railed to him about you questioning him. Nussbaum was very upset. He then called me and told me to call you off."

"But why? Did I do something wrong?" Sam asked. Neither one of them said anything. The question just hung in the air.

Johns shifted his weight a little and settled back into his chair. His furrowed brow gave Sam the impression that he was weighing some sort of decision. After a few quiet moments had passed, he spoke, "What I am going to tell you Sam is in confidence. It must be off the record." She had no reaction and remained silent. "Nussbaum is being considered for an appointment by the governor to his newly formed 'crime commission.' He wants this appointment more than life itself, or so it seems. He wants the chairmanship so he can hobnob with the political powers in Madison and get his face on television. He has touted the murder-free statistics and low crime rate in Monroe as the cornerstone of his argument for the appointment. It also appears that he has a good chance of getting the chairmanship."

"However, if any suspicions about Ellen's death reach the news media, his chances would be dead in the water. A suspicious death in Monroe would cast doubt on his character after all his bravado and flamboyancy. The Monroe Press wouldn't intentionally do anything to derail him, but if any hint of a scandal got to Madison, well . . ." Johns paused.

Sam was listening intently. "But what if—" she started to say.

Johns cut her off in mid-sentence. "I know. What if Ellen's death wasn't of natural causes? Then what? Tell me again about Gregory's reaction to your question about Ellen's death," Johns asked.

"Well, he looked startled, you know, like he wasn't expecting the question. The tiny muscles in his right eye were twitching and his face got instantly red. I wasn't accusing him of anything. I was just giving him information about Ada. I could see that he was very upset when I left him standing beside his car."

"What do you make of that?" Johns asked.

"I don't know. During lunch he was very much in control. At times, he hesitated before answering my questions. His body language seemed strained. I thought that the interview was hard on him. But then again, to give him the benefit of the doubt, maybe he had been through a rough patch with Ada and all her suspicions and was just tired of the whole thing. Maybe he thought it was all behind him or just maybe he was suffering from a "mens rea."

"What's that?"

"Sorry. In one of my classes at the University, my professor told us that it was a Latin term for a "guilty mind.""

Johns smiled at her. "When are you meeting with Ada?"

"Nothing definite for now. We still need to make a time."

"Let me know how your visit goes. If we are chasing ghosts here, then I don't want Nussbaum in a worse state than he is already in."

Sam looked at the ceiling and then straight at Johns. She got his attention. "Do you want me to back off?"

Johns hesitated a moment. "No. We have to follow the law wherever it takes us."

Sam nodded. She got up to leave and turned back to him. "You just have to love politics and politicians." Johns laughed. "And by the way, Neuberger is waiting for you at the front desk."

CHAPTER 14

Ada busied herself in her kitchen, slicing and cutting up cheeses. She was looking forward to her meeting with Sam. For the first time in a long time, she felt that she had met someone who could give her the answers she so desperately needed.

A strand of gray hair swayed back and forth lazily on her forehead as she worked. The sun was shining in brightly through her Swiss-lace-covered windows. The coffee was perking away and the aroma wafted throughout the kitchen to her delight. She had many fond childhood memories of growing up on a farm to the smells of perking coffee.

Her mother had had a blue porcelain coffee pot in their kitchen that welcomed in the dawn of each new day with robust aromas. As a child, she remembered her grandmother's old wood cooking stove in their kitchen, standing beside her mother's newer oven. For nostalgic reasons, her mother would occasionally stoke a fire in the old fire box and put the coffee on to perk. Ada's memory of that old cooking stove was a treasure in and of itself. Her mother told her many stories about her grandmother and the awesome meals that were prepared on that wood stove. Grandma cooked three meals a day, baked bread, and made cakes and pies. And the wood stove heated the kitchen during the cold Wisconsin winters. Ada often wondered why her mother romanticized the past when life seemed so much easier in the present.

Earlier, she had made some lemon bars that were perfectly arranged on a glass serving plate that sat near the gurgling coffeepot. As her practiced hands worked at cutting up some aged Swiss, Cheddar, and Gouda, she looked at the clock. Detective Gates would be there soon.

She had a big old-fashioned kitchen with high ceilings and a round oak table in the middle of the floor. The table was made of solid oak by local Amish craftsmen, with pedestal legs and claw feet. On this beautiful table, she had set two places for lunch. She loved the kitchen and had spent many wonderful hours there when Ellen owned the house. As they drank gallons of coffee together, they laughed at the many absurdities of life. The bond of female friendship was never stronger. They were more like sisters than good friends. What cemented their friendship were failed relationships with men. They promised to be true and to trust only one another forever. No more men!! Woman Power!

Oh God, she suddenly thought. How she missed Ellen! She was so sweet and kind and had a dry sense of humor. If Gregory hadn't sold her Ellen's house, she didn't know what she would have done. She could still feel Ellen's presence everywhere. She felt a slight tug on her heart; *"Special and dear memories,"* she said to herself. She gently wiped away a tear that had rolled down her cheek like a droplet of water from a warm summer's gentle rain.

Her radio was tuned to the local AM station, and she soon found herself humming along with some of the tunes featured on the Swiss Hour. They were playing a few of her favorite songs that her mother taught her to sing as a child. She felt a warm glow in her cheeks as she listened to Chuejerbuelied, Maeritrummel, Meyeag, and Schoeni Zyte.

After the music stopped, Ada finished up in the kitchen. Ellen's sudden death had taken the very breath of life from her. She needed closure to move on. But she could only do that once she was convinced of the true cause of Ellen's death. She owed it to Ellen. Peace and closure is what Ada needed, and she hoped that Detective Gates could help her. "And what about Keith?" she asked. It constantly niggled at her.

Satisfied that lunch was ready to serve, Ada went into the living room and sat down. She had a framed picture of Ellen on a lamp stand near her couch, and she looked at it. The picture was taken on Ellen's forty-fifth birthday on a trip they took to the Wisconsin Dells. Ellen was wearing a grotesque flowered hat and oversized sunglasses and she was laughing at the camera. It was a great trip, and they remarked on it several times. Ada kept the hat, and it was now one of her prized and treasured possessions.

Ellen had helped her through two of the darkest hours and chapters of her life. That is why Ada felt so strongly that she owed it to Ellen's memory to find out the truth.

When Ada was eighteen, she fell in love with a young man two years older than herself. His name was Daniel O'Neil. She was a freshman and he was a junior at the UW Platteville. After they started dating, she developed a passion for him that kept her hormones raging and lightheaded. The only problem they shared was that they both had very similar personalities. They were very opinionated, strong-headed, and stubborn. They argued a lot, but their lovemaking after an argument was fierce and very satisfying. Their relationship fell into a pattern of arguing and then making up. It bothered Ada that Daniel seemed to thrive in this kind of relationship of control and verbal combat. He made mention of marriage several times, but she had her doubts. She thought she loved him, but how could she be sure?

After one of their arguments, Daniel set out on a Friday night with some of his buddies to spend the weekend at a friend's cabin up north. Ada was very upset about this abrupt departure. After all, he just left without so much as a good-bye, a phone call, or anything. Her roommate suggested that they go to a frat party that same night and have some fun drinking and dancing. "Just what I needed," Ada told herself.

She got very drunk at the party and danced the night away. She laughed a lot and felt very much alive. Toward the end of the evening, the booze had lost its taste, and a little voice inside her told her to stop drinking. That was the last thing she remembered.

The next morning, she awoke and felt chilled. She was dreaming that a freight train was racing through her dorm room. As she reached for the covers, she discovered to her horror that she was lying naked in a strange bed next to a naked snoring man. She screamed. She freaked out. She had never done anything like this before. She got up and hastily looked for her clothes. The nausea came on fast. She spotted the bathroom and made a beeline to the porcelain god. Her head was pounding and she felt awful. After she came out of the bathroom, she scanned the bedroom again for her clothes. She couldn't find her bra, but her panties, skirt, and blouse were piled on the floor next to the bed. Her penny loafers were on the floor next to the front door. She struggled into her panties and skirt, and she put her blouse on inside out. She didn't care. She needed to get out of that stifling room. She picked up her shoes and carried them out with her. The snoring opportunist never moved. He was out like a light.

Once outside, she got her bearings and headed back to her own dorm. Her head was throbbing, and her stomach churned as she made her way back, stopping only once to vomit in the bushes. She felt terrible. "What have I done?" she asked herself over and over again. Back in her bed with a wet washcloth on her face, she had the sensation that the room was spinning.

A severe headache was starting to kick in again. She dreaded seeing Daniel. *Someone is going to tell him!* she feared. *I need to tell him first and beg for forgiveness*, she agonized.

Sunday night, she went to his dorm to wait for his return. The boys were late getting back. A few other friends also gathered to wait for them. She nervously looked around to see if she could recognize the snoring man, but he wasn't there. At 8:00 p.m., the news came that there had been a very bad car accident. Ada felt the breath punched out of her. Later that night, it was confirmed that Daniel had been killed along with the other students. She immediately called Ellen.

The guilt of the argument they had and not saying good-bye haunted Ada. Also, her indiscretion was unbearable. She spent innumerable hours talking through her grief and guilt with Ellen. After Daniel's funeral, only the passage of time and Ellen's patience made life bearable again. After she graduated, Ada vowed to herself that she would not have another relationship. Men would find her attractive and ask her out, but the scars etched on her heart that fateful night ran too deep. Besides, falling in and out of love wasn't for her.

Her second meltdown occurred as she was approaching thirty-two. Ada's biological clock was ticking and she was panicking. She did a self-assessment of her life and didn't like the picture she was seeing. She was feeling very lonely and she urgently felt she needed a soul mate.

She knew a guy, Ned Andersen, who farmed outside Monroe with his parents. He was single and never married. The family farm was prospering, and they seemed to be very successful business people.

Ada became obsessed with the idea that Ned was the right one for her. She plotted and planned and got to know him better when she volunteered to serve on the Agricultural Days Committee with him. Ned was good-looking and enjoyed her advances. A combination of her loneliness and Ned's availability led Ada into a raging and passionate love affair with him.

In her opinion, Ned drank too much, but she overlooked this detail and projected unrealistic marriage projections on him. After all, she could change him. *Couldn't she?* She thought that Ned could give her the love that she so desperately needed.

Ellen was now living with Ada after her return from Chicago and cautioned her to reconsider her decision. But Ada wasn't to be deterred. She was very strong-willed and was convinced that she could make it work.

But after Ned left her standing at the church altar, Ellen once again came to her rescue and stayed true to her. The bonds of their friendship carried the day. Ellen never judged her. She was there when Ada needed her.

Ada awoke from her reverie when she heard the sound of the door chimes. She stood up, straightened her dress, and went to answer the door.

"Hello, Detective," she said pleasantly.

Sam followed her into the kitchen and sat down in the chair that Ada had motioned her to. It was Ellen's place at the table. She poured the coffee and gave a cup to Sam. As they engaged in small talk, she placed the cheese tray on the table and the bars in front of Sam. She then sat down.

"If you don't mind, would you call me Sam instead of Detective?"

Ada laughed. "Of course I will, my dear, my mistake." Ada settled back in her chair and took a bar and chewed slowly. Then she picked up her coffee cup and took a sip. Sam thought that she was thinking about a way to open up their conversation.

"How do you like the coffee? Is it too strong for you?" Ada asked.

"No, it is wonderful and the bars are delicious."

"It is my mother's recipe. My father said that she made the best bars in Green County and that no sweet was safe around him. Lemon was his favorite."

Ada carefully replaced her cup on the table. "Isn't this a grand old table? Ellen inherited it when her mother passed. The table became the gathering place for her friends and family at the old farm place. When Ellen's spinster aunt died, she left this house and a sizable amount of money to Ellen. It was a gift that Ellen badly needed at the time in order to get back on her feet and out of my house." Ada paused and slowly took another sip of coffee. "Well, anyway, Ellen could sit here and talk and entertain for hours and never run out of coffee. We played a lot of Euchre around this table on Saturday nights." Suddenly Ada looked very sad. After a few moments, she gathered herself and looked at Sam. "Look, Sam," Ada began, "I want to tell you a story and I would appreciate it if you would hold all your questions until I am finished, okay?"

"Is it okay with you if I take a few notes then?" Sam responded in a friendly voice.

"Sure, that would be just fine with me."

She watched as Sam retrieved a small yellow notebook from her shirt pocket and a ball-point pen. "Okay, I am ready."

Ada took another sip of coffee and launched into her story. "On the night that Ellen died in this very house, I was with her until six forty-five. She had invited me to supper before my meeting at seven o'clock. There was a special meeting a city hall on land use in the city, and I wanted to give my opinion on its effect on the environment. I am very passionate about the environment, and I was ready to speak my piece.

"Well, anyway, Ellen served Schwinebraten with mashed potatoes, a real farm supper. For dessert, she made an Apple Kuchen that we passed on, since the meal was so filling." Sam looked at her with a puzzled look.

"Pork roast and apple cake."

"Okay, thanks."

"She was in good spirits, and we talked about taking a short trip on Sunday after church to Pendarvis House in Mineral Point. After the tour, we planned to have a picnic lunch in one of the parks. Ellen also commented about Gregory having a girlfriend that he had denied with a shrug during his last visit. You see, Gregory's right eye has an almost imperceptible twitch when he isn't telling the truth, and Ellen had noticed it."

Sam jotted down a note in her notebook.

"After that, she said she was feeling pretty good and that the heart medicine that Dr. Gehringer had prescribed for her was working wonders. Mentally, she was slipping a little, and her memory had little lapses, so she had taken to writing short notes to herself. Gregory had observed this decline and told her that he was worried about her, but Ellen assured him everything was fine. We ended our little chat and that was that. We hugged and I left for my meeting. After the meeting, I went home and I went to bed." So far, Ada's voice was fairly flat and monotone as if she had repeated her story many times before.

"The next morning, I tried calling Ellen but she didn't answer. I thought it strange and went by to see her. I rang the doorbell and knocked, but no answer. The door was locked. I looked in the side window, and I noticed that the light from her prized Tiffany lamp was on in the living room. I could also hear the faint sound of the television set. My first thought was that maybe she had fallen asleep in her favorite chair. I knew she had hidden a key to her house under a flowerpot on the front porch, so I let myself in. To my horror, I found her slumped over dead in her chair."

Ada paused and sat quietly. A tear escaped from her eye and spilled down her cheek. She reached for a Kleenex that was tucked under the sleeve of her blouse and gently dabbed her cheek. "Sorry," she said. "I immediately phoned the police department and then just stared at her. I couldn't take my eyes off her. I couldn't believe it. Her death didn't make any sense to me. I thought for sure that an autopsy would be performed to determine the cause of death. But that old senile Dr. Gehringer signed the death certificate as heart failure. I went to Gregory and requested that he order an autopsy, being that he was her son. He said that his mother had had a very good life and he didn't want to contradict the good doctor, who he had known for years. I wrote lots of letters to city officials and made a general nuisance of myself but all to no avail. I couldn't believe that a happy and optimistic woman could just up and die like that. You see, an autopsy would have put my mind to rest. But I experienced a range of emotions that went from rage to resentment and then to despair. You see, I had a strong feeling of emptiness in my sorrow and grief, and I thought my flowing tears would never end."

She paused again for a moment, and then her voice perked up as she continued. "Suddenly it seemed like déjà vu when Keith died. I was in the Swiss Pin Bowling Alley on the Thursday night before he died. I was at the bar talking to the owner about scheduling a date for a Sunday afternoon bowling event for charity. Keith came up to the bar and ordered a couple of beers. He looked pretty tipsy to me. He noticed me standing there and told me how happy and proud he was that his son Brad was accepted to the University of Wisconsin. He offered to buy me a drink. I declined. He bragged about his son until his beer order arrived, and then he disappeared back into the smoky din. I remember saying to myself how proud he must be. He certainly seemed very happy. Brad was the first Kranenbuhl in his family to go to college. The very next day, I heard that he had died from a heart attack. Again, I couldn't believe it. I had just seen him and talked to him the night before. Keith seemed very happy and in good health. I ran into Mary Tollakson on the square, and she told me that Dr. Gehringer had signed the death certificate, heart failure."

"Now, Sam, I don't believe in coincidences." Ada was staring straight at Sam with conviction in her voice. "I think something is wrong here that needs to be investigated. I am an eyewitness to seeing two normal and healthy people one day, and the next day, they are both dead. And their deaths were only a few months apart. There is something here that I am not seeing, and I can feel it in my bones. It's like a sixth sense that won't let go. It just plain doesn't feel right to me!"

Ada paused. She seemed exhausted. She stared at her coffee cup for a while and then she took another lemon bar. A silence fell between them.

Sam shifted in her chair, "Do you have anything concrete to offer other than your suspicions?"

Ada sighed, "I think it was the rush to judgment on the part of Dr. Gehringer. He signed both death certificates as heart failure based solely on their past health histories. Even though he was treating them both for heart conditions, they were doing well enough physically. I think it was just a rush to judgment. A quick 'yes or no' can bypass the truth sometimes. The middle ground of doubt was ignored by him, and he isn't even a trained pathologist. I think if the medical examiner had done a forensic autopsy on them, he may have found something different. I have heard that an autopsy takes about two hours. What is two hours when determining the actual cause of a person's death? Then we would know for sure. At least, that's what I think."

Sam's imagination sprang to life. She felt a little rush of excitement. This wasn't the conversation she was expecting. Ada was obviously a very intelligent woman who had given much thought to her suspicions. And Sam had to agree with her about coincidences. She remembered that Sergeant Oliver told her that during a criminal investigation, pay particular attention to any coincidences, because they could eventually lead somewhere. It may not be apparent at first, but don't ignore them. *Could there be something here then?* she asked herself.

"What do you think about Gregory? After all, he denied your request for the autopsy" Sam asked.

"Well, I watched Gregory grow up. He seemed to take after his Uncle Ben." Ada saw the questioning look on Sam's face. "Marge's husband," she said. Sam nodded. "Ben owned his own business and some of his business practices were rumored to be a bit shady. I questioned Marge about this, but she pretty much ignored my inquires into the matter. She claimed she didn't know what his business dealings were, but she shared with me that she had some of the same concerns. Gregory spent a lot of time at Ben's store during his teenage years and enjoyed working there."

"Was Gregory well liked in school?" Sam asked.

"He was a loner for the most part and didn't have any close friends. He didn't date much, but he really fell for a classmate in his junior year. She was very good-looking. He asked her out on a date but she refused. After that, he became a teenage stalker. The girl was well aware of this and made fun of him. I don't think he ever got over it. The embarrassment was devastating.

"His aunt and uncle wanted him to go out for sports to be more accepted by his classmates. But instead, he joined the high school bowling team. He bowled five three-hundred games and was written up in the Monroe Press for his achievement. That feat has never been surpassed."

"How did he do academically?"

"Well, he was a straight 'A' student and finished second in his class. Here again, he was very smart, but just didn't seem to fit in. I think he was very relieved to graduate and go on to college."

"What about your autopsy concerns? Did it bother you that Gregory just let it go?" Sam asked again.

"I think the timing of Ellen's death must have been awful for him. In a relatively short period of time, he lost his aunt and uncle and then his mother. I never really pressed him as much as I would have liked too. I had to respect his grief. But on the other hand, I just can't let it go. I used to lie awake at night just thinking about it. And then when Keith died, well, it just got to be too much."

Ada seemed to be getting tired, but Sam just had one more question. "Can you tell me about Gregory's relationship to his mother?"

"It was very difficult for him. Ellen abandoned him as an infant and didn't come back into his life until he was a teenager. At first, he was very cold toward her when she was trying to overcome her alcoholism. He wanted to know who his biological father was, but she couldn't tell him. The sad truth was that it could have been any one of four or five different college guys. The alcohol had taken control of her life. She was looking for love, but instead, she only got sex. I tried to help her but failed.

"As time went on, Marge tried to convince him that even though his mother had made some terrible mistakes, she really did love him. Gregory never bought into this. However, he did start to treat her with a little respect, and as she grew older, he would come from Milwaukee and help with some chores around the house."

Sam looked at her watch and was surprised to see that she had been there for an hour and a half. "One more question, Ada. Are you telling me that you think that the two deaths are connected?"

Ada paused, "I don't know. I have thought a lot about it, but I always draw a blank. It doesn't make any sense to me. But I just feel there is something there."

"Okay," Sam responded. "I need to get going." She pushed back her chair.

"Will you think about our conversation today? I would like to know if you think it has any merit." Ada asked softly.

"Yes, I will give it consideration and thank you for asking me here today. The coffee and the cheese and the bars were delicious."

Ada led her back into the living room and then paused next to the chair that Ellen had died in. She pointed it out to Sam. "A constant reminder," she said.

"Why don't you get rid of it?" Sam asked.

"Actually, I thought Gregory would take it along with the Tiffany lamp, but he said no. He had no interest in it. In fact, he wouldn't even sit in it after Ellen's death. When I made him a fair offer for this house, I told him I wanted all Ellen's things to stay. I told him I didn't want an estate auction. He agreed to my terms, except for the lamp, of course."

Curious, Sam thought. "Just one more thing, Ada. Do the initials J.S. mean anything to you?"

Ada's eyebrows came together and her brow wrinkled as she was thinking. "Well, the only person that comes to mind is Julie Stryker."

"I don't think I know her." Sam said.

"She works at The Blumen Keuner Shoppe on the square." Sam made an entry into her notebook.

"Thank you again for inviting me, Ada."

As they made their way to the front door, on the table next to the door was an envelope, which she picked up and handed to Sam.

"What's this?" Sam asked.

"It's Ellen's obituary from the newspaper. I had an extra copy and I thought if you saw her picture and read it, she would seem more like a real person to you. My grandmother had an old saying that comes back to me more and more these days. She said that you can't 'unbake' the bread. Maybe, when we finally get resolution to Ellen's death . . ." her voice trailed off.

Sam smiled at her. "My dad used to say, "Sam, you can't unring a the bell." Ada nodded.

She thanked Ada for the envelope and warmly shook her hand. Then she quietly exited the front door. Standing on the porch, she felt exhilarated. "Maybe things are beginning to pick up at last in Monroe."

CHAPTER 15

Gregory anxiously and quickly paced around the floor in his living room apartment. He was clearly agitated. Earlier that day, he had had his annual performance appraisal at the hospital. It hadn't gone well. His supervisor, Helen Stewart, pointed out mistakes in his paperwork that normally would have been letter perfect. "What is causing these mistakes? I don't understand, Gregory," Stewart asked him. Gregory didn't respond. "This isn't like you. You are a top performer here, and you have always been an exemplary employee." She paused; no response from him as he sat staringlooking at the evaluation form. He didn't say anything.

"Are you under some kind of stress? It doesn't appear to me that you are concentrating on your work." Stewart was trying to be as low key as possible during the interview. She was well aware that these annual appraisals can cause anxiety, even among top performers. Gregory sat as passively as he could, listening to the criticism of his work, and tried kept his cool.

He looked up at Stewart and offered a response to the questioning. He lied and told her that he was taking a new medication, a prescription drug. The side effect of the drug was causing him to have insomnia. The lack of sleep was causing him difficulty, and at times, he had trouble concentrating on his work.

Stewart couldn't believe what she was hearing. The word malpractice was ringing in her head. She had attended many seminars on the exposure of lawsuits for malpractice and this was a textbook case, if she ever heard of one. She was about to say something when suddenly Gregory's stomach felt queasy and he became nauseous. His face turned pale, and he was unable to catch his breath. He put his head between his knees.

Stewart immediately became alarmed at this abrupt change in his appearance. After a few moments, he seemed to recover. "Are you okay?" she asked. Gregory nodded. Then they agreed that Gregory should take the rest of the afternoon off. They both also agreed to reconvene the next week to finish the evaluation. She offered to help him if he needed it. "More time off, perhaps," she offered.

Gregory quickly agreed and left work straight away. "I'll be in touch," he said as he exited her office.

Back in his apartment, he paced nervously around the room. His mind was in overdrive, and the more he paced, the more exhausted he became. After his interview with Detective Gates at the Yellow Iris, he hadn't been able to sleep. Those recurring hellish nightmareish dreams in the cold damp cellar with the freakish ghost haunted his nocturnal sleep. He was becoming more and more fearful of going to sleep at night. But when he finally drifted off to sleep, he tossed and turned and moaned and screamed. Every time his screams woke him up, he was in a fierce sweat. The tormenting dreams were emotionally draining and troublesome. The suddenness of waking up screaming was also driving him crazy.

His supervisor was right, of course. He was under severe emotional distress. After all his masterful plotting and planning of the murders, the unforeseen consequences surrounding the deaths were making him a wreck. The justification for these murders was getting more and more blurred. He had to admit that he was no longer in control of his life. This whole affair was driving up his blood pressure and heart rate and was affecting his breathing. The fear of getting caught and going to prison was slowly driving him mad.

He tried to sit down, but he jumped up again. His nerves were getting the best of him. As he paced, he looked at his mother's Tiffany lamp and felt a pit in his stomach. His meeting with Gates had really unnerved him. The police are trained to catch murderers in their lies, and he was convinced that she would eventually catch him. The overwhelming fear and realization of getting caught and going to prison terrorized him. He could never survive in that environment. Was he really unaware of the imbroglio that surrounded him? The rush of adrenaline and the ego boost he felt after the murders had long since disappeared. His only option now was to plan his escape and to disappear forever. Thank goodness Wisconsin wasn't a death penalty state.

He went into the bathroom to wash his face. Looking into the mirror above the sink, he saw a face looking back at him that he didn't recognize. The face seemed to have aged twenty years. It was the face of a stranger. He looked like hell. He needed a haircut, and the bags under his eyes were drawn and hideous. He had lost weight and his face was thinner. Whatever happened to the simple and mundane routine of eating, sleeping, working, and being in control? The predictability of it all got him out of bed in the morning. But now he was a nervous and shattered mess.

The realization that he was now stuck in this surreal drama of murder and survival depressed him. The reasons for his actions made less and less sense to him. *What have I done?* he questioned himself. *What right did I have taking those lives? Was there a little ticking time bomb in my brain that went unnoticed and undetectable just waiting to go off? Did the thought of Ellen's money set it off?* But now, the fear of getting caught was overwhelming and draining his soul. The more he tried to rationalize his actions, the more confused he got. What was so simple in the beginning had now transformed him into a neurotic freak.

Calling Roger Nussbaum in Monroe had been a mistake. Gates's unexpected question about Ellen's death caught him completely off guard. He wasn't expecting it. Her question had angered and haunted him the entire weekend. He lost all sense of reason and control by making the call. He called Nussbaum Monday morning before thinking it through. If he was Detective Gates, he would certainly question his motives. *"Does she really suspect me, or was she just passing along some information about Ada's concerns?"* He had lost his temper. He would have to be more careful in the future.

He went into the kitchen and grabbed a bottle of beer from the refrigerator. Normally, he didn't drink very much, but now he needed it. He removed the cap with a bottle opener, took a drink, and headed into the living room and sat down. He needed to get his life together. He needed a strategy and a plan to put all this behind him. As he settled into his chair to think, the phone rang. He knew immediately who was on the other end of the line.

"Hello, Gregory," Ada said cheerfully. "I have some good news. Detective Gates, oops, I mean Sam, came by to visit me this afternoon."

Gregory started to feel tightness in his throat and in his chest.

"We had a nice chat about my suspicions concerning Ellen's death, and guess what? She seemed interested. More than I can say about those uppity politicians at city hall, if you know what I mean. Well anyway, she said she would have a think on it and get back to me. Isn't that wonderful, Gregory? I feel now that I have an advocate."

"Did she ask any questions about me?" Gregory nervously asked.

"Now that you mention it, she was curious about your childhood. I filled her in as much as I could. Was that okay with you? It didn't occur to me to ask you first."

"Yes, it's okay. Did she have any other concerns about me?"

"Well," Ada paused for a moment, "she wondered why you didn't ask for an autopsy after Ellen's death. But I assured her that you were grieving and wanted closure."

"Did she accept your explanation?"

"Sure, why wouldn't she?" Then Ada remembered something else. "Also, as she was leaving, she wanted to know if the initials J.S. meant anything to me. The only person I could think of was Julie Stryker."

"Who is that?" Gregory asked.

"Oh, I don't think you know her. She works at the Blumen Keuner Shoppe on the square and has only been living in Monroe a few years. Well, I need to get going, Gregory. One of my favorite TV programs is coming on in a few minutes."

"Good bye, Ada, and thanks for the call." Gregory carefully replaced the receiver on the phone and cradled his head in his hands. "Oh God," he whispered to himself. "Gates is going to figure this out! I need to start planning my disappearance now!"

He went to the sofa and sat down. The phone call seemed to calm him somewhat. His destiny was now sealed. He knew that Gates was on to him and would arrest him for murder. He felt caught in the eternal loop of lies and paranoia. It was like he was trapped in the hamster's cage without a means of escape! That infernal wheel just kept spinning and spinning!!

CHAPTER 16

It was 6:00 a.m. when Sam rolled herself out of bed. She had awoken fifteen minutes earlier and turned off the alarm clock and watched the minutes tick by until six o'clock. She didn't need the alarm to wake her today. As she slipped out of bed, her loose-fitting, flowered, cotton pajamas flapped about her as she hurried to the bathroom to freshen up. She felt excitement and exhilaration.

She had rented a small one-bedroom, second-floor apartment with a garage on Twenty-first Avenue after moving to Monroe. She liked the location because it was close to the police station and she could easily walk to work. The surrounding neighborhood and streets were very quiet, which suited her. The apartment consisted of a living room just big enough for a sofa, TV, stereo, and an easy chair. Luckily, the sliding glass door off her living room faced the inner court of the apartment complex and not the street. From her balcony, she could look down on the common area and see a gazebo, colorful flower beds, and a manicured lawn.

Her kitchen could comfortably fit one person. Her bedroom was cozy with a double bed, a chest of drawers, and a large walk in closet. On her chest of drawers were a picture of her parents and a picture of Dan Oliver with London's Big Ben in the background. She really liked the picture of Oliver, and it reminded her of her sojourn to England. She often thought about her internship there.

She put on an oversized white terry cloth robe and made her way to the kitchen. She brewed a fresh pot of coffee and drank a glass of orange juice. Then she went into the living room and sat on her sofa, waiting for the coffee to perk.

After the previous day's visit with Ada, she had come home and dug out a chalkboard and easel from her closet. She had brought the board and easel with her from her time at the Silver Bay Police Department. After setting it up next to the TV, her thoughts turned to Oliver. She missed him. The letters they wrote to each other were very superficial. The tenor of the letters was that of two friends just staying in touch. But as time slipped away, she wondered if she would ever see him again. She thought he was a very bright police officer and appreciated his many insights into police investigation. And now she was ready to launch herself into a case of suspected murder based solely on the intuition of the beloved friend of the deceased.

After two hours of thinking and writing things down on the chalkboard the night before, she had decided to wait until morning to review her work. As she now sat looking at the board, the aroma of the perking coffee wafted into the living room. She got up and poured herself a large mug and found a stale donut to munch on. Back on the sofa, she stared at the notes on the board.

Oliver had told her to never forget how dangerous it is to make arrests based only on suspicions. A rush to judgment can blur the truth. Oliver had his own chalkboard in his office at the Yard and had written at the top "Who Killed Cock Robin?" He explained to her that in the nursery rhyme, the sparrow confessed to the murder. But did he do it? A fly said he saw Cock Robin die; so what about the fly's only one good eye? What good would a one-eyed fly be on the witness stand?

Defense lawyers have a reputation of cross-examining eyewitnesses to the point where the fly would probably have a mental collapse or breakdown. In the end, he would probably question whether or not he was a fly at all! But on the other hand, a good investigating officer would always want to have the facts. Then he could prove motive, means, and opportunity and not take the word of a fly! Oliver's animated explanation amused Sam, but she also saw and remembered the wisdom behind it.

Sam's board was two and a half feet high and three feet long. It seemed too big for her living room. With chalk in hand, she had drawn a vertical line down the middle of the board and a horizontal line at the top like the capital letter "T." At the top of the board, she had written the word "Pagan."

She had decided to treat Ada's suspicions as a murder case to help her clarify her own thinking. If the two deaths turned out to be natural, so much the better, but she needed to take this analytical approach. Oliver had a theory that the unknown murderer always needed a name when trying to solve a case. He would make up a name and go with it until the true identity of the killer was revealed. Sam chose the name "Pagan" because to her, murder always represented the darker side of human nature. On the other hand, she had to be mindful about her initial thoughts about Gregory and couldn't use his name. She needed to remain neutral and not bias her investigation.

On the left-hand side of the board, she had written Ellen Johnson. She then scotch-taped the obituary and picture that Ada had given her to the side of the board. The picture in the obit must have been taken when Ellen was in her thirties. Sam thought that she was very beautiful. Then she had written on the board: "Death certificate—heart failure," "Doctor G. signed it," "No autopsy," "Sudden death—otherwise healthy except for heart," "Gregory declined autopsy request," "Gregory was sole beneficiary of Ellen's estate," "Gregory wouldn't sit in chair Ellen died in," "No crime scene," and "If a crime was committed, medical experts were needed to determine the cause of death." She had also written the word "premeditated" with a question mark.

Since this assumed murder didn't appear to be a crime of passion, Sam reasoned that it had to be calculated and planned in advance. It took a certain intelligence to plan and carry out such a dark deed.

On the right-hand side of the board, Sam had written the name Keith Kranenbuhl. Fortunately, she had saved all her old newspapers and found his obituary and picture, which was now taped to the right-hand side of the board. Sam had written: "Death certificate—heart failure," "Doctor G. signed it," "Sudden death—otherwise healthy except for heart," "No autopsy had been requested by Stacy (the wife)," "No crime scene," and "If a crime was committed, medical experts were needed to determine the cause of death." The word "premeditated" had a question mark behind it.

As she gazed at the board, she could immediately see the similarities between the two suspected murders. "Interesting," she said out loud.

If Pagan had murdered them both, what was the connection? The similarities between the two deaths went beyond coincidence. Of course, Sam needed more than Ada's intuition to prove anything. The deaths were nine months apart. Other than both victims having hereditary heart problems, what did they have in common?

She brought out a yellow legal pad and made some notes. She needed to talk to Stacy to learn more about Keith. She needed to ask if Stacy still had the heart medicine bottle Keith was using before his death. She needed to ask Stacy about an autopsy. This one would be tricky, and she didn't know how to approach it. She didn't want to freak her out with that request and add another burden to her grieving heart. She would have to discuss it with Chief Johns. Maybe if some interesting stuff turned up making the death look suspicious, the request for the autopsy would go easier. Dealing with someone's emotions during the grieving process is a very tough thing to do.

Sam put down her pad and she was satisfied with her work. She then planned out the rest of her day. She would get dressed, have breakfast, and report her findings to Chief Johns. Then she would call Julie Stryker at the Blumen Keuner Shoppe to set up an appointment for the next day. Sam felt energized. For the first time since coming to Monroe, she felt she had a challenge. She could put her investigative skills and imagination to good use. She also decided to drive to the cemetery to visit the graves of Ellen and Keith. She felt that being there, next to the graves, could help personalize the victims. Just like the picture that Ada had given her, they were becoming real people once again.

But before she could do any of that, she had to check in with her mother. Sharon was always on her mind, like a shadow that constantly followed her. Sam knew that she had to do something to make her mother's situation more manageable. She would shortly need 24/7 care. If Sharon was to be in a safe environment, Sam felt it her duty to make it happen. It wouldn't be easy, and she was dreading the thought of her mom going into a nursing home to atrophy into one of "societies discards!" As soon as Sam said it, she cursed herself. The strain was getting to her.

CHAPTER 17

Sam slowly drove her car through the entrance to the Green Lawn Cemetery and crept along the narrow asphalt road and parked next to Keith's freshly dug grave. The cemetery was located on the southeast corner of Monroe. The afternoon sun shone on her face as she got out of her car. About fifty yards away, she saw another smaller cemetery with signage over the arched entrance that read "Holy Cross Cemetery." The Catholics were buried there.

The afternoon sun had a certain magical quality to it in this sacred place. The overgrown maple trees filtered the sunlight, giving it a surreal effect on certain parts of the cemetery and the grave markers.

Her earlier meeting with Johns went well. He listened intently to her recap of the meeting with Ada and agreed that she should pursue her inquires. However, he once again cautioned her to go slowly and to proceed only with the facts that she was able to ascertain. She assured him that she would proceed with a certain amount of anonymity.

As she stood quietly by the grave, she took Keith's obit out of her pocket and looked at his picture. She thought his smiling face had a slight trace of mischievousness into it. As she reflected on the circumstances of his death, another car pulled up about one hundred feet away.

An elderly gray-haired woman got out and carefully walked over the uneven ground to a grave. Her sad-looking face and wire-rimmed glasses had a haunting but yet familiar look. The woman held a bouquet of freshly cut flowers in her hand. She stopped at her destination and bowed her head for several moments. Then she kneeled down and gently placed the flowers at the foot of the headstone. After that, she sat down on the grass and was very still.

Sam's heart went out to her. The deceased was gone but not forgotten. There was love surrounding this woman. Sam was mesmerized. She couldn't take her eyes off her. She saw the woman wipe away a tear. Then she struggled somewhat to get to her knees. The woman then pulled up a couple blades of grass and put them into her pocket. Once on her feet, she walked slowly back to her car and drove off. Sam tried to hold back her own tears. Visiting a cemetery can evoke strong visceral emotions. *Did the woman feel a sense of comfort or peace or hope by visiting the graveside?* Sam wondered.

Her thoughts went immediately to Earl. Her visits to his graveside were troubling. The cemetery where he was buried was located on the edge of the city limits of Silver Bay. It was in a remote location by some standards, and it had fallen into a state of disrepair.

The cemetery board was broke and struggled for money to maintain it. The walls and pavement were crumbing, and the headstones were tilting. The grass was spotty at best and the wind blew in debris. Kids had vandalized some of the headstones and monuments. They showed little to no respect for those souls who lay at rest. The police theorized that part of the damage was from kids practicing dark rituals at night as part of some cult. Whatever the reason, it made Sam very sad. Perhaps some day, she could move his remains to Monroe. Green Lawn Cemetery seemed like a garden to her.

Ellen's grave was about twenty feet from Keith's. The breeze picked up a little as she turned and walked toward it. She passed a few headstones with immigrant names on them. As Sam drew nearer to the grave, she could see a bouquet of dried-up flowers at the base of the headstone. She surmised that Ada must have left them there.

Sam took Ellen's obit from her pocket and stared at it. She could hear the songbirds singing as she read. "So, this was the woman that Ada felt so passionately about," she said to herself. "And here she is, buried beneath my feet."

Suddenly, Sam felt emotionally down, as if a dark cloud hovered over her. She lamented that she didn't have any close women friends, like Ellen and Ada's friendship. Some of her college friends found jobs in Madison after graduation. She would visit them when she could, but to have a soul mate? She realized and reaffirmed that her life was pretty narrowly focused on her job and the care of her mother.

She would date from time to time, but no one special was in her life. Most of the guys she met were at first intrigued that she was a police detective. Then their interest in her rapidly decreased when she refused to tell them sordid stories about murder and sex crimes. She accepted the fact that dating a cop would be tough, given the long and odd hours when working on a case.

The only person she felt comfortable with was the grandfatherly Pastor James. She trusted him because he was a good listener and seemed to always say the right things when she needed to hear them.

Looking around the cemetery, Sam remembered a woman she once interviewed as part of a case. She wouldn't go into a cemetery alone. She always took a priest with her when visiting grave markers. She believed that if any of the sleepers weren't at peace, then their spirits would haunt the cemetery. She never went into a cemetery at night. The priest was her protection.

Now, as she looked at Ellen's grave, she wondered if Ellen was at peace or was her spirit unsettled; *for that matter, how about Keith?*

Her visit to Green Lawn had given her a strong desire to get to the truth. Just like her quest to find Earl's killers, she was impassioned to get started. As she turned to go, a cool breeze suddenly blew across her face and she became chilled. She hurried back to her car!

CHAPTER 18

Julie Stryker was lost in thought as she arranged flowers for a twenty-fifth wedding anniversary celebration in the rear room of the Blumen Keuner Shoppe. She was the only employee of the owner, Betty Brown. She liked working at the shop, and they got along very well. The day before, Detective Gates had called her and asked if she had known Susan Peterson, Pastor Carl's wife? She confirmed that she and Susan were close friends until her death. Then the detective asked if they could meet briefly to clear up some details of an inquiry that she was working on. She said that she only had a few questions for her and would she be so kind to meet with her. Julie suggested the Coffee Bean Café on the square. The coffee there was delicious and the pastries were made fresh daily. Julie checked with Mrs. Brown and got the okay to meet the detective at 1:00 a.m.

As she finished the arrangement, Julie was both curious and puzzled. *What could this be about?* she thought to herself. Numerous thoughts went through her head. *Was she the witness to a crime and didn't know it? Or was she in some kind of trouble? What was this meeting all about anyway?* She was sure that she would find out. At 10:45 a.m., she bid Mrs. Brown farewell.

"Take all the time you need, dear. Things are a little slow today," she said as Julie exited the front door to the sidewalk.

"Thanks," Julie replied as she disappeared through the door. Once outside, it was a short walk along the ornate red-brick sidewalk to the "Bean." She had worn her light blue floral dress for the meeting, and her hair was done up nicely. She wanted to make a good impression. It was a nice day, which made her short journey pleasurable.

Julie Stryker had only lived in Monroe nine years. She was originally from

Denver, Colorado, where she had worked for the Global Insurance Company after graduating from college. She was employed as an underwriter.

Shortly after she started, she met Jason Stryker, another new hire. He was from Monroe, Wisconsin, a state that she had never visited. Jason was also fresh out of college and had moved to Colorado for the job and the adventure. He was a real "go getter" in the insurance business, and he soon turned heads at the office signing up new clients. He also turned Julie's head. They dated for about a year and then got married in Denver.

Soon afterwards, Jason realized that his heart really wasn't into living in the West anymore and wanted to move back to Monroe. He talked this move over with Julie, and since she was in love, she agreed.

Then one day, the chance for him to return to Monroe presented itself. The Voegeli Insurance Company of Monroe added Global to their line of products, and at the same time, they were looking for another employee. One of their employees had retired after forty years, giving Jason the opportunity that he had been looking for.

Julie was hesitant at first about moving away from the Denver area, but eventually, she felt that she needed to support Jason. His enthusiasm to move back to the Midwest was infectious. Julie had fallen in love with his parents and extended family on their visits back to the Wisconsin. She also felt that the move would give her more life experiences. She was told that she needed to become a Green Bay Packer football fan to be fully accepted by the family. She felt she could manage this because she had absolutely no interest in football. Her own parents weren't too happy about the announced move, but blessed it anyway, much to Julie's relief.

After Jason started at Voegeli Insurance, Julie landed a part-time job at the Blumen KeunerShoppe. It was only to be temporary until she found a full-time job. But shortly after Julie started, she discovered that she had a natural talent for flower arranging. Mrs. Brown also observed this and hired her on full time.

Once they were settled in Monroe, Julie quickly fell in love with the farms and pastoral setting in Green County as well as the friendly people. She was readily accepted by Jason's parents and siblings. She was warmly welcomed by his extended family as well and was shortly enmeshed in all their ceremonies, celebrations, and family dramas.

Her marriage to Jason was going great, and they started talking about starting a family of their own. Jason wasn't much interested in any church affiliation, but Julie found St. Michael's Catholic Church to her liking. Jason had no objections when Julie wanted to raise their future children in the faith. She was a regular attendee at Mass and she really liked Father Bernard.

But then tragedy struck. One day, Julie heard from her sister-in-law that some girl named MaryAnn Newman had moved back to Monroe. She didn't know how to take the comment or why should she even care? It wasn't long before a family secret came bubbling up to the surface. Jason had been engaged to MaryAnn! They had both graduated from Monroe High School the same year but attended different colleges. Their high school romance had turned into long-distance dating and a marriage proposal from Jason. Shortly thereafter, MaryAnn met another guy who was in law school and broke off her engagement to Jason. She gave him back his ring and broke his heart.

Jason had left this detail out of his past when he and Julie were dating. As it turned out, the boyfriend-turned-lawyer married MaryAnn. But after a few years of marriage, their marriage started to unravel. He started divorce proceedings against her. During the trauma of her marital breakup, MaryAnn learned that Jason had moved back to Monroe from some of her friends. The fact that he was married didn't seem to bother her. When her divorce became final, she moved back to Monroe and moved in with her parents.

She then contacted Jason and went after him with a white-hot passion. The family was horrified and warned off Jason, but he wouldn't listen to them. He suddenly turned cold and indifferent to Julie. When Jason didn't come home at night, she felt sick and depressed. He wouldn't even talk to her. He had become a stranger.

Julie was left reeling and feeling bewildered and abandoned. She blamed herself. Jason's family rallied around her and offered emotional support. They all remembered when MaryAnn dumped Jason and the emotional pain he went through. The best thing he did was to move to Colorado and marry Julie. No one understood why this was happening.

Julie lost weight. She never thought or even considered the possibility that Jason would cheat on her. The final blow came when Julie arrived home early from work and found them in bed. She packed up her things and moved out of their house. She moved into an apartment over the Blumen Keuner Shoppe that was owned by Mrs. Brown.

After the divorce, Julie settled into a routine of work and being with her friends. Jason's family kept in contact with her and offered support and help whenever she asked. Also, her church friends rallied around her and helped her through the shock of it all. There wasn't very much marital property to divide up, but after the divorce, Jason starting sending her a check every month. The only reason for the money that Julie could think of was guilt, and Jason wasn't even Catholic! After the divorce, Jason and MaryAnn moved in together but never married. Whenever she was asked about the divorce, she would always say, "Life isn't always fair."

When Julie arrived at the 'Bean', she requested and got a privacy booth facing the square. A few old ladies from her church smiled and waved to her as she was being seated. She picked up the menu card and waited for Gates. Since coming to Monroe, she had learned to appreciate the coffee and pastries there. The different coffees listed on the cardboard menu had her in a state of anticipation. She had tried them all as she slowly read down the list. She mouthed the names, "Almond, cappuccino, caramel cut, chocolate raspberry, crème brulee, hazelnut, Irish cream, Swiss chocolate, almond and mocha."

Suddenly, Julie felt someone's presence and looked up from the card. She saw a smiling Detective Gates looking back down at her. She blushed. "Sorry about that," Gates said.

Julie jumped to her feet and shook Sam's hand. "I am Julie Stryker and you must be Detective Gates."

Sam noticed that she was about five feet six inches tall with chestnut, medium-length hair. She had a nice figure and cute, bright, sparkly brown eyes. Sam immediately liked her.

"Thank you for meeting with me on short notice," Sam said. "Please sit down. And please call me Sam."

"Well, okay, Sam," Julie said hesitantly. The waitress came over and they both ordered a cappuccino and a Danish pastry. After the waitress left with the order, Sam started with some small talk about the weather and Monroe. She wanted Julie to be at ease before she launched into the reason for the meeting.

When there was a lull in the conversation, Sam pulled the photo of Gregory out of her shirt pocket and handed it to Julie. It took Julie only an instant to look at it and laugh. "Where in the world did you get this?" she asked.

Sam told her about Pastor Carl finding the picture among Susan's stuff and was curious about it. The picture had your initials on the back. Julie turned it over and smiled and handed it back to Sam. "If you are asking me about the picture, I can certainly fill you in," she said.

"Any help that you can be will certainly be appreciated," Sam replied. The coffee and Danish arrived. Julie took a sip of the aromatic coffee.

"Well, I first met Susan at the Blumen Keuner Shoppe. She would come in and order flowers for her church. Mrs. Brown gave all the churches in Monroe a fifteen percent discount, and Susan took full advantage of that. After a while, we got to be good friends and we would have lunch together. She often invited me over to her house to enjoy her flower garden, which was very beautiful. She had a real talent for growing things." She paused and sipped more of her coffee. Sam sat silently eating her delicious roll and sipping her coffee. As Julie told her story, Sam could see the bond of friendship that the two women shared.

"Susan was very interested in my life story, and she thought it was just terrible the way Jason, my former husband, had treated me. I tried to convince her that I was perfectly happy with my single life. And that my church work and my friends kept me plenty busy. That's all that I really needed. I didn't want or need another man complicating my life. But Susan wouldn't hear of it. She constantly pointed out to me that I needed a man to complete my life. You know, to make it whole. I totally disagreed with her, and we had some interesting spirited but friendly debates and discussions about it." Julie took a breath. Sam was intently listening and didn't interrupt.

"Well, anyway, one day, she walks into the Blumen Keuner Shoppe with that picture. She showed it to me and told me that the name of the man in the picture was Gregory Denton. She explained that he grew up in Monroe and was now living in Milwaukee. And most importantly, she had it from a reliable source that he wasn't married. I asked her where she got the picture of him. It was almost comical the way she described taking it out of the second-floor window at her house without him knowing it. We had a good laugh over that. Susan tried for about a week to get me to reconsider my stance on men and, in particular, Denton. She even volunteered to set up a chance meeting. But I said no.

"Then one day, a customer of mine was talking to Ellen Johnson in the Blumen Keuner Shoppe, and the woman asked her about Gregory. My ears immediately perked up. The customer told Ellen that she had heard that Gregory was dating some girl named Kitty in Milwaukee. Ellen looked surprised and her eyes got very big. Then they walked over to the corner of the Shoppe near the front door, and they started whispering. I couldn't wait to call Susan with the news. That was the end of Gregory Denton and the matchmaking, that is, until you showed me his picture today."

Sam had sat very still, listening to her every word, and when she had finished, she asked, "By any chance, you wouldn't know Kitty's last name?"

"Sorry, no. I really wasn't interested." They sat in silence for a while.

Then Sam asked, "Why didn't you move back to Colorado after the divorce?"

Julie shifted slightly. "You know, I have had others ask me that. The only thing that I can come up with is that Monroe really grows on a person. It is a special place. It has a small town, home town charm. The friendly people who live here care about one another, and that feeling of inclusiveness is wonderful. In fact, I have more genuine caring friends here than I ever had in Colorado."

They finished their coffees and Sam thanked her for the meeting and paid for the coffee and Danish. She needed to get back to Pastor Carl to put his mind to rest, and then report back to Chief Johns. As she was leaving the 'Bean', she thought that Julie's response for not going back to Colorado left out one very important piece. *She was still in love with Jason and thinks that one day he will come back to her!*

CHAPTER 19

Chief Johns sat behind his desk holding the telephone receiver to his ear. He had the look of a man who was totally bored. He played with a pencil by spinning it around on top his desk. Nussbaum was animated in his conversation while, Johns grunted a couple of times to acknowledge that he was still on the line and listening.

Sam had called him earlier that morning for a brief meeting to give him an update on her progress, but his day was booked solid and she couldn't get in to see him. But she insisted, so Johns caved and told her no more than fifteen minutes. She gave him a short summary of her suspicions concerning the two deaths. He especially listened to her plea that only an autopsy on Keith would settle the matter. Johns pondered for a while and tried to think through the consequences of this request. Then he agreed that they should visit Stacy Kranenbuhl and try to explain the situation to her. Hopefully, she would consent. He then asked Sam to set up the appointment. But as for now, Roger Nussbaum had him on the line and was boring him to death as his voice droned on. His phone calls to Johns had become a daily occurrence and a nuisance, to say the least.

After Sam had left his office, he had to admit he admired her tenaciousness. She showed a real passion for her work and had the imagination to back her up. He wished that more of his other officers where like that. When Sam first came to the department, he had his doubts. But there was something special about her, and he had grown to respect her intelligence. She had that intangible that set her apart. Maybe being the daughter of a decorated police officer had something to do with it.

But for now, it seemed to Johns that Nussbaum needed a good listener, and being in a position of power, he took advantage of the chief. Nussbaum was very excited today because a scandal had surfaced in the law office of his chief rival for the chairmanship. The scandal had something to do with payoffs and political favors. Good stuff, to Nussbaum's mind. He was now asking the chief for anything he could think of that could harm his chances and derail him. Johns assured him that all was well. But he left out any references to the work that Sam was doing. He didn't want the embarrassment if Sam's intuition on the suspicious deaths didn't pan out. However, on the other hand, she was sussing out a very interesting theory of a possible double murder, and that couldn't be ignored. He needed to keep her investigation quiet for now.

Johns mind wandered off again as Nussbaum went on and on, first to the mess on his desk and then to the rumor that Nussbaum was trying to whiten his teeth in preparation for his new television persona. The rumor at the local barber shop was that he was also slowly turning his graying hair back to an auburn color using hair dye. Johns smiled to himself, thinking about this gossip as he sat still and quietly listened to Nussbaum telling him how great he was and that he intended to make the state of Wisconsin even bigger and better. "We will be on the world map and leading the nation in crime reduction once I am appointed," he rambled on.

"So you think it is a sure thing?" Johns asked. "The chairmanship, I mean."

"After the press is finished with my rival, it should be a slam dunk for me!"

There was a pause in the conversation and Johns said, "My grandfather once told me that when racing down a football field with the ball for a touchdown, always be aware of the other team's players and where they are on the field. If not, you may not make it."

"I didn't know that your grandfather played football," Nussbaum quickly responded.

Johns looked to the ceiling and rolled his eyes, thinking to himself *Why bother? He has really lost it.* Finally, Nussbaum had another call coming in and hung up. Johns got up to stretch his legs and went to get a much-needed cup of coffee.

He suddenly felt tired. "Did the call from Nussbaum cause this?" Then he reflected on his visit to the doctor yesterday. The news wasn't good and the lecture afterwards wasn't a surprise. He was forty pounds overweight, had high blood pressure, high cholesterol, and his waistline was apple-shaped.

His doctor told him that diet and exercise was the answer. Medication wasn't the answer.

Johns's main problem was the stress of the job. His wife had talked him into quitting smoking which wasn't helping either. In the summer, he seemed to live on beer, brats, and cheese. Also, the Swiss Bakery on the square beckoned him with cream puff pastries, dark chocolate, and his favorite cookie, Spitzbuben, two butter cookies with strawberry filling made like a sandwich. He knew that he needed to do something about his weight, but there were no good solutions. "Whatever," he told himself.

Back at his desk, he reviewed again the notes Sam had given him. As he read through them, the case that she was building seemed compelling. But at the moment, it was all circumstantial and only centered on her own suspicions and Ada's intuition. Sam needed hard evidence, and she was convinced that she would eventually come up with it. Johns also felt that the key to solving the case was the autopsy. That would be a tough one to get the permission he needed. If no poison was found in either Ellen or Keith's body, then the deaths were as reported—natural causes. But what if poison was found?

CHAPTER 20

Brad Kranenbuhl yelled down from his second-floor bedroom, "Where's my favorite red T-shirt, Mom?!" Stacy was in the kitchen and could tell from the tone of his voice that he was excited and agitated. She went to the bottom of the stairs and called back up to him that it was dirty and in the wash bin. Stacy heard his bedroom door slam, and a few moments later, he flew down the steps past her. "You know that's my favorite shirt! You know that I feel better when I wear it! Please wash it today, okay!" he ordered her as he dashed out of the front door and down the porch steps. Before she could say anything else, he was gone.

Stacy shook her head and went back into the kitchen to get ready for her visit from Chief Johns and Detective Gates. Since Keith's funeral, she had relied heavily on Brad and Pastor Carl to help her through her days of sadness and grieving. Her tears came easily as she remembered the good times with Keith. And now, no matter when she called Pastor Carl or went to visit him, he always had time for her. Brad was also hurting and trying hard to manage his own broken heart. He missed his dad terribly. In fact, she had never felt closer to Brad than during their grieving. But they also had their moments. Life-altering tragedies do that to families, and theirs was no exception.

As she prepared the food, Stacy remembered how happy and upbeat Keith had been about Brad going to the University of Wisconsin. He had a bounce in his step and often felt giddy about it; the first Kranenbuhl to go to college. Brad was living the dream, his dream. And as an added bonus, his new heart medicine had minimal side effects. From all his exuberance, he boasted that he would outlive all his siblings and cousins and live to be one hundred and one!

For the first time in a very long time, it seemed to Stacy that Keith had stopped worrying about the heart disease that had plagued his family. He talked more about his hopes and dreams for Brad and his college graduation party in four years. It was going to be something really special. That's why the suddenness and the shock of his death totally devastated her. Going from the heights of joy and optimism into the pit of sullen sadness and loss was almost more than she could manage.

Since his death, everyone had been very kind and generous to her. Her refrigerator still had food in it that her family, neighbors, and friends had dropped off. No matter how much she protested, the food just kept coming. The ladies at the church really went overboard on casseroles. She started attending church again, which she found very comforting. Even the bank president was very kind, giving her time off to attend to things.

Detective Gates had set up the appointment for 10:00 a.m. Stacy went to the square earlier that morning and bought some fresh pastries from the Swiss Bakery. Keith had made jokes about cops and donuts, and it made her smile to think about that now. She was brewing fresh coffee in the kitchen, and the aroma wafted throughout the house.

She left the kitchen and went into the living room to wait. As she passed by the mirror in the hallway, she took a quick glance at herself. She was wearing blue jeans and a cream-colored blouse and sandals. She originally thought that she should dress up for the visit but she changed her mind. She just felt more comfortable in her casual clothes.

Her blonde hair was tied in a neat bun, and she adjusted her glasses. She noticed the wrinkles under her eyes that she had tried to cover up. "Oh well," she sighed. She was wearing the fourteen-carat gold neck chain that Keith had given to her on her birthday. She remembered how she got on his case about spending so much money. But he only laughed and claimed she was worth every cent and carat! "Memories," she said to herself. She made her way to the living room and sat on the living room sofa. While sitting there waiting, she tried to think of a reason why the police wanted to see her.

The doorbell rang at precisely 10:00 a.m. She jumped up and answered it. She immediately recognized Sam from church and smiled at her. "Please come in," she said. Chief Johns followed them into the living room. After she seated them, she asked if they would like some coffee and pastries. Then she disappeared into the kitchen.

Sam surveyed the room and noticed bowling trophies on the fireplace mantel and scattered around the room. There were gold-toned team trophies and individual trophies. *"Quite impressive,"* Sam thought. *"There must be between twenty-five to thirty trophies scattered around the room.*" It reminded her of some kind of religious shrine.

Stacy returned with a wooden tray offering up of steaming coffee cups and pastries and set it down on the table in front of Johns, located between the two sofas. As he reached for his cup of coffee, his eyes fixated on the cream-filled puffs and he sighed.

"Cream or sugar?" Stacy asked.

They both declined. "Black is just fine," Johns said.

Sam started the conversation by asking how she and Brad were doing. Stacy assured them that they were holding up okay given the circumstances, but at times, it was very difficult. Then Sam pointed to the bowling trophies. Stacy leaned back in her seat and sighed. "Keith loved bowling. He was too small in high school to make the sports teams. He and his friends tried out for the teams, of course, but in the end, he was always cut. He was told that he was too slow, but he felt his size was the real problem. Then he discovered that size didn't matter in bowling. It wasn't a glamorous sport, but he was good at it." She paused and waved her arm around the room. "And now you can see the results of his passion to be good at sports!" Then she laughed. "My mother always told me this collection of bowling trophies would end up in a garage sale someday."

No one said anything. Johns felt this was a good time to start the intended conversation. "Thank you for seeing us," he began. "As you know, my name is Chief Johns and this is Detective Gates."

Sam smiled at her and thought, *Oh God, what a beginning.*

Johns paused for a moment and said in a soft voice, "If it is okay with you, we have a few questions concerning Keith's death."

Stacy looked at the chief and then at Sam and caught her breath. She turned a little pale. She felt light-headed.

The chief gave a quick glance at Sam and continued. "I'm sorry . . . I didn't mean to alarm you. I apologize if I came across that way." Johns waited a while for Stacy to compose herself. "We have some questions that are only a part of police procedure when dealing with a sudden death. We just want to verify some of the details. That's why we are here today."

Stacy looked at him with a puzzled look on her face. "I thought Keith's death was very straight forward. Didn't Dr. Gehringer sign the death certificate as heart failure? Do you not agree with that?" Stacy asked.

Johns shifted his weight a little on the sofa. *This conversation wasn't getting off to a very good start,* he thought.

"Can I have another cup of coffee?" Sam asked.

Stacy immediately responded, "Oh yes," and retreated to the kitchen.

"Do you want me to take over?" Sam whispered to Johns.

"No, I need to take the lead on this," he whispered back. "I'll try another tack."

Stacy returned with a pot of coffee and poured Sam a cup. Then she put the pot on the serving tray.

After Stacy re-seated herself, she looked at Johns.

"As part of closing a case on a sudden death and writing up the paperwork, we just need to touch all the bases," he began again. "I assure you that our questions are purely routine and not intended to be anything other than that."

"Okay," Stacy said.

"Would you, by any chance, still have the heart medicine bottle that Keith was taking at the time of his death?"

Stacy's face changed expression and she had a quizzical look about it. "Yes, I think so. I think it is still in his jacket pocket. Shall I get it for you?" Stacy got up and went to the front hallway closet and opened the door. Johns followed her. She reached in and grabbed Keith's Green Bay Packers jacket. Before she could reach into the pocket, Johns took the jacket from her.

"Just routine," he said, "and if it is okay with you, I will bag the bottle."

Stacy looked alarmed and a little startled as she watched Johns put the bottle into a plastic bag. "What are you going to do with the bottle?" she asked.

"I am going to have it analyzed in Madison just to be sure that it wasn't tampered with," Johns replied. "Just routine stuff, Mrs. Kranenbuhl, and nothing to be concerned about. I will let you know the results once I have them." Stacy didn't say anything. She only nodded.

Back on the sofa, Johns asked her if she had noticed anything peculiar in Keith's behavior over the past few months. Stacy sipped her coffee and thought about his question for several minutes. She couldn't take her eyes off the little bottle that Johns had placed on the coffee table.

Johns wondered whether or not she was deciding to tell him something, a concern perhaps that she wanted to keep to herself. He didn't rush her and glanced over at Sam, who was intently watching Stacy's face.

Finally, Stacy spoke in a very low and slow voice. "Yes, there was one thing," she began. "Keith and his buddies went to a bowling tournament in Milwaukee a few months ago. Nothing unusual in that, I guess. He had been going to those tournaments for several years. It was a chance for the guys to get away from their wives and to have a good time. You know that sort of thing. Well anyway, when he got home, he was pretty excited. He said that he met a girl named Kitty Kleppe, who knew someone from Monroe. Other than that, he didn't say much except that it seemed to me that he suddenly stopped worrying about how we were going to pay for Brad's education."

Sam threw a quick glance at Johns, who was listening intently to Stacy.

Stacy continued, "At any rate, he stopped talking about it. I asked him several times about his change of attitude, but he just said he had a plan. He also said that 'Good things can happen to people when opportunity comes knocking and you just have to be ready for it.' I asked him what he meant by that, but he just smirked and walked away."

Stacy paused and took another sip of coffee. Sam was on the edge of her seat. *Kitty Kleppe*, she thought to herself, *how interesting!*

Stacy looked at Johns, who sat in silence and said nothing. "Shortly after his return from the bowling tournament, Keith starting taking mysterious trips to who knows where the first Saturday of each month. He was very secretive about these trips, and he always seemed to have extra money on him when he returned. At first, I thought he was gambling or something. Then one Saturday after he returned, I searched his pants pocket after he changed, and I found five one-hundred-dollar bills. I couldn't believe it—all that money! I confronted him about it, and he hit the ceiling. We seldom argued, but this one was a real burner. I accused him of keeping secrets and having an affair and anything else I could think of. He assured me that nothing like that was going on and to trust him. He said that I really had to trust him on this one and to just to let it go. We never spoke about it again, but it did put a bit of a strain on our marriage." Stacy sighed and relaxed a little and then sat back on the sofa. She looked like a person who had just unburdened herself.

Sam nodded at Stacy and asked, "Did Keith ever bring up Kitty's name again?"

"No, he never mentioned it."

"Did Keith ever tell you who the person was that Kitty knew from Monroe?"

"No. In fact, he would get very agitated if I brought it up, so I just dropped it. But, it did worry me. We never had any secrets between us until then."

"When did he start making these Saturday trips?" Sam asked.

"Well, it was shortly after he came back from that bowling tournament. I can't remember the date or exactly when."

"And you have no idea where he went on those Saturday trips?"

"No. He would always leave about the same time, around 8:30 in the morning and get back home about 11:00."

They sat in silence for a few moments when Johns suddenly stood up. He picked up the bagged bottle. "Thank you for your time, Mrs. Kranenbuhl," he said. "We need to get back to the office."

They all said their good-byes and Stacy showed them to the door. "Now don't forget to tell me about the bottle," Stacy said.

"No, I won't," Johns replied.

They thanked her again for the coffee and pastries. "They were delicious," Johns said as the door closed behind them. Sam gave him a little grin.

Once back in the patrol car, Johns said, "Are you thinking the same thing that I am thinking?"

Sam hesitated briefly and responded to his question, "We have a lot of unanswered questions here, and I could easily jump to some conclusions."

"I want you to get in contact with this Kitty Kleppe and interview her," Johns said. "Ask her what she told Keith that got him so excited and perhaps killed. I will send Keith's medicine bottle to forensics in Madison to test for prints and poisons." As they pulled away from the house, Sam looked back and saw Stacy staring at them out of her living room window. She looked very sad.

CHAPTER 21

Sharon lay sleeping on her worn, floral, living room sofa. She made gentle snoring sounds as she slept. Her head was resting comfortably on her bedroom pillow and her arm was draped over the edge of the sofa. She was fully dressed, wearing her flowered-print cotton dress. Her naked feet pushed up against the armrest of the sofa. It was 9:30 a.m., and the sun was shining brightly into the room.

About two weeks ago, she found that she couldn't sleep at night. She started to imagine hearing strange noises in the dark. In fact, familiar things seemed very strange and frightening to her. Those noises were disturbing, and when she turned on the lights to investigate, the light seemed to be too bright and hurt her eyes. Then she got herself into the habit of standing by her living room window after dark and peered into the night.

She blamed Sam for her loneliness. It was as if Sam had abandoned her and left her destitute. After all, she couldn't move out of the home that Earl had created for them. He would never forgive her for that. The anger she felt was centered in the "life is not fair" genre. "Why did Earl have to die?" was her mantra. She constantly reviewed her life and his death with regret. She was also jealous of Sam's youth. Sam was young and seemed to have everything. On the other hand, she was old and had very little at the end of her life. In the scheme of things, she considered herself old, dull, unattractive, and boring.

During the nightly vigils, her bare feet felt cool against the hardwood floors. Years of wearing cheap but fashionable pointed-toed shoes had taken its toll. In old age, her feet had gone from active feet to aching feet.

As she looked out into the darkness, she was looking for anything suspicious. Earl had told her many stories about criminals who roamed the streets at night. The streetlight near her house gave off an eerie light sometimes and played tricks on her, especially, when the wind blew the tree branches. The moving shadows at times looked like people. She thought she saw a person, but then she wasn't sure. The darkness and the dancing shadows distorted her sense of reality. "Is that a person I see or just the shadow of a swaying tree?"

Also, the lights from a passing car would unnerve her. The car headlights would cast weird-looking shadows into her house. Then her imagination would turn them into strange unexplained images. "Is a car going to stop in front of my house?" she anxiously asked herself.

After a while, she would leave the window and wander about the house. She was afraid to turn on the lights, just in case someone was outside looking in. Moving about the house scared her. As a child, she had gotten up to go to the bathroom at night, and her elder brother jumped out of the darkness and scared the life out of her. Her screams woke up the entire household. She never got over it. And now, years later, as she moved silently from room to room, she expected some dark figure to jump out of the darkness and attack her. In the darkness, she wasn't in control and wasn't able to detect danger, which left her feeling very vulnerable. She was afraid of the unknown.

When she was ten years old, her brother once teased her about seeing a hole in the wall of their basement cellar. Having no flashlight, he dared her to put her hand into the hole. The thought of it sent shivers up and down her spine while he laughed hysterically.

After checking all the rooms and the door locks to make sure that she was alone and safe, she went back into the living room and sat on the sofa. All this nocturnal activity and agitation wore her down and eventually she exhausted herself. She rationalized that if she went to sleep on the sofa, the darkness would pass, and she would be okay in the morning.

Suddenly she moved her arm as she stirred and opened her eyes. She had to reorientate herself and remember where she was. As she struggled to get up from the sofa, she was a mess. She hadn't changed her dress in several days, and her gray-white hair had taken on the life of an unkempt straw scarecrow. She went into the bathroom to wash her face. She looked at herself in the mirror. Her face looked wrinkled with sagging pale skin around her eyes and mouth and below her chin. Her drawn face told her that she had lost more weight. She looked very thin and frail.

After her self-assessment, she made her way to the kitchen. A half-opened bottle of vodka was open on the kitchen table. She opened the refrigerator and glanced inside. She saw a salt shaker and a carton of orange juice. She thought that was strange because yesterday she found a carton of milk in her kitchen cupboard. She took the orange juice over to the kitchen table. She found a clean glass in the cupboard and made herself a drink. The screwdriver tasted great.

After Sam's conversation with Yost concerning the vodka, Sharon's supply was cut off. The only way to get the vodka now was to have it delivered by the local beverage mart. They were only too happy to make the deliveries. She always paid in cash. But she always insisted upon a special delivery time, when Yost was not at home. Sharon knew her routine by heart.

Since she was having trouble writing checks due to her hand tremors, Yost would cash her social security check for her, not knowing the real reason why she wanted the cash. On this point, she felt very clever in tricking her.

Yost was checking in on her every day now and that made her very agitated. She didn't think that Yost was in the best of shape physically to be checking up on anybody. She was old like her. Yost would tell her that she needed better hygiene because she smelled bad. Sharon ignored her.

She also told her to wash the dishes. Sharon told her not to bother coming over to check on her, but Yost still came anyway. Sharon was certain that Yost was reporting back to Sam on what she saw. Also, Sam's friend, Pastor James, was calling her frequently on the phone but she always hung up on him. After all she was okay, wasn't she? Even Sam's phone calls were irritating. Why did she always have to call during one of her favorite TV programs?

As Sharon sat at her kitchen table, she sipped her drink and thought about Earl. She remembered his drinking stories and the way he laughed. He once told her that vodka was the choice of drink among oil workers in Asia or someplace like that. They would take their morning orange juice and mix in a little vodka and stir the drink using their dirty screwdrivers. He claimed that's how the name "screwdriver" came about. He also told her that the name Bloody Mary referred to the blood-like color of the tomato juice.

When she ran out of orange juice, she would switch to tomato juice and a Bloody Mary mix for her morning pick-me-up. She really missed Earl and all his wonderful stories. It seemed strange to her that she could remember his funny stories but forget where she laid down her reading glasses.

As of late, she couldn't remember what day of the week it was. She got extremely irritated and frustrated when she wanted to watch one of her favorite TV programs and had the wrong day. She seemed to be drifting through time, and all the days of the week were the same. She couldn't distinguish one day from another. She couldn't remember the last time she had eaten. But she could remember her mother saying, "There comes a time in every woman's life when a vodka tonic . . ." she couldn't remember the rest.

After she finished her drink, she stood up and felt light-headed. She tried to sit down again but fell to the floor and blacked out. The next thing she remembered was Yost holding her head in her arms, asking her questions.

CHAPTER 22

After the interview with Stacy, getting Kitty Kleppe's phone number was much easier than Sam expected. The manager at the Swiss Pin Bowling Alley made a few calls to Milwaukee for her and was able to get Kitty's number. She then called Kitty from the police station.

Kitty answered after the first ring. She sounded pleasant enough after Sam identified herself as a police detective and told Kitty the reason for the call. Yes, she knew Gregory Denton and would be happy to meet with her. So they arranged to meet at the Ten Pin Bowling Alley on Wisconsin Avenue. Sam was a little surprised how relaxed and calm Kitty was on the phone. She didn't ask any questions. *Was she trying to be cooperative or just coy?* Sam asked herself.

Sam was sitting in her living room in her bathrobe and slippers. She was drinking a cup of coffee and looking at the chalkboard. In a few minutes, she would be leaving for Milwaukee to interview Kleppe. She was really excited. The pieces were starting to fall into place. "The game's on," she said to herself. She felt pumped up. She once again studied the obituary pictures of Ellen and Keith on her easel. Could she really be on the cusp of solving their murders and validating Ada's suspicions? She certainly felt a visceral sensation in her gut.

As she surveyed her working outline on the easel, she grabbed a piece of chalk and drew a line through the name "Pagan" and wrote in Gregory. "It just has to be him," she told herself. But she was also very aware of a warning that Oliver had preached to her. Sometimes cops will theorize a crime, and instead of investigating a case based on the facts, they will spend a lot of time and energy attempting to prove a theory. Many innocent people have been wrongfully convicted by overzealous investigators. Sam cautioned herself to be careful and to use her own good judgment.

With chalk in hand, she made some additional observations and wrote them down. 1) Were Keith's mystery trips, to who-knows-where, somehow tied in with Gregory? 2) Gregory was a pharmacist—poison? 3) Would Stacy agree to an autopsy? 4) Too many coincidences!

She had just finished her coffee when the telephone rang. It was Janet Finley, her roommate from college. Just hearing Janet's voice took her back to her college days.

After graduation, Janet went to work for a law firm in Madison. She excelled at her job and very quickly became the office manager. As students, she and Sam would hang out with their friends at the "State Street Grill" located near the capital. The bar was small in that it could accommodate only about twenty-five people. It was the perfect setting to have a beer, eat bar food, and listen to music being played on a jukebox. She thought the cheeseburgers and fries were the best she had ever had in the state of Wisconsin. The fries had a hint of garlic. The noise level at the bar was normal and the dress casual. It also had an outdoor patio with tables and chairs that Sam especially liked. The cigarette smoke in the bar area always irritated her eyes.

After moving to Monroe, Sam reconnected with Janet. Janet told her that about ten of their college friends found work in Madison after graduation and that they still hung out together at the bar to socialize. After hearing this, Sam joined their group because it was a distraction and it got her mind off her problems. It also gave her the opportunity to go out on the occasional date.

Also, if Sam was in the mood for some casual sex, this was the perfect venue. Janet told her about a little trick that she used from time to time. "If you see a guy you like, just hike your skirt up over your knee and smile." This ploy seemed a little too simple and obvious. *Guys have to be smarter than that,* she reasoned. She was wrong.

Sam didn't have any problem with recreational sex. It satisfied a need to relax and to get caught up in the notion of romance. However, if she felt any kind of emotional entanglement coming on, she simply dumped the guy. At this stage in her life, that was all she required.

The reason for Janet's call was that a guy named Doug Herlinger had asked about her.

"Who is that?" Sam asked.

Janet explained that the last time Sam was in town, this Doug guy chatted her up at the bar. He was an accountant and tried to buy her a "brandy old fashion." Sam had to really concentrate. She told Janet that she must have had too many beers and didn't remember him.

"So, he made that good of an impression," Janet joked.

Sam told her that she was working on a case and didn't know when she would be in Madison again. She told Janet to tell Doug that she was too busy to see him.

After she hung up, she got dressed. She checked the time and was ready to leave when the phone rang again. "Who could that be?" she asked herself. Two calls in the same morning was a bit odd.

"Hello," she answered.

Pastor James was on the line. He told her that Sharon had fainted and had fallen in her kitchen, but she was now resting comfortably in the hospital in Silver Bay. He told her the story of how Mrs. Yost found her and called the police and ambulance. Then Yost called him to relay the story. That's why he was calling her. Could she come to the hospital as soon as possible? Sam assured him that she would drive right over. Pastor James said he would wait at the hospital until she arrived.

After they hung up, Sam called Johns and explained to him about the emergency. Then she called Kitty to reschedule their meeting. Sam quickly packed an overnight bag and left for Silver Bay. Her thoughts were both chaotic and depressing as she sped east along the highway to Silver Bay. As she drove, her thoughts faded in and out of a dense fog, charged with anger and concern. *Why didn't Yost call me?*

CHAPTER 23

Gregory's tense white knuckles were choking the telephone phone receiver as he listened intently. He was gripping the phone receiver so hard that his left hand was cramping up. After he hung up, he slammed his fist down on the top of his kitchen table so hard that silverware scattered everywhere. "Damn it!" he shouted as the pain made the rapid ascent through his hand to his wrist and up his arm. He was alone in the kitchen. Then he went into the living room and sat down in his armchair and stared into space. He was gently holding his hand. The phone call had unnerved him!

Kitty called him to tell him that a Detective Gates from Monroe called her and wanted to interview her about him. Gates had some questions that needed answers. Kitty asked Gregory what it was all about. He told her he didn't know.

"Don't lie to me!" Kitty shouted into the phone.

Gregory paused and turned pale. "I am not lying," he said rather weakly.

"Look, am I mixed up in something that you did or not? Am I in any kind of trouble?"

Gregory tried to reassure her that she was okay and not to worry. As he told her that, his mind was whirling. *How did Gates learn about Kitty? When they were dating, did he tip his hand or say anything to her that would implicate him in the murders.* He felt faint. He had shortness of breath and was sweating. *Was he having a panic attack?* He needed time to think! He told Kitty to say whatever she wanted to Gates. He had nothing to hide. Then he asked her to call him after the interview and tell him what happened.

"You bastard!" she yelled into the phone. "Screw you, Gregory!" and she hung up.

The phone call started to sink in and resonate with him. He was still sweating. As his mind raced, he reasoned that Gates had somehow figured out what he had done. He had been so careful, but Gates was putting the pieces of the puzzle together. *But how?* he questioned. *A female detective?* he laughed. But she was now slowing circling above him like a vulture, waiting to take away his last gasp of freedom.

He was angry at himself. In all his planning, he didn't calculate the odds of getting away with murder. *Was he living in a vacuum? Why didn't he factor in the unintended consequences? What was he to do?*

Then suddenly, he had clarity of mind that made him relax. He felt much calmer. His path now became very clear. He must act and act quickly. His only option was to leave Wisconsin and disappear into Canada. It would take only a few days to cash in his savings and leave the country. He could probably live for a year or two or three on the money he inherited from his mother. A new identity and a new start!

Gregory felt energized. He changed into a pair of blue jeans and a T-shirt and got out a yellow legal pad and pencil. He needed to map out his plan and put it into action. No way was he going to sit around and wait to be arrested. The thought of going to prison terrified him. He was sure he wouldn't survive there!

He retrieved his road atlas from his bedroom closet. After opening it to Canada, he studied it as it lay on his kitchen table. *Such a big country,* he thought to himself. *Getting across the border was no big deal. His driver's license was all that was required.*

As his eyes focused on the multi-colored provinces of Canada, he seemed to put himself into a trance-like state. Gregory's mind was churning. His options seemed endless. After all, Canada was a very big country, and he could very easily get lost in it. His somber mood had changed. He felt good as he perused all the possibilities for his escape. The idea of vanishing into the vast unknown landscape of Canada gave him hope. It gave him something to look forward to. He needed to end this nightmare he was living, move on, and leave it all in the past! He went to the refrigerator and grabbed a beer.

CHAPTER 24

haron wasn't in a very good mood when Sam got to the hospital. She was giving everyone trouble. Sharon seemed disoriented and confused. Her doctor recommended that she needed to be sedated. After talking it over with Pastor James, Sam agreed. The decision was made in order to keep her a couple of days in hospital for observation and evaluation. Both a physical and a mental checkup were to be done. The next step seemed obvious to Sam, but she needed a doctor's recommendation.

Mrs. Yost had volunteered to watch over the house and to tidy things up. She assured Sam that she would keep an eye on the place. Pastor James said he would look in on Sharon every day. Sam wanted to stay with her mom, but the reality of her condition was very clear to her. Sharon was being cared for, and there was little else for her to do. She tried calling Phil, but couldn't reach him.

So after signing all the appropriate forms and bidding farewell to everyone, Sam left for her childhood home. She intended to spend the night in the house of her youth.

Entering the house, she felt a little strange. She was alone and the place had a different feel to it. Memories came flooding back as she looked at the pictures of her family and the familiar furnishings. She suddenly felt very sad.

She made her way to her old bedroom, which was pretty much the same as she had left it years ago. The house was haunted by memories. As she prepared for bed, she remembered the times when her parents tucked her in and told her not to be afraid of the dark. Nonetheless, she had a very fitful night full of crazy dreams. The next morning, she was up early and left for her meeting with Kitty. Sam had called her to reschedule their appointment after she received the call from Pastor James concerning Sharon. Kitty was okay with the new meeting time.

Sam arrived early at the Ten Pin Bowling Alley on Wisconsin Avenue in Milwaukee. She noticed that the light behind the "n" was burned out, making it the Ten "Pi" Bowling Alley. She seated herself in a dimly lit eating area near the front of the bowling alley. It was 10:30 a.m. on Saturday morning. The bowling alley opened at 9:30 a.m. The sound of clunking bowling balls hitting the slick, oiled alleys filled the lounge.

She noticed a couple of families bowling; parents and kids having a good time. Also, there were several teenagers bowling, laughing, and having fun throwing gutter balls. She saw an adolescent kid playing a pinball machine on the opposite side of the food lounge. From his manner and the way he attacked the machine, Sam thought that he must be a pinball wizard of some kind.

Sam hadn't eaten since yesterday, and she wasn't hungry now. Her mind was jumping back and forth between her planned interview with Kitty and her concerns for Sharon. The idea of a nursing home weighed heavily on her.

Her night in the old house was troubling. Life was good and uncomplicated before Earl died. She didn't have a care in the world. But his death came crashing over her like some tragic wave that knocked her down and then receded. Now she felt burdened by the responsibilities of her job and caring for her mom. After Earl's funeral, Pastor James told her that the way we cope with death is the same way we cope with life. *Could that be true?*

Sam was looking in the direction of the front door when she saw a slender, petite woman with long bottle-blonde hair wearing oversized sunglasses come through the door. Sam instinctively waved to her. The young woman took off her sunglasses and waved back. Then she walked with slow deliberate steps as she made her way to Sam's table. *Interesting walk*, Sam thought.

She was dressed in very tight blue jeans, open-toed sandals, and a light blue, see-through, silk blouse. The blouse was unbuttoned at the top, exposing two very large breasts supported by a thin bra. She was loaded down with gaudy jewelry on her ears, fingers, and wrists. Sam immediately noticed her bright red-painted fingernails.

Sam stood up and asked in a pleasant voice, "Kitty?"

The woman smiled and said, "Yes."

Sam stuck out her hand and Kitty grabbed it. "Please sit down and thank you for seeing me."

As she sat down, Sam caught a slight whiff of the perfume that Kitty was wearing. The scent was "Parisian Nights." It was very expensive and well out of Sam's price range.

Sam's initial thought as she observed Kitty was that this over-the-top, self-indulgent look, resembled a character out of central casting. This was going to be a challenge. She wondered if a real person was hiding under the makeup and mascara.

She asked Kitty if she wanted something to drink. Sam waved the waitress over and Kitty ordered a Coca-Cola. While waiting for her pop to arrive, Kitty played with her sunglasses. She seemed a little nervous as she stared at the table. Her blue eye shadow seemed to dominate her face.

Sam briefly explained why she had to reschedule their meeting and the urgency of her mother's sudden illness. Kitty seemed mildly interested at her explanation. Nevertheless, Sam's folksy approach seemed to put her somewhat at ease.

After her drink arrived, Kitty took a sip from the glass and looked at Sam. She had a quizzical look on her face. Sam sensed that Kitty was ready to have a conversation.

"I have a couple of questions concerning Gregory Denton," Sam began. "We are clearing up a case and we hoped that you could help us fill in some of the blanks."

Kitty swallowed hard. "What case is that?" she asked. She now fully realized that she was part of the case. Her intense desire to know what Gregory had done was the reason she was here. She tried to steady herself.

Sam said she couldn't comment on the case.

"Why?" Kitty asked.

Sam then innocently shrugged her shoulders and said that she couldn't talk about it. "Police procedure was confidential." Her answer seemed to both irritate and satisfy Kitty.

"How did you meet Gregory?" Sam asked.

Kitty gave her a little wry smile. She hesitated a bit as if thinking about how much information she should give the detective. "Just woman to woman?" she asked.

"Sure," said Sam.

"Well, I guess I should give you a little background on myself."

Oh great, Sam thought, *here I am asking about Gregory, and she wants to talk about herself. This could be a long morning.*

"I was a cheerleader in high school, and I was a very pretty and popular girl with the football players, if you know what I mean. After high school, I dated a guy from the University of Wisconsin named Tim Collins, who told me that he was going to marry me once he graduated. We lived together three years. I worked as a secretary to help support us. We had a great time together, and his friends were always telling him how lucky he was to be dating me. He constantly talked about earning big money after graduation, so we dreamed big dreams. After graduation, he landed a great job in New York City in the financial district. He was going to send for me once he got settled in. And you can guess the rest." Kitty paused and took a sip from of her drink. Sam just looked at her and didn't say anything. She also noticed that when Kitty talked, she would touch her breast.

"Well, after that heartbreak, I learned my lesson. My mother had warned me about him, but I didn't listen. After all, I was in love. Well, so much for love and romance and happy endings, if you know what I mean!"

Sam noticed that her face tightened up and had an angry tension about it.

"I learned my lesson. Put yourself first and get what you can out of life. That's what I learned! So I started looking around for men with lots of money."

Sam leaned back in her chair. She could see a very angry woman sitting across from her. Obviously, she was used as a sex object by this Tim guy, and now she was out for revenge against all men. *How did Gregory fit into all this?* she asked herself.

Kitty continued. "I quickly learned how to put my moves on them. I joined a fitness center and got into great shape. I read about breast implants in those Hollywood magazines, and now you can see the finished product. My two new friends sure know how to turn heads!" Kitty laughed at her little joke.

"I also got blonde highlights in my hair. I had my teeth whitened and bought expensive perfume. After all this hard work, the investment paid off. I started going to upscale bars where young professional businessmen hung out after work. My plan worked to perfection. I found that I was being hit on from the get-go."

However, after a couple of dating disasters, I soon became very selective with whom I hooked up with. I only sought out men who were quiet and shy. The aggressive and loud ones were only looking for one-night stands and a quickie. I learned that the quiet ones wanted a good-looking woman at their side, and they were willing to pay for the privilege. I became a real asset to their egos and they paid full price. After all, I was now a high maintenance woman!" She laughed out loud. The kid at the pin ball machine turned and looked at her.

"From the money these guys were giving me, I could supplement my job earnings with a new car. I also had money to burn on a new fancy apartment and new clothes. I also learned that in order to keep the guys interested, I had to keep them off balance and guessing as to when the next sexual favors would come. It is great fun! You should try it."

Sam nodded. *Okay, let's bring this bravado to an end,* she said to herself.

But Kitty continued. She was on a roll. "I tried dating married guys for a while but it got too complicated. I thought it would be a simple and safe way to upgrade myself, but a couple of them thought that they had fallen in love with me. They wanted to leave their wives and bratty children. No way. So I settled on unmarried types. I would take them on very nice sexual rides and then take their money. If I got bored with them, I would move on."

Kitty paused. All this self-centered arrogant talk had left her exhausted. Sam stared at her. This was way too much information.

"Okay, so tell me about Gregory," Sam said.

Kitty shifted in her chair and started again. "I met him at the After Five Bar downtown. I flirted with him using my usual eye contact and winks. After a couple of tries, I got his attention, and he finally got up the courage and bought me a drink. Then we struck up a conversation. He was ripe for the picking. I asked him a zillion questions about himself, and once he started talking, he wouldn't shut up. We exchanged phone numbers, and before long, I had him in bed, his bed, of course. He called me every day and started sending me flowers and expensive gifts. I had him hooked.

"He had one interesting hobby, though. He liked to bowl. I bowled a few games as a kid growing up here in Milwaukee, so I went along with his little sport. It turned out that he was pretty good at it. He had a high bowling average. In fact, he bowled on a league here. I would come and watch him if I didn't have anything better to do, if you know what I mean."

"Did he ever talk about his family or did you ever go to meet any of them?" Sam asked.

"He was pretty quiet about it, but he did say that both his aunt and uncle were dead."

"Did he ever talk about his mother?"

"Yeah, he didn't like her very much. After hearing the story about his abandonment, I thought he should grow up and get a life. We all have tragedies in life and we need to get over them. You know what I mean? But I kept those thoughts to myself."

"Okay," Sam said.

"He also shared some stories about growing up in Monroe, but he never took me there. Look, don't get me wrong, I was not in this relationship for the long haul. Eventually, he would figure out his cash flow problem with me and find a reason to dump me. Or, I would dump him if something better came along. I am always trolling."

"So, who dumped who?" Sam asked.

"I met a guy who liked to travel and had lots of money. He was older than I would have liked, but what the heck! Money is money. When I told Gregory that I met someone else, he went sort of crazy. He told me that he loved me and he was going to come into some serious money soon. I blew that off. It was a line I had heard before, and I wasn't buying it now. He was in it for the easy sex and he didn't want to lose that. Well anyway, we split up. I would see him occasionally in bars after that, but we both knew the relationship was over."

Sam thought for a moment and asked her if she ever had any concerns or problems while dating Gregory.

"One night after making love, he told me about working in his uncle's pharmacy in Monroe. He was bragging about how easy it was to cheat his customers by substituting off-brand drugs and prescription drugs, and then charging the higher price. I told him that wasn't very nice. Then I asked him how he would feel if that happened to him. 'The cost of doing business,' he crowed.

"Then I laughed and told him that the condom he just used was defective. I had poked a hole in it. He sat up in bed and stared at me. His face burned red as he got very angry. Being the drama queen that I am, I told him that I really wanted to have his baby and to marry him! He hit the roof! He got very upset. In fact, I felt a little afraid of him. To calm him down, I told him it was a joke. You know, like the cost of doing business! It took him a week to get over it. But after that episode, I never really felt comfortable around him again. What a temper!"

Kitty paused and sat back in her chair. Sam pondered whether or not to ask her a personal question. She looked at Kitty and asked her if she could ask a rather personal question. Kitty shrugged.

"Do you think that you will ever fall in love again?"

Kitty was unfazed by the question. "Look, the men I date have the minds of children. They are not equipped to see reality or the big picture of romance. Their brains are in their penis, if you know what I mean. They have absolutely no perspective on their own personal pain after the breakup. For instance, some of them think they are in love with me, but their thought process gets all twisted up with lust. All this new steamy and red-hot sexual passion for me gets confused in some bizarre logic of love. They are utterly convinced that their feelings are shared by me. But when the breakup comes, and it always comes, the train wreck of their egos is laughable. They call me. They send me gifts. They beg me to get back together. Men have this need to control, and once they lose it, it tears away at the very fabric of their masculinity." After Kitty finished speaking, she laughed and sat back in her chair and smiled. "Did I shock you?" she asked.

Sam had no comment. "So tell me about Keith Kranenbuhl," Sam said.

"Who is that?"

"The guy you met at a bowling tournament from Monroe."

Kitty laughed, "Oh, him. I had met some of Gregory's friends during my bowling phase, and one of them asked me to be a sub at a tournament. I told him that I would. He was good-looking and I am always trolling . . . sort of a habit. Well, anyway, we were bowling against this team from Monroe, and I asked that guy Keith if he knew a Gregory Denton. He said that he did.

"We were hitting the beers pretty hard and I asked him if Gregory had won the betting sweepstakes. He laughed and said not that he knew of. I told him that when we were dating, Gregory told me that he was going to be very rich very soon. He just laughed at my comment and that was that."

"Is there anything else to add?" Sam asked.

"No, that's about it, except that I got a painful blister on my thumb from bowling in that damn tournament."

Sam pushed her chair back and stood up and thanked Kitty for meeting with her. After they shook hands, Kitty walked toward the front door rolling her hips with each step. The kid at the pinball machine was staring at her with his mouth open.

As Sam watched her exit the front door, she wondered if Kitty contacted Gregory about her meeting. *Of course she did!* She answered her own question.

CHAPTER 25

Jordan Kosack, age twelve, and Wade Mathias, age twelve, squirmed anxiously in their chairs at a table in the interview room at the Monroe Police Department. On the table in front of them was a stack of license plates. The room was windowless and their parents sat quietly on a row of chairs along the wall behind them. Mr. and Mrs. Kosack sat expressionless. They both stared at the floor like prisoners awaiting jail sentences. Mr. and Mrs. Mathias held hands and looked at the back of the heads of the two boys and occasionally glanced at each other and slightly shook their heads. A uniformed police officer was standing in the corner of the room looking at his fingernails. They were waiting for Detective Gates in order to start the interview, and she was delayed in a briefing with Chief Johns.

The two boys eyed each another and started to giggle. The rough voice of Mr. Kosack broke the silence in the room. He told them in a loud voice to shut up! The Mathias couple jumped at his outburst as well as the police officer. The boys immediately stopped sniggering and looked down at the table. The officer turned away and smiled. Both parents looked very upset and nervous.

At half past ten, Sam entered the room and sat down across from the two boys. The uniformed cop nodded at her, folded his arms, and leaned against the wall. She opened the file folder in front of her and didn't say anything. She just stared at the two boys, who were sweating and looking very nervous. She glanced at the parents and they nodded back at her.

She looked again at the two boys with disgust. The boys stared back. "So tell me about these license plates," she began. The boys remained silent.

"Okay, let me tell you a couple of things. Number one is that one of your

153

best friends, your buddies, called the police station and dropped a dime on you. Do you know what that means?"

No response.

"Does that surprise either of you? I mean, does it surprise you that you may know one decent and honest person? A person who respects the law and what it stands for!"

The boys showed no emotion and stared down at the table. Wade looked as if he was going to cry.

"That means you should either zip your lips or pick friends who aren't so honest."

No response from either boy.

"When we got the phone call at the station, the mysterious caller said that he had seen the license plates in Jordan's room. When Officer Stamm went to your house, Jordan, he talked to both of your parents. Did you know that?"

Jordan winced.

"Your parents told him that they knew nothing about the license plates or the complaint, but they were more than willing to show the officer your bedroom. And what did they find?"

Jordan stared at his hands which rested on the table. Sam slammed her fist down hard on the table, and the license plates flew up in a sudden clatter. Everyone in the room jumped! Jordan looked like he was going to faint. He stole a sideways glance at Wade, who was in shock.

"Who stole these license plates?" Sam shouted.

The room became deathly quiet. No one said anything.

"Okay. Tell me about the license plates. Whose idea was it anyway?"

Wade opened his mouth as if to say something, but not a word or a sound passed his lips. He looked helplessly at Jordan. Jordan quickly glanced back at his parents. Their facial expressions were vacant and frozen. They just glared at him. He turned back to Sam.

Jordan started to speak in a voice barely above a whisper. "It all started when Wade spent the night at my house. We could see the streetlights on the square from my bedroom window. In fact, the whole square was lit up. Just for fun, we started timing the police patrol cars as they circled the square, and pretty soon, we knew almost to the minute when they would drive by. We thought it would be great fun and a rush to sneak out of my bedroom window to steal a license plate, you know, just to see if we could get away with it. My parents never checked on us anyway."

An audible grunt came from Jordan's dad. Sam shot him a glance and he looked away.

"Besides, we only planned to take the front plate and not the back plate."

This time, the moan came from Mr. Kosack. Sam let it pass.

Jordan continued, "So we tried it one night and it was easy. We had thirty minutes to pull it off. Then we expanded our zone to one or two blocks off the square. I wanted to hang the plates up on my bedroom wall, since it was my idea. If my parents saw them, they never asked me about them." Jordan looked at Wade for confirmation but Wade looked sick.

"So that was it?" Sam asked.

"Yes, that's about it. We are very sorry about it. In fact, after we saw your ad in the 'police blotter' asking for help, we decided to give it up. It just wasn't a challenge anymore."

The police officer at the door smiled.

"So, what do you think I should do to the both of you for punishment?" Sam asked.

They looked at each other and shrugged.

"Well, I could turn you over to the DA, and he could prosecute you for theft, or I could recommend community service. Of course, you would have to return all these plates to their proper owners and apologize." Sam paused and looked at the boys and then at the parents.

No one said anything.

Suddenly a strange look appeared on Mr. Kosack's face, and he started to squirm about in his chair. His wife looked at him and whispered to him to sit still. The strange look on his face quickly became one of pain and contortion. He began to sweat. *Oh shit,* he thought to himself as he grimaced.

Earlier that morning, he was busy and missed breakfast. So before he left for the police station, he quickly made a sandwich for himself. He heated up some leftover Braunschweiger sausages and ate them with a slice of Limburger cheese, some raw onions, and brown stone-ground mustard smeared on rye bread. His makeshift breakfast was delicious as he wolfed it down. The only thing missing was a beer. But now the pressure of that hasty meal was building in his stomach and moving very fast into his gastrointestinal tract. He knew what was coming. His wife was now staring at him full face with a look on her face that screamed, "Don't you dare, you idiot!"

He tried desperately to get into a more comfortable position. But he was helpless to stop the inevitable. The pressure was building, and it was rapidly becoming intolerable. He desperately tried every means available that he could think of to delay the ticking time bomb in his pants. His wife's eyes were now laser locked on to his eyes. Her jaw was set and her eyes were staring a hole through him. No one else seemed to notice his plight.

He grimaced again and twisted his body into another contortion to be comfortable, but it was too late. The rush of gas came with a vengeance! The fart exploded from his body with hurricane-force winds, and the sound ripped through the room like the unwarranted intrusion that it was. The sound was loud, fast, and ferocious as it echoed around the small room. Mrs. Kosack screamed and slugged her husband as hard as she could in the arm. Everyone turned and looked at her poor husband. He had the unmistakable look of a very naughty five-year-old boy looking down at his shoes with a very red face. "Sorry," he said to no one in particular.

Suddenly, Wade started to laugh and then Jordan joined in. The boys were shaking and laughing so hard that tears were cascading from their eyes and flowing down their cheeks. They were holding their sides for all they were worth. The wave of laughter from the boys quickly turned into a long stretch of coughing and gasping. They were both doubled up in their chairs.

Sam couldn't help herself and started laughing at the boys, who were visibly out of control. Mrs. Kosack and the Mathiases joined in the revelry. The officer at the door had a very big grin on his face. The only one not laughing was poor old Mr. Kosack, who sat in silence cursing his breakfast.

Once they regained control of themselves, the room quieted down. Wade spoke up for the very first time. The farting-dad episode had taken the tension out of him and out of the room. He looked at Sam and said, "Did you know that the devil drives a black sports car? Ain't that something?"

Sam quickly looked at him. "What do you mean by that, Wade?"

"Yep, Jordan and I went out as usual one night and spotted the car that the devil drives parked under a streetlight. Isn't that right, Jordan?"

Jordan nodded.

"The street was too well lit up to lift the plate, so we thought we would go back later and snatch it. But by then, the car was gone."

Sam straightened herself up in her chair. Her mind started processing this new information. Suddenly she tried hard not to show her excitement. "How do you know that the devil was driving the car?"

"By the license plate, of course," said Wade proudly.

"Are you sure that it was the devil's?"

"Well, I am pretty sure," he responded. "Isn't that right, Jordan?"

Jordan shook his head up and down. Then he said, "At Sunday school, they taught us that the number 666 is the devil. The sports car had a 666 on the license plate. Actually, the number was S49-666. And the plate was maroon with white lettering."

"How did you know that?" Wade asked.

"Because I am smarter than you!"

Both the parents laughed.

"Do you remember what night that was?" Sam asked. Her mind was racing. She remembered that Gregory's license plate at the Yellow Iris had triple sixes on it.

"Oh, it was a Thursday night, because both our parents go bowling, so it wasn't too hard to sneak out." Jordan said.

"Just to be clear," Sam said, "when did this happen again?"

Jordon looked at Wade, "On a Thursday night about four or five weeks ago, I guess." Jordan shook his head again. "I can't remember exactly."

Sam needed to end the interview quickly. Gregory told her that he hadn't been to Monroe since he sold the house to Ada. Now she needed to verify Gregory's license plate. She thanked the parents for bringing the boys in and told them that the assistant district attorney would be in contact with them. In the meantime, she told the boys to return the plates and that officer Stamm would accompany them just to make sure all went well and the plates were returned to the proper owners. She told the parents that her recommendation to the DA would be community service. Both the parents and the boys seemed relieved as they left the police station.

Sam hurried to the front desk and asked the officer on duty to run Gregory's plate. It only took a couple of minutes. Sam retrieved a pen from her pocket and her hand shook slightly as she wrote the plate number on a piece of paper, S49-666. She could feel the excitement building inside her body. She thanked the desk officer and then raced down the hallway and into Chief Johns's office. She now had two eyewitnesses that put Gregory's car in Monroe the night before Keith Kranenbuhl's death!

CHAPTER 26

Chief Johns sat in his unmarked police car reflecting on the murder case that Sam was involved with. Earlier that morning when Sam had briefed him on her meeting with Kitty, she told him that Gregory had talked about coming into money before his mother died. She also told him about Kitty asking Keith if it was true about Gregory coming into a lot of money. The coincidences were too much to ignore.

She then told him that after the interview, she went back to the Silver Bay Hospital to check on her mother. She found her sedated. She then conferred with the doctors and drove back to Monroe. It was late when she got back.

Continuing her narrative, Sam told Johns that after getting ready for bed, she had sat in her living room and reviewed the notes on her easel. She was convinced now, more than ever, that Gregory was Pagan. She could just feel it, a sixth sense; and now, she was convinced.

The next step was to convince Chief Johns that Stacy needed to agree to exhume Keith's body and test for poisons. Since Gregory was a pharmacist, it was no great stretch of the imagination that he would have ready access to any poison he wanted or needed.

The pieces of the puzzle were rapidly falling in place. She surmised that Gregory poisoned his mother for her money. Then Keith found out from Kitty that Gregory expected to come into a lot of money before his mother died. Keith must have put two and two together, and that sum total led to his own death. On that point, she was sure she was correct. She also felt that the chief needed to be was on board as well, or at least she hoped so.

Chief Johns was on board. He decided to meet with Stacy at her home. He telephoned her for the appointment. The question he needed to ask her would be too painful to answer if she had been asked to come down to the station. She needed familiar surroundings and privacy. Her grieving and sadness had to be respected. Johns knew that as people try to heal, the last thing they need is any doubt cast upon their departed loved one. After all, cemeteries are supposed to be "resting places" for the dead and should not be disturbed.

Stacy told Johns that her son was up north visiting relatives for a few days so she would have to meet with him alone. Their appointment was set for 2:30 p.m.

It was 2:00 p.m. and Johns sat alone in his unmarked police car at Pleasant Park, located approximately three blocks from Stacy's house. He had left the station early to get away from all the noise and chaos because he needed some time to think. It was a very nice sunny day as he watched several children playing on the jungle gym bars and the slides.

His thoughts were about Sam. He admired her stick-to-it attitude. She was obviously very intelligent, and she seemed to sort things out pretty well using her instincts. She was the first person to take Ada seriously concerning the deaths of both Ellen and Keith. The local perception about "Crazy Ada" had clouded his own objectivity in the past.

However, now that Sam had pursued her own line of inquiry, her theory about the deaths being too coincidental was making sense. It was becoming more and more obvious to her that Gregory Denton was in some way connected to the deaths.

If, in fact, they were both poisoned as Sam strongly suggested, then the deaths were premeditated. *But why?* That was the question that needed to be answered. Commissioner Roger Nussbaum wasn't going to like this turn of events. But that didn't really bother Johns or concern him at the moment. Bringing a killer to justice had to trump Nussbaum's political agenda. He sighed as he tried to reason out the exhumation question. Stacy would need a credible explanation. Something that made sense and something that she could cling to. A suspected homicide based on circumstantial evidence was a stretch. He thought about other exhumations to use for examples in suspicious deaths but decided to pass on them. That is, unless he felt it appropriate to get the permission he needed. He also wondered if Stacy would object on the basis of some religious beliefs. He doubted it, but he needed to be prepared anyway. He glanced at his watch, started the car, and drove off.

As he pulled up in the front of Stacy's house, he could see her looking out the living room window. He made his way up the steps. Before he could ring the doorbell, she opened the front door. She welcomed him in and then led him into the living room and sat across from him. He sat on the same sofa as their last meeting.

This time, Stacy offered no refreshments. She had a very concerned look on her face as she searched his face, looking for any clues for the visit. But his face remained unexpressive. He was acutely aware that her emotions and feelings were very fragile, and he had to respect that.

Johns began the conversation by thanking her for seeing him again and gave her a brief explanation of how the investigation was going. He tried to be as vague as possible. Then the crucial moment came. He looked into her eyes and said in a very flat, low, monotone voice, "We have reason to believe that Keith's death may not have been of natural causes."

Stacy gasped and slumped back in her chair. She stared at the floor and turned pale. Her eyes and mouth were wide open, and her eyebrows were raised. He gave her several minutes to absorb this information.

"We have our reasons to pursue this line of inquiry and we need your help." He paused again and watched for Stacy's reaction.

After a few moments, she asked softly, "Did you find anything suspicious in Keith's heart medicine bottle?"

Johns knew this question was coming. He had rehearsed his answer. Even though the lab found nothing during their examination of the bottle, he had to cast some suspicion on the medicine bottle without deliberately lying to her. It was important to the case to get her permission for the exhumation and autopsy.

"The report that came back from the toxicology laboratory in Madison raised some concerns for us," he said. "But I can't comment on them at this time." He paused again to let his words sink in. "I hope you can appreciate the sensitivity of our investigation."

He could see that he had her full attention. Her eyes welled up, and a tear rolled down her cheek. She seemed to be fighting back the torrent of tears that were starting to blur her vision. She reached for a tissue and blotted the tears. At the same time, she was intently following Johns's explanation.

"We think that Dr. Gehringer may have rushed to judgment on the cause of death."

Stacy gasped.

"So, just to be sure of the facts, we need your permission to do an autopsy on Keith's body." Johns paused again to let her take in this new information.

He didn't want to rush or panic her. Stacy sat frozen to her chair and was very quiet for some moments.

"So what are you saying?" she asked.

"I am asking permission to establish the exact cause of death," he said.

Then another moment of silence followed as she sat very still. Johns felt sorry for her. This was a lot for her to process.

"How do you think he died?" Stacy asked.

"We are not certain and we don't want to speculate. This is a very delicate matter and we can't go on assumptions. With your help, Stacy, we can clarify the facts concerning Keith's death and put all of our minds to rest." Stacy sighed and stared at the floor again.

"Is this the only way?" she asked softly.

"I am afraid it is."

"What do I have to do?" she asked.

"I have an autopsy consent form with me that will need your signature."

"Then what?" she asked.

"We will exhume Keith's body, and the medical examiner will do the autopsy."

Stacy's face turned pale. She felt ill. She was in a cold sweat. She was having trouble breathing and getting her mind around this information. She felt faint. She wished that Brad was home to hear this.

"Do I have to be there when they exhume his body?" she asked.

"No."

"How soon will I know the answer as to the cause of his death?" she asked.

"We will notify you immediately," Johns said.

He then took the consent form out of the folder he was holding and showed it to her. She looked at it with suspicion. As she read, she couldn't comprehend what she was reading. She had to trust Johns. Her hand was shaking.

He handed her a pen and showed her where to sign. Her hand was trembling so badly that Johns thought that she might drop the pen. But she managed to sign the consent form. She handed the pen and form back to Johns and asked him, "Can I tell Brad?"

"We would appreciate it if only you and Brad know about this. We don't want to set off any wild speculation in Monroe. After all, it's a police matter for now."

"Okay," Stacy replied weakly.

Johns got up and Stacy remained seated. "Thank you," Johns said. "After this ordeal is over, you will know the reason Keith died, and it will put your mind to rest."

Stacy nodded.

"I will show myself out," he said.

No response from Stacy.

As Johns exited the house and headed for his car, he knew what he must do. But first he needed to call Sam. She would be excited.

CHAPTER 27

essica Hannes sat on her living room sofa with her bare feet tucked under her. She held the telephone in her lap. She was wrapped in her bathroom robe and was slowly drinking a cold beer.

She was alone in her house. Her husband, Ted, an insurance salesman, had business in Brodhead and wouldn't be home until 11:00 p.m. Jessica worked as the office manager in the Green County Medical Examiner's Office with Dr. Ken Anderson. She also did work for the Green County Coroner, Dave Dickerson. Her office was located in the basement of the hospital. Next door to her office was the morgue where autopsies were performed.

She was surprised and shocked when the autopsy request for Keith Kranenbuhl crossed her desk. In all her years at the coroner's office, she had never seen a request like this one. Dr. Ken told her that the exhumation and examination were confidential and not to tell anyone. Chief Johns had insisted upon the confidentially of it. She agreed to the chief's request for confidentiality.

She stared intently at the phone on her lap. In fact, she had been holding the phone for several minutes pondering whether or not to make the call. She was a loyal employee of Dr. Ken and never did anything to betray his trust, but this was different. She knew that if Ted were home, he would advise against the call. So she had to decide for herself. With a hesitant hand, she picked up the phone and dialed.

Ada was washing dishes when the phone rang. She went into the living room and answered it. It was Jessica. Ada had known Jessie all of her life. They were second cousins, but they weren't especially close friends. Jessie was four years behind her in high school. After graduation, Jessie went on to college. She graduated from University of Wisconsin, Platteville, with a degree in business administration and a minor degree in biology. After college, she got a job in the Green County Coroner's office and worked there all of her career.

"I am calling you in the strictest of confidence, Ada," Jessie barely whispered. "You can't breathe a word to anyone about what I am going to tell you."

The nervousness in Jessie's voice was apparent to Ada. "I won't say anything, Jessie. You can trust me," she replied. "What's up?"

"It's really important that you keep this call confidential. I promised Dr. Ken that I wouldn't say anything."

"I promise," Ada replied.

"Well, I thought that you would like to know that we received a request today to exhume Keith Kranenbuhl's body for an autopsy."

Ada gasped and sat down heavily on a chair next to her. She felt light-headed and her body tensed up.

Jessie continued, "I know that you have publicly questioned Keith's death and apparently the police are looking for answers as well. I shouldn't be telling you about this. Dr. Ken told me to keep this information confidential. I have always thought highly of you and the way that you openly challenge the system, especially if you think you are right. I admire the way that you have been especially outspoken about your opinions and beliefs. So, I just thought that you should know about this."

Jessie paused. Ada remained silent. Jessie's hands were shaking. "So I just thought I would call and let you know. Remember, not a word to anyone, okay?"

Ada assured her that she wouldn't say a word to anyone. Then on impulse, she asked Jessie to call her if they found anything that would lead to a suspicious death. Jessie paused for a long moment and then agreed to call her. Ada thanked her and hung up the phone. Her heart was racing. She felt exhilarated! She felt exonerated! "The police have found something!" she said to herself. "Thank God for Detective Gates!"

Jessie sat quietly on the sofa after she hung up. *What have I done?* she questioned herself. *I can't tell Ted. He would be furious. I have betrayed Dr. Ken.* She suddenly felt very guilty. *After all the years of trust between colleagues . . .* she couldn't finish her thought.

Her thoughts then shifted to Ada. At family reunions, Ada always challenged her male relatives by making them face up to their biases against women. When she demanded that one of them get her food or a beer, they scoffed. When she reminded them that women were people too, they scoffed. She told them that a woman president would straighten out the country. She also told them that women should be equal to men in every sense of the word!

This rancor mostly confused the men, and they didn't have any comebacks except for using four-letter words. The women who were listening remained silent but often inwardly cheered as Ada made her points.

Jessie was taken with her outspokenness and honesty. She didn't have the courage or will to stand up for her own rights. If she did, Ted's expectations of a good wife would throw their marriage into turmoil. She thought that Ada was ahead of her time. She also thought that "Crazy Ada" wasn't so crazy. It seemed to Jessie that men were always telling her what to do. Her phone call to Ada could be the first step to more independence. *After all, what harm could be done by letting Ada know? She would find out anyway.* Jessie felt better as she finished her beer.

CHAPTER 28

Gregory sat his kitchen table. It was late at night. He had a yellow legal pad in front of him reading over his notes. His recurring nightmare had broken into his otherwise peaceful night's rest and altered his sleep. He felt like he was going mad. That she-devil ghost standing at the bottom of the stairs, staring at him as he stared back at her was unnerving. Her cold hand on his foot still sent him into a screaming frenzy. And no matter how many times he blew his nose, he couldn't get the musty smell of that ghastly basement out of his nostrils. *What's wrong with me?*

He hadn't returned to work since his evaluation. His phone call to his supervisor was short and to the point. He was taking personal leave for personal reasons. She approved the request.

Gregory's tired eyes perused the yellow pad. Then he closed them briefly in order to think. He had listed all the things he needed to do before escaping into Canada. His research into the ten provinces had been thorough. He could almost name them by heart: Ontario, Quebec, Nova Scotia, New Brunswick, Manitoba, British Columbia, Prince Edward Island, Saskatchewan, Alberta, and Newfoundland.

He decided that Ontario was the best option. Its capital city was Toronto. The province had the second largest land mass and the largest population. In fact, Toronto had over one million people and was culturally diverse. He logically concluded that if he tried to disappear into a remote area of Canada, he would stand out and people would ask questions. Monroe came to mind. But if he relocated into a densely populated area, where people tended to keep to themselves, he could become anonymous and lose himself in the crowd. The city of Toronto was circled three times on his notepad.

He had already made arrangements at his bank to close all of his financial accounts. He would cash out at approximately one hundred thousand dollars. The money would be more than enough for him to get a fresh start. Walking out on his apartment wouldn't be a big deal to him, but leaving behind his beloved Corvette would be very difficult and traumatic. He loved that car more than any of his other possessions. He had spent many enjoyable hours driving around in it. The car was a part of him, and the thought of parting with it brought him sadness and anger. His obsession with the car seemed to control him like the worship of a divine diva.

After he collected his money, he would have to park his beautiful car for the very last time in the underground parking garage. The police would probably impound it and sell it off to some punk who wouldn't appreciate her. It wasn't fair. He felt like he had earned the right to have a beautiful and expensive car, and the thought of abandoning it was horrid.

Thinking about his car brought back memories of Kitty and the rides they took together. He thought that he loved her, but in the end, she had just played him. But he was smitten. He would have given her anything she wanted. He had never met a girl like her before. She totally consumed him. Looking back on it, it was all about sex. He was paying for sex. Even now, after all that had happened between them, he would go back to her in an instant. Whenever he ran into her at a bar with someone else, it seemed strange to him. He felt that she should be going home with him.

After their brief encounters, the memories of them dating seemed wasted. The breakup had thrown him into such a tailspin that he hadn't had sex with another woman.

So there he was, dating Kitty and soon to be inheriting a large sum of money from his mother's estate. He was on top of the world. Life couldn't be any better. Then the crash came. He lost Kitty, and now he was desperately trying to save his own life. The enormity of his situation was sucking the air out of him. He couldn't breathe. If he left the apartment to get some fresh air, he was paranoid about the people who passed him on the street. *Why are they looking at me?*

His thoughts then shifted to what clothes to take in order to travel light. The phone rang and he jumped. *Who could that be?* He picked it up on the second ring. It was Ada.

"Hi, Gregory. Did I wake you?"

"No," he said. "It's the middle of the night," he murmured to himself as he listened.

"I have great news for you!" she shouted into the phone.

"What's that, Ada?"

"I have just received word that an autopsy is going to be done on Keith. Isn't that wonderful?"

Gregory's hand tightened around the phone receiver like he was choking it. He instantly turned pale.

"Why are they going to do that?" he stammered.

"I don't know. Maybe they are looking for a suspicious cause of death. As you know, I never believed Dr. Gehringer's report. That old quack should have retired years ago! But I do think I need to take some part of the credit for the autopsy. I think that I finally convinced Detective Gates that there was something suspicious about Keith's death."

Gregory couldn't speak. His free hand was furiously rubbing against his cheek. The phone went silent.

"Aren't you excited, Gregory?" Ada asked. "Isn't this great news?!"

He gathered himself and said, "Do you really think that they will find something?"

"Oh yes, I can just feel it in my bones. Just like Ellen's death, I really need to know the truth and now I can almost smell it!" Ada said again with excitement.

Gregory thanked her for the call and hung up. His future was now sealed and cast in the finality of his plans to flee the country. The dreaded realization of it all hung over him like the blade of a guillotine. His felt his heart beating to the pounding pulse of the terror that filled him.

Before Ellen's death, his life seemed to be so benign and innocuous, but now he was paying a terrible price. The demons that were haunting his hellish nightmarish dreams were now surfacing. He had to take control of himself and his future! He couldn't take his next breath for granted. He was afraid. He needed to take action and escape into Canada without delay.

CHAPTER 29

On the afternoon that Keith's body was being exhumed, Sam got a call from Dr. Simonson in Silver Bay. Her mother had had another episode and possible stroke. He requested that she come right away. She told Johns about the emergency and then immediately left for Silver Bay. Johns told her that he would call her after he got the autopsy results. Sam told him to call the minute he had the results, regardless of the time. She gave him the phone numbers for the hospital and her mother's house.

She now sat alone in the waiting room of the hospital. It was after 9:00 p.m. and visiting hours were over; she felt exhausted. Sam called Pastor James when she arrived at the hospital. He said that he would come over later that evening.

After Sam arrived at the hospital, her hopes of seeing Sharon immediately faded. The doctor was running tests and had her hooked up to a machine. He asked Sam to wait. Now she sat alone in the waiting room, gazing up at a few pastoral pictures of grazing cows, red barns, and deer in a corn field.

She perused through some magazines to occupy her mind, but she couldn't concentrate. Her thoughts soon turned to the plight of her mom and then to her murder case. She hoped that Pastor James would be there soon.

She felt anxious and very much alone. Just sitting around and waiting started to get on her nerves. She was a woman of action. She needed to be doing something! She felt guilty just sitting and doing nothing. She considered calling Johns but thought better of it. He was going to call her when he found out something, so why bother him now? She felt that her case was breaking wide open and she should be in Monroe. But she also needed to be with her mom. Johns had told her to go to Silver Bay and that he would call her at the hospital once the autopsy results were in. It wasn't her first choice, but she had to settle for that. The stress of choosing between tending to her mom and doing her job was troubling to her.

To occupy her mind, she revisited the case in her mind. As she stared blankly at the opposite wall, she reconstructed her theory of what had happened to Ellen and Keith. Once again, just to be clear in her own mind, she needed to go over her suspicions that Gregory was, in fact, "Pagan" and the murderer.

For whatever reason, she surmised that Gregory had poisoned his mother. Was it for her money or something else? The murder had to be calculated and premeditated, being that Gregory was in Milwaukee when Ellen died. Being a pharmacist, he would have easy access to poisons. He also knew the family history of heart disease. So Gregory must have reasoned, and rightly so, that Ellen's death certificate would read heart failure and probably wouldn't be challenged. By inserting the killer toxic capsule into her heart medication bottle, it would only be a matter of time before she unwittingly took it, and Gregory would be safe with his alibi in Milwaukee. He counted on Dr. Gehringer writing "heart failure" on the death certificate. And his plan seemly went off without a hitch. Brilliant, he probably thought.

But sometimes, there are unforeseen consequences. He didn't foresee Ada's love and passion for his mother or her tenacious questioning of the cause of Ellen's death. But then again, luck was on his side when Ada and her suspicions were generally ignored by the authorities.

Then what about Keith? The chance meeting between Kitty and Keith was very unfortunate for Keith. He was a smart guy, and he rightly guessed that Gregory had something to do with Ellen's death. When he confronted him, Gregory probably had no choice but to pay him the blackmail that he demanded. The last thing Gregory needed was Keith going to the police. But once again, circumstances and fate intervened. Keith's son being accepted to the University of Wisconsin had put additional financial pressure on Keith.

What did Keith tell Stacy? "Don't worry about the money for Brad's education, I have a plan."

Keith must have figured that he had an easy out. After all, Gregory was rich and drove a fancy car. He wouldn't miss the money. So the obvious solution was to get more money out of Gregory. Sam reasoned that the killer capsule that ended Ellen's life was tried again on Keith. He probably thought that he had nothing to fear since Gregory was in Milwaukee and no apparent threat to him. But he underestimated Gregory's capacity for murder.

And once again, Gregory underestimated Ada and her stubborn determination. "I don't believe in coincidences," Ada had told her.

The circumstantial evidence seemed solid to Sam. If Keith's autopsy revealed poison as the real cause of his death, along with Wade and Jordan's statements about Gregory's car being in Monroe the night before Keith's death, the police could make an arrest. All she needed to do now was to wait for the phone call from Johns.

As she sat back in her chair, she started to feel a sense of calmness. There could be no other explanation. She was confident that her theory of the murders would be confirmed, and she was also sure that justice would be served.

Suddenly, she became aware of a figure that was standing over her. She looked up and saw the smiling face of Pastor James looking down at her. She also noticed the clergy badge on the lapel of his sports jacket. "A penny for your thoughts," he said.

Sam laughed. "Sorry about that, police business."

Pastor James sat down next to her. "How's your mom doing? Any news?"

Sam then refocused her attention on him and filled him in on her mother's condition. They sat in silence for a while, and then Pastor James offered to get them some coffee. He left her and retrieved two cups from the canteen in the cafeteria. As a clergyman, he was very familiar with this extended waiting game in hospitals and was preparing himself for a long night.

After he returned, he asked Sam if she wanted to talk about her murder case but she declined. Pastor James thought she looked very tired and worn out. Her eyes looked sunken and strained. She was dealing with a lot of stuff. They both sat in silence sipping their coffees. It was a comfortable silence. They knew each other well enough to feel comfortable just sitting together.

After some time passed, Sam looked at Pastor James and asked him why he became a pastor. She was wondering if he was called into the ministry or just happened into it by chance or some other circumstance. Her question was purposeful, and she was hoping his reply would get her mind off her immediate concerns and transport her to another place.

"You know, I never even thought about asking you that question. I hope I am not being too forward or personal. My dad is the reason that I am a cop, but I never asked you why you are a minister," she said.

Pastor James smiled at her and then laid his head back on the sofa. He immediately recognized her need for a distraction. He slowly started to tell his story with his eyes narrowing, looking into empty space as he traveled back in time in his mind.

"It was in my junior year of college," he began. "I was very involved with a Christian youth fellowship group at the university. As you know, I was raised in a very conservative church, and my parents made church attendance mandatory. The fellowship group at the University reminded me of the many good times I had at my home church. We sang songs and laughed a lot. I wasn't sure what I was going to do after I graduated from college. My degree was in history. I felt I could always teach, but that was about as far as my imagination would carry me."

"At one of our fellowship meetings, a woman missionary from a church in Alaska came and gave us a talk on summer mission work with the Alaskan natives. She talked about the beauty of Alaska and the adventure of the last frontier wilderness. She talked about the wild untamed animal life there. She spoke of moose, bears, and bald eagles. She painted a spectacular and romantic picture in golden words and images. She hooked me like a fish. I signed up that night."

"All my travel expenses were prepaid and I left for Alaska in May after final exams. I was assigned to the Ungalik tribe, who lived in a small village near the foot of Mt. McKinley."

"There were three students in our little mission group, and we soon found ourselves living in pretty primitive conditions. Outdoor plumbing quickly took the shine and glamour and romance out of the adventure. My job was to instruct young native children in English and to learn about their culture. After the summer, I was to write a paper about our sojourn for credit and share the experience with others." Pastor James glanced over at Sam who appeared to be interested and lost in his story. She smiled back at him as he continued.

"After the shock of my new surroundings wore off, I needed to make the best of my situation. The cultural differences between the tribal people and us were amazing. The slower pace of life in the village had a very soothing rhythm to it, and I had trouble adapting at first. Being a high-energy guy in constant motion, I had an especially difficult time slowing down my own pace of life.

"The villagers were very respectful of one another and of me. In fact, they were very accepting and didn't seem to mind when I complained about this or that. I found that the kids were very charming, respectful, and always on time to their lessons. They would bring me little gifts, and I started to have naive fantasies about a teaching career in Alaska.

"After I got settled into my daily routine, I noticed that an elderly gentleman would come into my classroom. He would just sit in the back of the room quietly and observe. He didn't say very much and seemed quite content to watch. The kids just ignored him, you know, like he wasn't there. After some inquires, I learned that he was the local village shaman. I surmised that he was probably checking up on me. If the kids didn't mind his presence, why should I?

"Then one day while on one of my daily walks around the village, I brushed up against some bushes and I broke out in the most irritating rash. I couldn't stop the constant itching and scratching of my legs and arms. The shaman was called in, and after a brief examination of my condition, he rubbed some local herbal ointment on the rash that gave me instant relief. It smelled awful and made my nose hairs tingle. I asked him what it was, but he just held up his hand and smiled. 'Tribal secret,' he said.

"After that incident, the shaman and I got to know each other better. He spoke excellent English, and we had some interesting discussions about our spiritual and cultural differences. He told me that it was important for the kids to get to know me. I represented a side of life that these kids would never experience first hand. Eventually, our discussions turned more and more toward spiritualism. His spirituality was tied to mother earth and all that she offered.

"I tried to speak to him about my faith in God. I told about my limited life experiences trying to live a life of faith. In fact, the more I talked to him, the more I felt intimidated by him. He asked me questions that I couldn't answer, and that bothered me. He asked about life and death issues and how my faith dealt with them. I just rambled on, trying desperately to remember the main points of the numerous sermons that I sat through on the subject. I should have paid more attention.

"If he was amused at his novice, he didn't let on. He then asked me to describe God. Once again, he didn't have much to say as I stumbled through my lame and limited explanations.

"He displayed a certain calmness and quietude about himself that caused me to become relaxed and introspective when I was with him. I had never felt this peacefulness with another human being.

"I soon found myself doing self-examination questions of my own faith journey. Can you believe it? All of this questioning of my beliefs was taking place in the remote reaches of Alaska! And my tutor was the local shaman!

"My parents wouldn't have believed me if I tried to explain what was happening to me. The thought that I was being tutored in the faith by the local village shaman would have been too much for them. My other companions thought my strange behavior concerning the shaman was a mystical quest of some kind. They teased me about it. But I ignored them.

"The shaman told me that a sign or revelation would occur in my life that would guide me to the truth. He said that it came to him as a young man while on a bear hunt with his father. I quizzed him about that, but he ignored me.

"The day before our group's departure back to the lower forty-eight, the shaman beckoned me to take a walk with him along a wilderness trail. It was a misty, rainy, and foggy day, but the thought of a walk through the forest with my new friend would be exhilarating. He had never asked me to take a walk with him before.

"I put on a rain jacket and hat and boots. We easily made our way through the underbrush along paths that moose and other wildlife had trampled down. I had no idea where we were going, but it was a gradual uphill climb, and I had to keep looking down to maintain my footing on the wet foliage and rocks.

"After a couple of hours of walking single file, the sun suddenly broke through the overcast clouds, and the path we were on took an abrupt left turn and stopped. We found ourselves at the precipice of a steep valley looking directing across at Mt. McKinley.

"Obviously, the shaman had been there before. The grandeur and the beauty of the mountain were both spectacular and overwhelming. The bright sun shining off the snow-capped peaks took my breath away. My body seemed to float as I stared at the majestic view. Sounds kind of weird, doesn't it?" Sam nodded.

"Both my mind and body sensed that we were in a sacred place. The shaman had told me that certain places have sacred auras about them, and looking out from this place, I felt a sense of holiness.

"As I took in the view, the hairs on the back of my neck tingled and a strong feeling of awe came over me. The sun felt warm on my face. I took off my hat and a soft breeze blew through my hair. I suddenly had a keen awareness of this place. I could clearly hear the sounds of nature. I heard the birds twittering their ancient songs and the chatter of ground squirrels. I had a very strong visceral feeling of being one with nature.

"It was during this moment that I suddenly felt very close to God. I also felt a peacefulness that I had never experienced before. Then, in a vision of clarity, I knew what I was going to do with the rest of my life. The translucency of my mind and body and soul instantly fused together. This transformation was forged into an enduring resolve to become a minister. For the first time in my life, I felt that I was complete and whole. I bowed my head and said a silent prayer. I was totally oblivious of my companion. During this time of enlightenment, he hadn't made a sound.

"After a while, I turned to him and saw that he was staring at me. He just smiled, and we both knew that something special had happened on that mountain. We made our way back to the village. We never spoke about the experience or my feelings about it.

"Our group departed the village the next day. In our own individual ways, we were all changed. The Alaskan experience had touched us. When I got back to school, I set my sights on seminary and I never looked back."

Sam was totally engrossed in Pastor James' story. She said softly, "You knew it. You just knew it, didn't you? Standing on that mountain with the shaman, you knew that your life was changed forever. Have you ever second-guessed your decision to be a minister?"

Pastor James looked at her, "No, I haven't," he said. "It was a calling. God was calling me into the ministry by revealing to me his creation and majesty. Isn't that remarkable? It was the most single significant event of my life. It only took a matter of minutes, but it changed me forever."

"Awesome," Sam said. "What part do you think the shaman played in it? Do you think that was the same place where he found his own truth?"

"I don't know, but I wouldn't be surprised. He probably saw something in me that I wasn't even aware of. Kindred spirit or something like that," he said. They both fell silent and let their thoughts take over.

The night nurse opened the waiting room door and announced that Sharon was awake and that Sam could see her now. Sam and Pastor James followed her to Sharon's room. She was lying very still on her bed staring at the ceiling.

"We had to sedate her," the nurse said. "She had been very agitated and confused but she is okay now." Sam thanked her. The nurse told Sam if she needed anything just to ring the buzzer. Sam took a seat next to Sharon's bed and gently squeezed her hand. No response. Pastor James took the seat on the other side of the bed.

Looking at her mom made Sam very sad. She looked so thin and tired. Her face was sunken in, and her eyes bulged out a little as she stared at the ceiling. Sam felt as if she was looking at the beginnings of a death mask. She felt a tear roll down her face. She realized that Earl's sudden and tragic death had started her mother on her own death journey.

Sharon couldn't come to grips with her loss. She had isolated herself into her prison of grief with no chance of parole. Looking at her now, the next step was very clear to Sam. She would have to bring her back to Monroe and put her into a nursing home. It was very evident that Sam couldn't care for her by herself.

Pastor James asked her if it was okay to say a prayer. Sam bowed her head as Pastor James prayed for Sharon, Sam, and the whole family, including Phil. He then thanked God for his many blessing and to give them all strength and courage to face the future. The prayer was very comforting to Sam as she sat silently holding her mother's hand. She wondered if her mom could appreciate it.

She heard the door open behind her and looked around. Dr. Simonson motioned her to follow him. Once in the hallway, he asked her and Pastor James to follow him into his office. The consultation was brief and went as expected. The x-rays taken of Sharon confirmed a small stroke. No surprise. They all agreed that it would be in the best interest of Sharon to go to a nursing home after she left the hospital. She needed the 24/7 care that only a private nursing home could provide.

Pastor James looked at Sam. Sam nodded back and mouthed the word, "Monroe."

In the hallway afterward the meeting, Pastor James offered to take Sam out to get something to eat at an all-night diner. Even though she was exhausted, she accepted. She just needed to get away.

During their light meal and conversation, Sam was unaware of the phone ringing at Sharon's house.

CHAPTER 30

D r. Ken was seated at his desk in the autopsy lab in the basement of the Monroe Regional Medical Center. Since the city of Monroe is the county seat, all autopsies whether forensic or coroner-related were done in the lab. He still had on his white lab coat and footies, filling out forms. He felt exhausted; just another twelve-hour day. Keith's body was laid out on the dissecting stainless-steel table behind him. If he wasn't good friends with Chief Johns, this examination could have waited until morning, but Johns was in a hurry.

The state-of-the-art lab was the result of Madison politics. Quid pro quo favors in the state assembly created the funding for the lab. It featured an examination theater, refrigerated vaults, and three small offices; one for the medical examiner, one for the county coroner, and one for the office manager. Normally, autopsies were requested by families whose loved ones died in hospital to find the actual cause of death. This requested examination was the first one in the history of Monroe to determine if a murder had been committed. That was the urgency, and Dr. Ken also felt a rush thinking he was part of a criminal investigation.

His autopsy assistant, David Wagner, was out of town on funeral leave after his mother-in-law passed away. So, that meant that Dr. Ken had to do the autopsy by himself. This also meant that he was responsible for the cleanup and sanitation of the autopsy tools.

Fortunately, the lab had the testing equipment needed to do the requested toxicology testing for poisons. He collected the biological specimens he needed from the body. Not knowing what he was looking for, he screened for several varieties of poisons, hoping that one of them would be correct.

As he waited for those results, he put Keith's body away, scrubbed down the lab, and methodically cleaned the enterotome, skull chisel, surgeon needles, rib cutters, scalpel, toothed forceps, bone saw, and vibrating saw. As he filled out his paperwork, he was probing for the unanswered question that Johns needed for his investigation. Only Keith could provide the answer.

Normally, the cause of death is found in one of five causes: natural, accident, homicide, suicide, or undetermined. Johns had asked him specifically to look for any evidence of poison. Dr. Ken had read Keith's death certificate, but he also knew that statistically approximately one-third of all death certificates were incorrect. He didn't want to make any mistakes, so he did a complete autopsy, focusing on any myocardial infarction (heart attack) evidence.

As he filled out his report, he highlighted three items: A fatty liver (excessive alcohol intake); partial blockages in the heart area (not the cause of death); and poison with a question mark. He would finish his report once the test was completed.

He was exhausted. As he leaned back in his chair, he suddenly looked up from his report and laughed out loud. Earlier that evening, he asked Johns if he wanted to view the autopsy procedure in person. Johns turned pale and he nearly fainted. The shocked look on his face now amused Dr. Ken in his tiredness. During his career as a policeman, Johns had witnessed violence and blood of the most egregious kind, but the thought of an autopsy made his legs weak. He respectfully declined and said he would rather wait for the results in the visitors lounge on the first floor.

Dr. Ken decided to review his notes just one more time to be sure. He had started with the external examination of Keith's body and was satisfied when he found no evidence of any physical trauma. Then he did the internal examination with a Y-shaped incision. He needed to inspect the internal organs of the body for any evidence of trauma or any other indicators of death. He was searching for traces of poison, but he didn't want to overlook any other probable cause of death.

He looked at his watch. The test analysis should be completed within the hour. Getting up from his desk, he closed his folder, took off his lab clothes, and headed to the stairwell that took him to the first floor.

Johns was napping in an armchair as Dr. Ken entered the visitors' lounge. He slightly nudged him, and Johns immediately woke up. "Did you find poison?" he asked.

"We will know in a few minutes. The analysis is in process."

Dr. Ken sat down in a chair across from the chief and said, "I found a fatty liver and a heart that wasn't in very good shape. Neither one of those conditions led to his death."

"So the death certificate was wrong," Johns concluded.

"Yes. Does that surprise you?"

Johns shook his head.

"We will shortly know if your theory on poison is correct. I found a very slight discoloration, but that could be from any number of causes."

Johns slumped back in his chair. "Thanks for putting in the extra effort on this one," he said.

"No problem. This will be a first for me in Monroe, I mean, the first murder investigation that I am a part of."

Johns smiled. "Me too," responded the chief.

Dr. Ken asked him about the case. Johns just smiled and said he couldn't comment on it.

Johns was tired. As they sat in silence, he did let it slip out that they had a possible suspect in Milwaukee, but that was all he said. Dr. Ken didn't pursue it.

They made some more small talk while waiting. Then, Dr. Ken looked at his watch and told the chief that he would be back shortly and disappeared through the exit door.

A couple of minutes later, Jessie appeared and greeted the chief. She told him that Dr. Ken had called her to come in and type up a report that the chief needed tonight. Johns told her that Dr. Ken would return shortly, so she sat down to wait. She picked up a copy of the Monroe Press on a table beside the chief and read the headline, "Roger Nussbaum named Chairman of Governor's Blue Ribbon Commission on Crime."

Back in the lab, Dr. Ken looked at his samples. He raised his head and said to himself, "Conium . . . the chief was right!" Just to be sure, he double-checked his analysis. He finished his notes and rushed back upstairs.

From the look on his face as he flew into the room, Johns knew the answer. Dr. Ken told him that he found poison in his lab sample, and that was the correct cause of death. "I guess you have your man. That suspect you mentioned in Milwaukee!"

Johns threw a quick disagreeable glance at Jessie. "Don't you breathe a word of this information to anyone!"

Jessie nodded.

Dr. Ken gave her the report and asked her to type it up and give a copy to the chief as soon as possible. She disappeared into the stairwell and headed down to her office.

"Is there a phone I can use to call Detective Gates?"

Dr. Ken took him to an office off the visitors' lounge to make the call.

Jessie went immediately to her office and quickly read over the notes that Dr. Ken had given her. After she finished reading, she typed them up on the official forms and took them back upstairs and gave them to Johns. She looked around, but Dr. Ken had already left. Johns thanked her and rushed out the exit door, leaving her alone in the visitors' lounge.

She made her way back to her desk. She picked up the phone and then she hesitated, leaving the phone receiver suspended in air. Her insides churned with the sense of excitement. A familiar conflict raged inside of her as she pondered on whether or not to call Ada. Her sense of betrayal to Dr. Ken was once again overwhelming. But her excitement at having the autopsy results in her hand and the powerful need to tell Ada was taking control of her mind and body.

Jessie's hand trembled as she dialed. Ada answered on the third ring.

"Ada, I have news," Jessie whispered breathlessly. Ada gave out a little gasp of air. "Dr. Ken found poison in Keith's body," Jessie continued. "It was conium, a type of poison that causes heart seizures."

The phone went dead as Ada processed the information. She was still trying to wake up.

"Ada, are you still there?"

"Yes," she responded weakly. "Is Dr. Ken sure?"

"Yes, he is. That's why I am here so late. Dr. Ken needed to give Chief Johns his findings tonight."

"Is the chief there now?" Ada asked.

"No, but he was waiting here for the results when I arrived."

"Did Dr. Ken do the testing in the lab?" Ada asked.

"Yes," Jessie replied. "I think Johns must have told him about his suspicions concerning poison."

"Were you there when Dr. Ken told the chief?"

"Yes, I was," Jessie replied, "and that's not all, the chief told me not to tell anyone. And he meant it!"

"Did you hear anything else between Dr. Ken and the chief?"

"They were speaking softly, but from what I overheard, Dr. Ken mentioned a suspect who lives in Milwaukee."

"What!" Ada screamed into the phone.

"Quiet down," Jessie said. "You know I could get into big trouble talking to you."

"Sorry," said Ada.

"I have to go," Jessie said and the line went dead.

Ada went into her living room and sat down heavily on her sofa. Her mind was racing. "A suspect living in Milwaukee? What could that mean?" she questioned herself.

Then a sudden rush of lucidity flashed before her eyes. "What a fool I have been!" she cried out. "Gregory!"

She felt flushed as she started to quickly replay the events surrounding Ellen's death in her mind. Suddenly, her eyebrows narrowed and then relaxed. The pieces were rapidly falling into place for her. She thought back on her intuitive suspicions about both Ellen's and Keith's deaths. She now saw Gregory in a totally different light. She could see clearly how Gregory's attitude about Ellen's death wasn't grief at all but fear. She felt betrayed and angry at herself for giving Gregory information about Detective Gates. She then shuddered as another thought slowly came into her mind like a dark storm cloud slowly making its way across a blue cloudless sky.

Marge had told Gregory that he was the sole beneficiary of his mother's estate. How did he process this information about his mother's "last will and testament?" In fact, how well did any of them know Gregory? Was he capable of two murders? But then, why was Keith poisoned? What did he have to do with anything?

Her panicky mind raced as she tried to sort out all these details. She felt hot and sweaty. But now she knew that she was right. Her suspicions were confirmed! She had been right all along! Her intuition was spot on concerning both deaths! They were murdered!

As she sat and fumed, she got angrier and angrier. "The bastard!" she shouted into the empty room. Her voice echoed throughout the house. Her muscles tensed up as she stared at Ellen's favorite chair across from her. Then she relaxed and suddenly felt tired and exhausted. "What am I going to do now? What am I going to do now?" She could barely speak above a whisper.

CHAPTER 31

G regory had awoken from yet another terrorizing nightmare. That ghoulish ghost from hell was still beckoning him to join her. She was coming after him. He was scared to go to sleep at night, and the lack of sleep was driving him crazy. But the good news today was that he was making his escape into Canada and that gave him hope.

After the disturbing phone call from Ada, he panicked. He knew that once the autopsy was completed on Keith, he would be arrested and charged. The day before, he had tried to dye his hair red. The plan was to change his appearance before he bolted for Canada. Something went wrong and he had orange highlights in his hair. He decided to wear a baseball cap on the trip to cover his mistake. If he was questioned about his hair at the border, he would make up some funny story that should be a good cover.

He hadn't shaved in a couple of days in order to give himself a scruffy look. Wearing faded blue jeans and a sweatshirt, he felt he would blend in with his fellow travelers. His trainers were fairly new and whiter than he would have liked but decided that would be okay. No one would really notice. He packed only one suitcase for his journey.

His thoughts turned to the bus station. The bus leaving for Toronto was at 11:00 a.m. and he would be on it. The thought of being safely on that bus, traveling at sixty miles per hour made him smile; first Chicago, then Detroit, and then into Canada. Freedom!! He felt a moment of jubilation.

His apartment was only thirty minutes to the bus station by foot, so he had plenty of time to get ready. But nevertheless, he felt he must hurry. The activity of getting ready, his movements, and action had calmed him somewhat. The constant motion helped him to remain calm.

Now, the last hours of readiness were at hand. He knew that the police

187

would be on to him, and he hoped to be across the Canadian border before they tracked him down.

In his pocket, he had a $100,000 cashier's check and about $1,500 in cash, all the money he had in the world. His only regret was leaving the Corvette behind. But it couldn't be helped.

Going to the bank to get the money had proved to be an ordeal. For one thing, leaving his apartment and being out in public, he made eye contact with total strangers and panicked. He sensed and then told himself that all those people could read him and knew what he was doing! Those thoughts were irrational and ridiculous, but it disturbed him so much that he almost cancelled his appointment and went home. But, he convinced himself to carry on getting his money. The bank employee he was dealing with must have suspected something because he wanted to know why he was closing his account and gave him strange looks.

Then on the way home, he spotted a gray-haired women walking in front of him. Her flowing hair was unkempt and scraggly. It freaked him out. His living nightmare was right in front of him in daylight. He sprinted the last two blocks, nearly knocking over a couple of people. Once safely back in his apartment, he drank two beers to calm his nerves.

In his more lucid moments, he questioned his motives for killing his mother. Was it for the money or something else much deeper? He also questioned his judgment in doing so. He convinced himself that he didn't want to do it, but he had an overwhelming desire or compulsion to do it. He didn't have answers to those questions, but his actions clearly put him on a path of no return. *Was hell his final destination?* he wondered.

Leaving the packed suitcase on the wall beside his bed, he went down the staircase to the underground parking garage. He wanted to see his black beauty one more time.

There she was, parked alongside about fifteen other cars. No one else was in the parking area. He was alone. As he stood admiring her, his thoughts turned to Kitty. They had enjoyed many pleasurable rides in his car. The thought of the wind blowing in her hair as they raced along rustic highways brought a brief smile to his face. He remembered the perfumed notes she sent him. He remembered drinking and laughing together. He remembered the sex and how good it was. "I am yours any time you want me," she said from painted lips.

Suddenly, he exploded. He slammed his fist down hard on the hood of the car parked next to his. A torrent of angry words spewed from his lips. "I am made out of flesh, bone, water, and blood!" he shouted. "I have emotions! I have a heart!" He couldn't hold back the tears. He slumped down beside his car and sat on the cold cement. He held his head in his hands. "She didn't care about me," he said to himself. "What was I? A meal ticket? Sex for sale. Is that all it was?"

It took him several minutes to compose himself. He got up and sighed. The reality of it all hit him very hard.

As he turned to go, he suddenly remembered a black heavy-duty flashlight in the trunk that he won at a bowling tournament. He had his name engraved on it along with the date and his tournament series (798), the best bowling series of his life.

He suddenly had an overwhelming urge to take it with him. He opened the trunk and grabbed it. The flashlight was heavy and about a foot long and held 4 D cell batteries. With flashlight in hand, he walked back up the garage stairs to his apartment.

CHAPTER 32

arlier that morning, Chief Johns finally got through to Sam at her mother's house. After her late supper with Pastor James, she went to Sharon's house to get some sleep. It was a restless night's sleep. Sam kept waking up thinking about her mom and how she was going to cope with her after she was discharged from the hospital.

Sam had just fallen into a deep sleep when the harsh ringing of the telephone abruptly woke her. When she heard Johns' voice, she immediately came to and was instantly wide awake. The sound of his voice took her back to Monroe and the case. He told her about the poison Dr. Ken found in Keith's body. He was working on a search and arrest warrant. He also told her that he was contacting the Milwaukee police department for assistance, and that he too was on the way.

Sam cut him off in mid-sentence. She was breathless. She told him that she was going to Gregory's apartment. Johns told her to be careful. Gregory had probably murdered two people, and he should be regarded as extremely dangerous. He ordered her to wait for backup once she got to his apartment. She said she would wait and slammed the phone down. She quickly dressed and splashed some water on her face and flew out of the front door and jumped into her car.

She jammed the gear shifter into reverse and hurriedly backed out of the driveway. She then jerked the shifter into drive and sped away. Turning north at the on ramp, she eased her way into the flow of traffic heading to Milwaukee. After a few minutes, she realized that she was passing everyone. The speedometer read 80 mph. Her mind was racing. She slowed her speed to 60 mph. Now she was in the flow of the traffic again.

She told herself to calm down. A cool head was needed. First, she needed to remember the directions that Ada had given her to his apartment. She knew Milwaukee well enough to approximate where she was going.

She needed time to think. Gregory didn't know that she was on her way to arrest him. She had the element of surprise on her side. Would the backup be there? If not, what would she do? What if she couldn't find the apartment? What if Gregory was already gone! Maybe someone in Monroe had called and tipped him off. All these thoughts were like shooting stars streaking across her mind. She was totally preoccupied as she sped along, ignoring the traffic around her.

As she approached the city limits of Milwaukee, the traffic slowed considerably. Her hands hurt. Only then did she realize that she had been white-knuckling her steering wheel. She was impatient. Her palms were sweaty. She maneuvered her car through the dense traffic, cutting off cars as she wove her way through the clogged arteries leading to downtown. She ignored the honking horns and laser-like stares from her fellow commuters. Her instincts had kicked in and she was on auto pilot, making all the right driving decisions without thinking about them.

The bright sunshine and the promise of another beautiful fall day in Milwaukee went unnoticed. Her mind was completely focused on Gregory. She repeatedly played the tapes of her conversations with him over and over in her mind. His detached attitude, his indifference to his family, and the cold and methodical way he talked to her all made sense. He was playing a part, like an actor, to fool her. He wanted to get away with murder! This condescending attitude made her angrier. She was getting too emotionally involved. She had to get herself under control.

After what seemed like an eternity, she turned onto East Juneau Avenue. After a couple of blocks, she slowed as she inched her way along the street to Gregory's apartment building and stopped. There it was! "Thank God for Ada's directions!" she exclaimed.

The hope of finding a parking spot on the crowded street was her first concern.

She glanced at her watch. The drive took only forty minutes. "Not bad," she murmured to herself. After pushing her way through all those morning commuters, the time seemed longer. She stared down the block. No where to park.

Then suddenly, she saw the rear blinker light of a car go on. As she sat and watched, a red sedan slowly exited a parking space. She was lucky. The space was directly across the street from the front entrance to Gregory's building.

She quickly parallel-parked. After she turned the engine off, she told herself to relax and to think and to pull herself together. This was the first time in her career that backup wasn't with her on the scene for an important arrest. She told herself that she would have to wait. She was jumpy and anxious. No other police cars were in sight. *Where is everybody?*

She looked up at Gregory's apartment. Ada had told her it was the corner apartment on the second floor of the brownstone and faced the street, Number 210. The building had three floors and took up half a city block. She didn't see any lights or movement in his apartment from her position.

As Sam sat in her car, she nervously fidgeted and her imagination was getting the better of her. *What if he was making his escape while she sat there doing nothing? Should she wait?*

She began to relive her interviews with him again. The one at the Yellow Iris Café made her even angrier. The more she thought about it, the madder she got. He played her. She needed air. She got out of her car and stood on the sidewalk. Then she paced back and forth. She went to the end of the block to try to get a better view of the apartment. Her nerves were finally getting the best of her. She stared at the apartment house and couldn't wait any longer. The adrenaline was pumping through her veins like a runaway freight train. The thought of arresting Gregory totally consumed her. She wasn't thinking logically. She was sure that every minute wasted was a chance for Gregory to get away.

She opened the trunk of her car and retrieved her gun. She belted the gun around her waist and pulled down the windbreaker jacket she was wearing to cover it. One last look up and down the street; no backup! She deliberately made her way across the street to the front entrance. The security front door was propped open with a small box, leaving a gap of approximately one inch; so much for security when a resident was too lazy to use his key. But it was a lucky break for her as she eased her way through the wired glass steel door.

She crossed the highly polished gray marble floors to the stairwell. The staircase would give her greater control of the situation once she reached the second floor door, a better option than the elevator. With her gun in her right hand, she cautiously moved up the staircase, not knowing what to expect. At the top of the open staircase, she saw that the hallway was deserted and quiet. She moved quickly and silently to Gregory's corner apartment. As she stood in front of his apartment door, she listened intently for any sounds inside.

She placed her head gently against the door to listen better to any sound or movement inside the apartment. To her surprise, the door moved with the light pressure she exerted. The only sound that she heard was softly playing rock and roll music coming from somewhere inside the apartment. She thought that surprise would be her best offense. She readied her gun and knocked on the door. No response. She nudged the door open and took a couple of steps inside. She wondered if he was even there when the sudden blow to the back of her head knocked her to the floor and rendered her unconscious.

She collapsed on the carpet. In his panic, Gregory tried to close the door as he struggled to drag her to the kitchen. Then he went back and grabbed her gun. He took it to the bedroom and threw it on the bed.

The weight of her body made it almost impossible as he tried sitting her up in a kitchen chair. He retrieved some duct tape from the cabinet below the kitchen sink and taped her arms and feet to the chair, then put a gag in her mouth. Sweating profusely, he hurried into the bathroom, ran the cold water faucet, and splashed the cool water over his face.

He was anxious and trembling. He needed to catch the bus at eleven, but he had a complication. Time was closing in on him. "What should I do about Gates? Do I leave her? Do I kill her?" His head throbbed with the beginning of a migraine.

Once he was certain that Gates was secured, he mopped the sweat off his face and went back into the bedroom and closed the door. He opened the suitcase, pitched in the bloodstained flashlight, and refastened the lock. He saw Sam's gun on the bed where he had thrown it. "I need to get out of here now!" he yelled at the wall. In his heightened state, he now expected the police to show up any minute to arrest him. He couldn't control the shaking and sweating. His heart was racing. He placed the suitcase back on the floor and grabbed the gun.

CHAPTER 33

Ada sat motionless in her car as she waited outside Gregory's apartment. After the phone call from Jessie last night, she couldn't sleep. Her agitated and fitful tossing and turning totally consumed her. At 4:00 a.m., she had finally got up out of bed, got up, slipped on her bathrobe, and made her way down the creaky stairs to the kitchen stove. She brewed herself a cup of coffee. As she sipped the hot black liquid at her kitchen table, she fidgeted. She felt the presence of Ellen's tormented soul. They had so many wonderful times together around this table. The visceral sensation she was feeling over Ellen's death was overwhelming. Apprehension and butterflies consumed her. Was Ellen trying to tell her something? But what?

"What should I do?" she asked herself. She had an impulsive and overwhelming desire to immediately go see Gregory and confront him. After her sleepless night, she needed to make a decision.

Taking her last sip of coffee, she went back upstairs and got out of her sweaty pajamas. She brushed her teeth, dressed, and was on the road to Milwaukee at 6:00 a.m.. It was a cool morning as she headed north. On any other day, she would have enjoyed the trip, but today, she had her mind on other things!

Now, as she sat and waited in her car across from his apartment, she tried to plan her next move. She was undecided. It seemed so perfectly clear what she would do once she arrived. But now she hesitated. Barging into his apartment and demanding answers didn't seem like the right thing to do. What if he got mad and attacked her? How could she defend herself? She needed to think this through more carefully. No one seemed to notice Ada as she sat quietly in her car.

Then suddenly, she saw Sam drive up and watched as she parked her car.

As she watched, she sat very still in her car. She felt the urge to get out and go to speak to Sam, but something stopped her.

From what she could see, Sam seemed very agitated, sitting there in her car. She seemed fidgety and nervous. Then suddenly, Sam got out of her car and stood on the sidewalk looking across the street at Gregory's apartment house. She walked to the end of the block and back again. Then she opened her trunk, took out her gun, and fastened it around her waist. She checked for traffic and made her way across the street and disappeared into the apartment building.

After several minutes passed, Ada got out of her own car. She locked it and waited for the traffic to clear and crossed the street. She entered the building through the same partially open front door. No sign of Sam. She guessed that she had already gone up to Gregory's apartment. She made her way to the elevator on the west wall, pushed the button, and waited.

Finally, it came. Two teenaged girls exited the small elevator engrossed in lively conversation. They didn't notice her. Ada jumped on the elevator and took it to the second floor. When the doors opened, she looked around. Satisfying herself that no one else was on the floor, she slowly made her way down the hallway toward Gregory's apartment. Her shoes made a clicking sound as she walked, and her breathing was labored.

She saw the door was slightly ajar. She listened and then peeked inside. She couldn't see or hear anything unusual. She pushed open the door and entered the apartment. She remained silent. As she gingerly walked down the short hallway illuminated by the early morning sunlight, she felt the blood pulsating through her head.

Midway down the hallway, she noticed that Gregory's bedroom door was closed. Another three steps and she looked into the living room. Other than the sheer curtains moving gently in the breeze from a partially opened window behind his sofa, everything seemed normal.

Then suddenly, she heard a slight groan. She spun around and took a couple of steps toward the kitchen and saw Sam duct-taped to a chair. Her head was hanging down limply with a gag in her mouth. Her hair was matted down with the crimson color of dark red. "Blood!" she gasped and put her fist to her mouth.

Gregory suddenly appeared from the bedroom waving Sam's gun over his head. His bloodshot eyes were wild as he stood staring at her. Ada froze; she couldn't move. She didn't recognize him at first. His appearance was altered, almost freakish. He had dyed his hair reddish-orange, and he looked very haggard and pale. He was disheveled, and he had the look of a wild man!

Shocked, Ada just stared at him in disbelief at what she was seeing. She couldn't move. Gregory spun around and looked at the open apartment door. He sprinted toward the door and slammed it shut. In an instant, he was back in front of her. He inched his way toward her as she slowly backed away from him. In terror, she fell backwards onto his living room sofa. She could see the blood rising in his face and sweat beads appearing on his forehead.

"Damn it! It's hot in here!" he yelled in a very high-pitched, squeaky voice. He quickly went over to the window, threw back the soft lacy sheer curtains, and fully opened the window. Ada could hear the sounds of the traffic below as soft cool breeze entered the surreal scene in the apartment. The curtain was waving in the breeze. Gregory returned to his position between Sam and herself and quickly looked at one and then the other like his head was on a pivot.

Ada's face was white with fright as she sat on the sofa staring up at him. She focused in on his small, beady, evil-looking eyes. His head moved mechanically from side to side. It was mesmerizing, like a predator animal getting ready to deliver the death strike! His eyes looked shiny and black to her, almost serpent-like.

Suddenly she felt disoriented, sick, dizzy, jittery. She felt trapped! She couldn't get away or shrink from the horror in front of her. Her heart was beating very fast, her hands were sweaty, and her mind was racing! She was staring death in the face! Then, suddenly, everything seemed to move in slow motion. She was conscious of the fact that her mind was analyzing the situation and formulating a plan. She had become very much focused.

Ada noticed that Gregory looked terrified as well. She quickly realized that she was dealing with a madman. This observation calmed her. She felt that she could perhaps now save her own life and Sam's using her own wits as she waited for his next move.

Gregory spun his body around and, in a high-pitched voice that she didn't recognize, shouted, "What the hell are you doing here? It's bitches like you and that cop over there that have screwed up my life!" His face was very red, his nostrils flared, and he was grinding his teeth. He looked like he was in pain.

He continued, "I had it made, you know! I had money! I had happiness! And I had a hot bitching lady! But no, that bitch cop had to start asking questions. She screwed with my head. I started having nightmares, for God's sake! And you know what, Ada? You were behind this! You just couldn't let it go, Ellen's death!"

Gregory couldn't stand still. He was dancing from one foot to the other, waving his arms about. The gun in his right hand looked like another of his body's appendages; attached, a surreal part of his arm and hand.

Ada summoned up all the courage and spit she had and fired back at him, "You stupid bastard! You killed your own mother and then you killed Keith!" She waited a moment for that to sink in and said, "What were you thinking? Have you no conscience or soul? And now, you have the balls to stand there telling me that you murdered two innocent and decent people for your own happiness! You are sick, Gregory! You are sick!"

Gregory stopped jumping around and stared at her. He bit his lower lip. Then he uttered a short hysterical laugh. "You call that woman my mother! She abandoned me, if you have forgotten that little detail. And you know perfectly well that my aunt raised me. Then, just like nothing ever happened, my loving mother comes back to Monroe and into my life when I am fifteen years old. I hated her for that! She pissed all over my childhood." He stopped talking and fell silent.

"So, what about Keith, then? Why did he have to die?" Ada shouted at him. Gregory jumped at the shrill loudness of her voice.

"Somehow, the bastard figured out that I killed Ellen, and he started blackmailing me! He had a nerve. I had to drive to Delavan once a month to meet him and pay the little shit. His attitude was appalling! He thought we should have breakfast and talk about the old times. Each time I gave him his $500, I told him to fuck off! And you know what he did? He just laughed."

"So why did you have to kill him?"

"Look, his brainy kid got accepted to the UW and he needed more money. Isn't that a crock of shit? He demanded that I give him the money or else. The greedy little swine got what he deserved!"

Gregory seemed to relax somewhat. His voice lost its high pitch. Justifying himself to Ada had a somewhat calming effect on him.

Looking past Gregory, Ada could see Sam stirring. It seemed to her that she had regained consciousness and was listening to them.

Suddenly, Gregory turned and looked at the clock on the desk next to the Tiffany lamp. It read 9:45! He immediately tensed up and his blood pressure rose again, causing his face to change color.

The panic of missing the bus was acute. He was losing control. His breathing became labored. He bent forward and wet himself. "What the hell!" he said, looking down at the stain. "I am going to miss the damn bus!" he screamed. "I gotta go now!" He spun around and pointed the gun at Sam. "First her, then you, Ada!" he shouted.

Sam lifted her head and stared at him. As she focused in on the gun barrel, she knew that she was looking into the face of death. She thought of Earl. "Jesus!" she said to herself.

Gregory was out of control. His outburst and wild talk started the adrenaline pumping once again through Ada's veins. His expression and the frenzied look said it all. If she was going to save Sam, she needed to act and act soon. She jumped up from the sofa, ran behind it, and screamed as loud as she could; she starting waving her arms wildly. Gregory spun around and stared at her.

Suddenly a stiff breeze blew in through the window causing the curtains to billow out behind her. Gregory froze in fright. He turned ghostly white. His eyes glazed over. He felt shortness of breath and tightness in his throat. *That cursed ghost had come to life! She was beckoning him! She was not more than five feet away!* His hand tightened on the trigger of the gun. He just stared at the bitch that had haunted his dreams! She was wildly waving her arms and screaming. Out of extreme fear, he took aim at the apparition and fired two shots. Ada instantly spun around and fell against the table holding the Tiffany lamp. It crashed to the floor with her; blood oozing from her body as she lay dying on the floor.

Sam struggled against her restraints. She was frantic.

Gregory started dancing around like a madman. He skipped and hopped around the sofa and sang a little tune, "Satan's bitch is dead. Satan's bitch is dead!" Then he screamed it over and over again. He began to laugh hysterically.

As the sunlight glistened off the broken pieces of colored stained glass, another stiff breeze came though the window, lifting the curtains up again. This time, he heard a rhythmic swishing sound, like the ghost was speaking to him. He panicked again and took another shot at the curtain. Nothing happened! The curtains continued to billow out. In his extreme frustration, he now felt like he was on the edge of insanity looking into the abyss.

He stopped moving and became very still. His head began to spin with the circles rapidly shrinking smaller and smaller. He felt as if he was in the center of a violent whirlpool plunging madly downward. Suddenly, his next move became crystal clear to him, a moment of extreme clarity. His mother was beckoning from beyond the grave.

From her torturous chair, Sam watched in horror as he stuck the barrel of the gun into his mouth and fired. His brains spewed out everywhere as he crashed to the floor.

Sam struggled to get free. Her head throbbed, but that didn't concern her. She felt helpless and frustrated through her tears.

Then she heard the apartment door crashing down and saw Chief Johns and Milwaukee police officers rushing toward her. As Johns worked to free her restraints, she felt the adrenaline leaving her body. She suddenly went limp and fell into his arms. He held her tight as the tears cascaded down her cheeks. "Oh, Ada," she moaned. "I am so very, very sorry."

EPILOGUE

Detective Sam Gates went on medical leave after being diagnosed with a concussion. She went into therapy for intermediate memory loss and was expected to make a full recovery.

Sharon Gates was released from the hospital in Silver Bay and entered a nursing home in Monroe. Sam put her house up for sale.

Ada Klausner was given a standing room only funeral service at the First Christian Church in Monroe. Police Chief Johns eulogized her for her spunk and bravery in saving Detective Gates's life. Roger Nussbaum was in attendance. Ada was buried in Green Lawn Cemetery.

Gregory Denton's body was claimed by a distant relative. He was cremated and his remains were taken out of state. No further information was available.

CPSIA information can be obtained at www.ICGtesting.com
Printed in the USA
LVOW120152060912

297546LV00002B/3/P